Traitors Within

A Michael Stone Series Novel

By James Rosone and Miranda Watson

Disclaimer

This is a fictional story. All characters in this book are imagined, and any opinions that they express are simply that, fictional thoughts of literary characters. Although policies mentioned in the book may be similar to reality, they are by no means a factual representation of the news. Please enjoy this work as it is, a story to escape the part of life that can sometimes weigh us down in mundaneness or busyness.

Copyright Information

Table of Contents

Chapter 1
Taking Aim

Incirlik Air Base, Turkey

It was hot and dusty as Michael Stone stood in the smoke break shack and took a long drag from his cigarette. He dropped it to the ground, putting it out with his boot.

Man, I needed that fix, he thought, and then he sighed. He knew he really needed to quit smoking one of these days.

As Mike exited the shanty, he looked off to the horizon. A storm was brewing. Faint glimpses of lightning illuminated the dark, ominous clouds in the distance. They needed to accomplish their mission soon if they were going to get the Reaper back before the nasty weather arrived.

Mike started walking back to the building where his motley crew was operating. He was anxious about this mission. A lot was riding on its success, including his reputation and nearly six years of work. As the lead officer in charge of the CIA's anti-ISIS operation in Turkey, this wasn't just about a drone mission; it was a step to pulling up the extremist organization from the roots.

For the last four months, Mike's team had been tracking a man they had identified as one of the primary financiers of

ISIS, a man who was acquiring large quantities of explosives for ISIS and selling ISIS-controlled oil and natural gas on the black market to foreign buyers. This arrangement had made his target extremely wealthy and well connected in certain circles in Turkey, Saudi Arabia, and Qatar. When one of Mike's other sources had informed them that his target would be getting married and hosting a large gathering at his home where other ISIS leaders would be present, Mike had worked aggressively to gain the approval needed to conduct this drone strike. Eventually, he had convinced his superiors to act. However, there was one caveat. Since this strike would be taking place inside Turkey, an allied nation, it would have to appear as if the attack was a car bomb and not a drone strike.

Since the formation of the Islamic State in Iraq and Syria, commonly referred to as ISIS, the CIA had created a counter-ISIS group, codenamed Task Force Torch. TF Torch's initial purpose was simply to monitor and identify ISIS leaders and as many of their members as possible. When their parallel mission to train and equip an opposition force to the Syrian government and ISIS had failed, TF Torch's mission had changed. They had become more of a direct-action unit, focused on eradicating ISIS on their own. The Special Activities Division had begun to take more direct action to go after the senior leaders of ISIS as well as key members involved in the organization and those supporting it.

As a senior paramilitary operations officer, Michael Stone had been a part of TF Torch from the very beginning. His team had worked hard, developing sources within the numerous refugee camps and then assisting those sources as they infiltrated ISIS directly. TF Torch had quickly made a name for itself as a team that could get things done, and Mike's ability to operate and think outside the conventional norms had separated him from his peers. Through expanded use of drones and continued access to the DoD's Joint Special Operations Command, they were starting to turn the tide on the war with ISIS.

Stone attributed most of their success to the close collaboration with the Kurdish Peshmerga, who were providing the brunt of the forces combating ISIS. Today's mission had been a multimonth collaborative effort between the CIA and the Peshmerga. It had taken years for one of their sources to infiltrate the ISIS leadership. Now that effort was about to pay off.

****

Walid Sattar al Sayed had tried to stay under the radar at the refugee camp in Turkey. He hadn't been particularly social, so it surprised him when a professional-looking man with a Saudi accent approached him.

"*Asalaam alaikum.*"

"*Alaikum asalaam*," Walid replied cautiously.

After a minimal amount of chitchat, the man came right to the point. "Walid, it would appear that you have fallen on tough times. You were clearly not taken care of or respected by your former employer."

Walid's eyebrows rose suspiciously, but he let the man continue.

"Unless I am mistaken, I heard that you used to work in the Syrian oil ministry. Yes? If so, then you may still have a number of contacts in that realm. Those connections are valuable to the men I represent. I'm wondering if you would be interested in selling oil on behalf of our organization. You would, of course, be highly compensated for your efforts," the man said with a smile.

Walid snorted. "I'm not so naïve as not to see who your organization is, or what you guys have been doing. I am not a fervent believer as you all are, and I don't want to be a part of what you guys are doing. I just want to sell oil and make a comfortable living."

The man nodded, as if he had anticipated this response. "Well, Allah has a use for people like that as well," he replied. "We are in the unique position of acquiring vast tranches of oil and need a way to sell it. We also need expertise to help manage the fields and ensure the oil continues to flow. Your compensation, as I mentioned before, would be quite comfortable. Is this something you'd be interested in doing?"

Pausing for a moment to think, Walid looked up at the Saudi, skeptical of his offer. "What would you guys do with the money? There's going to be a lot of it if you've truly captured the western fields."

Smiling, the man leaned forward. "Does it really matter what we do with the money so long as you are taking a cut?"

A short pause ensued before Walid shook his head.

"Good," the Saudi replied. "The money will be used for many things, chief among them salaries and acquiring better weapons and explosives. It's time this regime be moved to the ash heaps of history and make way for the true followers of Islam." The man puffed out his chest in pride.

Walid scratched at his beard for a moment. He knew these guys were bad business, but right now he had no business, and worse, government goons were still looking to do him harm. Finally, he answered, "Well, my own government discarded and tortured me. There is no love lost between us. I wouldn't mind the opportunity to get revenge for what they have done to me. However, I am not the most religious man, and I can't say that I agree with your brand of Islam."

Smiling, the Saudi responded, "That doesn't matter. Our organization is becoming like any other government. We're starting to identify the people who can help run the important political positions, even if we are still operating a shadow government. All we really need is someone who can help us discreetly sell our captured oil."

Now it was Walid's turn to smile. "That is something I can certainly do."

The two talked for a bit longer before they established how they would regularly communicate, where they'd meet and how they'd get Walid integrated into their process.

****

Prior to the Syrian civil war, Walid had been very happy in his position as a Deputy Minister in the Syrian Oil Ministry. However, in the fall of 2010, shortly after protests had broken out in Homs and Damascus, he had suggested to his boss that perhaps President Assad should try to work something out with the Syrian opposition group and end the bloodshed before it got out of control.

Several days went by, and then he was suddenly fired for speaking ill of the regime. His boss quietly told him it would be best if he left Damascus, since the regime was cracking down on dissidents. Believing he had done nothing wrong, he chose to stay in the capital city and try to ride out the controversy. Unfortunately, it was the first of many erroneous decisions he'd make. Two days later, in the dark of night, men from the political security directorate busted down the door to his apartment and arrested him for treason.

While in prison, Walid was tortured and interrogated for nearly a week. After several days, he managed to befriend one of the guards and bribed the man into letting him escape. Walid quickly fled to the Turkish border and was taken in as a refugee.

He had a brother who was a chemistry professor at the University of Aleppo. In normal times, he would have sought him out for help, but he didn't want to entangle his brother in whatever web he had become trapped in. Instead, he sent word to him of what had happened and warned him not to make the same mistake. He told his brother where he was going to be, in case he too had to flee. His brother had a wife and two little ones to care for, and Walid felt obligated to help should they need it.

****

Within a couple of months of meeting his mysterious new Saudi friend, Walid had become an instrumental part of funding ISIS and acquiring large quantities of explosives for the organization. He knew wholesale brokers who didn't have a problem buying oil and natural gas on the black market. These groups also had skilled engineers who could work the oil and gas fields, and the equipment to transport the oil and natural gas.

Because the transactions had to be done in cash or Bitcoin, all through multiple offshore accounts and front companies, it was easy for Walid to skim off the top without his masters knowing. After several years, Walid had become a very wealthy man and held some influence within the organization. As ISIS tried to firm up a more formal government, he became an indispensable leader behind the scenes. He started to envision himself as the possible future finance minister of this new government.

Walid was smart and cunning; he used his wealth to buy anonymity within Turkey. He paid off the right Turkish intelligence officers and military officers to keep his identity and location a secret. Through his contacts in Saudi Arabia and Qatar, he was able to secure a steady supply of explosives and other essential tools that his ISIS masters requested.

The Saudis and Qataris all had the same goal as ISIS— the destruction of the Shia government of Syria and Iraq, Iran's new proxy. The fact that Walid wasn't a religious zealot also played to his favor, as this put him more on par with these key allies' way of thinking. Though his ISIS bosses didn't condone his worldly behavior, he was too valuable a resource for them to make an example out of him.

****

Walking back from the smoke shack, Mike watched the storm clouds steadily roll in toward them, a wave of rain slowly drifting down to blanket the rolling hills below. Mike sped up his steps a bit. As soon as he reached the door, he pulled his access card out and swiped it, activating the keypad, then entered his six-digit code.

The door hissed slightly as it opened.

A wave of cold air pounded his face as he walked into the hallway. He quickly made his way back to a dimly lit room, which had numerous banks of monitors and two rows of analysts working behind them. This was TF Torch's nerve center, located in a nondescript building at the edge of the flight line on Incirlik Air Base. The CIA ran multiple drones out of this location, continually monitoring the situation with ISIS and from time to time carrying out a drone strike when the right opportunity presented itself.

An Air Force major signaled for Stone to come to his position. "Sir, the drone is on station. As you can see, the wedding reception is well underway. We estimate at least a hundred people at the compound." He zoomed in and out of the compound from a couple of different angles to give Stone a better picture of the area.

After examining the footage for a couple of minutes in silence, Stone looked at the major. "Have you confirmed the target is there?"

"Yes. Here's the image." The major pulled up a separate video file and clicked on it. It showed a few minutes of footage, following the target and his bride as they were eating at a table. From the angle of the drone, they could clearly identify the man. Facial recognition placed it at a 97% match to the pictures of Walid Sattar al Sayed they had on file.

Out of the corner of his eye, Stone saw a male get into a vehicle and leave the compound. "Who's that?" he asked, wanting to make sure the target was still there.

Scrolling back through the footage on a separate computer, one of the CIA analysts looked to see if they could catch a glimpse of the man's face. Fortunately, the man had looked up as several birds had flown by, and that had given them enough of an angle to grab a good picture. "Unfortunately, this guy isn't in our system, so we're not sure who he is. We just know he's not one of our targets," explained the CIA analyst confidently.

The major moved the main screen back to the live image of the reception before Stone could say anything else. Then he shifted his cursor over to another large screen on the side wall and opened another video file. "While you were grabbing a cigarette, we monitored six individuals who arrived about ten minutes ago. It appears that at least four of the individuals are bodyguards, but as you can see, we got a clear shot of the person they're protecting."

As Stone scrutinized the still image the major had just opened, he couldn't believe his eyes. It was Abu Muhammad al-Shimali. The Iraqi-born citizen of Saudi Arabia was a senior leader within ISIS. He was responsible for the facilitation of moving foreign fighters to and from ISIS-held territory and smuggling fighters into Europe, Britain and the US. The FBI had a five million-dollar bounty on his head.

"Do we have official confirmation of his identity?" Stone asked with a bit of excitement in his voice.

Another analyst, Jarred Miller, walked over to the major and Stone. Miller was one of the CIA's top analysts, and they had been lucky to get him on the task force. "I just got the results back from facial recognition. It's an 83% match. The guys back at Langley also believe this is him."

A second later, the secured phone to Langley rang. Jarred was closest to it, and he picked it up. Then he handed the phone to Stone. "It's the Director. He wants to speak to you," Miller said, a bit surprised.

Stone took the phone and lifted it to his ear. The Director told him in no uncertain terms, "Hit the wedding reception *now*. We want you to take out Walid, and more importantly, Abu Muhammad."

"Can I amend this mission to send in a capture team?" asked Stone.

"No," asserted the Director. "We want you to launch this strike immediately. Do not wait. We can't afford for you to miss Abu Muhammad. He's too high value a target to let him slip through our fingers, even if it means there will be collateral damage."

Turning to the Air Force captain flying the drone, Stone gave the order. "Fire!"

The captain activated his missile and locked on to what appeared to be a catering van parked near the courtyard where the reception was being held. Because this strike was going to take place in a friendly host country, the Reaper had been armed with a missile made of special polymers so that when it exploded, it would leave no trace of shrapnel or missile fragments. Stone had specifically ordered several of these missiles for his task force to use, in case they needed plausible deniability for a high-collateral strike.

The group collectively watched the feed as the missile raced toward its intended target. In less than a minute, the missile hit the van. The screen whited out for a brief second from the flash of the detonation. When the screen resolution returned, they could see that the van was gone, and so was most of the compound. The courtyard was a mangled mess of torn bodies and small fires.

Stone turned to address the group. "Great work, everyone. Not only did we get our target, it appears we got a bonus and hit their foreign fighter minister. I want a visual check of the survivors, if possible. We need to ensure that Walid and Abu Muhammad have both been eliminated. If you even think one of them survived, I want to know immediately."

After his impromptu speech, he left the room to head back to the smoke shack for another cigarette. This victory called for a celebration.

****

As Jamal searched the diaper bag for a fresh diaper, he realized that he hadn't checked to see if there were any extra ones in the bag before they'd left for his brother's wedding reception. Jamal pulled his wife and Walid aside and told them, "I will be back shortly. I'm going to drive to the store down the road and grab some diapers."

His wife didn't say anything but shot him a look that clearly communicated, "I told you to check the bag before we left."

His brother just smiled, and said, "It's not a problem, little brother. Just let me know when you get back. I have someone important I want to introduce you to."

Jamal nodded and then rushed off. While he drove down the winding road leading away from his brother's compound, their conversation played repeatedly in his head. He didn't know who his brother wanted him to talk to, but Jamal had told Walid in the past that he wanted nothing to do with his ISIS colleagues. Walid had always told him that he shouldn't believe everything that the Western media published, that they weren't as bad as they were portrayed. Jamal was nervous at the thought of what awaited him when he returned.

He grabbed the diapers as quickly as he could and then got in his car to return to the reception. As his vehicle came around the final bend in the road leading to the compound, he saw a bright flash. Then the windshield imploded, sending shards of glass flying toward his face. He lost control of the car and hit a tree. After that, everything just went black.

Chapter 2
Awakening

Gaziantep, Turkey

Jamal woke up two days later in a local hospital. At first, he was completely disoriented and unsure of where he was and what had happened. Then, as he sat there trying to eat the vegetable soup that had been placed in front of him, the images started to flood back. Suddenly, he experienced the accident all over again—there was the bright flash ahead of him at his brother's compound, the sound of glass shattering. He pulled his arms to his eyes, as if he could still shelter himself from the shards of the windshield that were flying at his face. He felt the car swerve beneath him and the brief moment of weightlessness that happened before his forehead slammed into the steering wheel. The airbag must not have deployed.

Jamal didn't have much time to process these memories before a doctor walked in and began to read over his chart. "How are you feeling?" he asked.

Jamal delayed for a moment as he assessed his body. "I have a bit of a headache, but otherwise, I'm feeling fine," he responded.

The doctor explained, "Well, you should have a headache. When you were brought to the hospital along with the other survivors from the wedding blast, you had a concussion, some abrasions on your face and hands, and a broken arm. Many of the others were not so lucky, I'm afraid. There were only thirty-six survivors."

Jamal realized for the first time that his left arm was in a cast. Suddenly, it throbbed with pain. Then panic set in. "Doctor—my wife, my children. Are they here? Were they injured?"

"I am so sorry to be the one to tell you this, but they died in the explosion," the doctor answered. "Your brother was Walid, correct? He also perished in the blast."

Jamal slumped down and began to cry. His family was gone. He was a man without a country, and now he had lost his family, too.

The day before Jamal was to be released from the hospital, a man in a suit stopped by his room. "I would like to offer my sincere condolences," he said. Jamal detected that the man's Arabic had a Saudi accent. "I knew your brother, Walid," the man continued. "It was a shame that he was killed in such a horrible way."

Jamal responded, "I was told it was a terrorist bomb that killed my brother and the rest of my family."

The man nodded. "Yes, it was a terrorist bomb—an American terrorist bomb," he explained.

Jamal was about to respond but stopped himself. He tried to analyze what he had just been told.

The man must have seen the look of deep thought on Jamal's face. "As you know, your brother had been selling oil and gas for our organization. This made him a target. We told him he needed to keep a lower profile, but he insisted that he was well protected in Turkey."

Jamal shuddered. He had suspected that he was speaking with someone from ISIS, and now he was certain.

The man continued, unhindered by the response. "You see, we have a person who works on the American air base. Our source informed us that an American drone had taken off roughly three hours before the explosion with two missiles. When it returned, it only had one missile. There were no other drone strikes in Syria or Iraq during the period that the drone was in the air—just the 'suspected car bomb' at your brother's compound."

The man let the information sink in for a minute. "Your government tried to kill you in Aleppo, the Americans just killed your family…now, we want you to come work for us."

Jamal was silent for a moment before he responded, "Why would I want to work for your organization? I adamantly disagree with your interpretation of Islam and what you are doing." He hoped that the man would not pull out a pistol and kill him.

Instead, the man just snickered before he replied, "It doesn't matter if you believe in our cause or not. We can provide you with the means to avenge the death of your family. If that interests you, then call me when you get out of the hospital and we will talk further about it." He placed a burner phone on the table near his bed, then nodded and walked away.

****

A week had gone by since the man in the suit had given him the burner phone. After settling his brother's estate with the local government and burying his wife, two children and brother, Jamal picked up the phone and called the only number programmed into it. It rang a couple of times, and then a man picked up.

"Yes," he said in a gruff voice.

"This is Jamal. I was given this number to call when I was ready to talk," he said. He wasn't sure if he was talking to the man in the suit or someone else.

"Someone will be in touch with you shortly," the voice responded briskly before abruptly disconnecting the call.

Jamal held the phone in his hand and stared at it for a moment. He was feeling impatient, his desire for vengeance burning within him.

The following day, a man called Jamal back on the burner phone. He picked it up on the second ring. "Hello?" he queried.

Without any pleasantries, the man on the other end replied, "Go to Café Rumist tomorrow at ten o'clock in the morning and order a coffee."

Jamal started to ask a question, but the line was already dead. He sighed. There was nothing left to do but wait.

Another restless night of sleep went by as his mind raced. He speculated what would happen at this meeting.

Am I being set up? he wondered. He kept contemplating whether or not that man would really have the ability to allow him to exact his revenge on those who had killed his family.

Jamal tossed and turned all evening, barely getting any sleep at all. However, the sun eventually rose, and it became time to head toward the café. By 9:50 a.m., Jamal was already seated with a drink and a pastry, trying to appear as normal as possible.

After a couple of minutes, the man in the suit from the hospital walked up from behind and sat down across from

Jamal. "*Asalaam alaikum*," he began. He had a warm and inviting smile, as if greeting a good friend and not someone he had only just met.

"*Alaikum asalaam*," replied Jamal as he took a sip of his coffee.

Smiling, the man declared, "I am pleased that you contacted me." He waved off the waiter, who had walked toward their table. "Now that you have settled your brother's affairs and buried your family, it is time for you to have your revenge. Are you ready?" he asked.

Jamal simply nodded his head, never breaking eye contact.

The man smiled. "Good. We have a plan for you. We want you to apply for political asylum in America. The Syrian government made a deliberate attempt to kill you and your family because you spoke up against the regime, and this has been well documented—"

Jamal interrupted, "—The Americans killed my family. Why would I want to apply for political asylum with them?" He clenched his fists in anger as he spoke.

Without missing a beat, the man replied, "Because the mission we have for you is *in* America. You possess a special skill set, one that we could use there more than we can here."

Pulling a folder out of his briefcase, he handed it to Jamal. "Inside the package, you will find a business card for Sheikh Ibrahim Eliamam. He is the imam at the Chicago Metro Islamic Center. He is also the doctor who runs the local medical clinic there. Make contact with him. He will know to expect you."

The still-unnamed man continued, "Once you are there, get settled into Chicago. Find a nondescript job and do not stand out or get in trouble with the police. Keep to yourself. Sheikh Ibrahim will introduce you to the other members of your team when and if he needs to." The Saudi spoke as if he was explaining to a new employee what his job duties were going to be.

Sitting back in his chair, then taking a sip of his coffee, Jamal asked, "What exactly do you want me to do?"

The man in the suit just smiled. "We want you to use your skills in chemistry. You will create a wide range of explosive devices for various uses."

Jamal's face betrayed his concern at this suggestion.

"Don't worry, my friend. Others will use what you have created, so you will not be at risk. You just need to produce the devices when asked. Of course, when you create these devices, you must be sure that you do not leave behind any evidence, such as fingerprints or traces of DNA. The Americans are very good at finding any errant remnants.

"The Americans have been waging war against the lands of Islam for nearly thirty years. They have killed millions of our people with impunity. That is about to change. You are one of the last pieces of the puzzle that will allow us to bring the fight to their lands; you will probably be the most important person in this effort. We don't ask you to be a part of our mission lightly. Now that you have committed yourself, we will do our best to protect you and help you succeed."

The two men talked for a couple of hours about how they would communicate. They would use a couple of specific chatrooms on the dark web ISIS had found and used as a cover. The man talked briefly about the dark web and how to access it using Tor and Privoxy, so his IP address could not be tracked. The man brought out his laptop and walked him through the process. It seemed simple enough. Though Jamal wasn't very tech savvy, he knew what Tor was and how an onion router worked. He felt comfortable being able to navigate inside the dark web to the areas he needed to. He could always watch YouTube if he had questions.

After several hours, the two men walked to the nearby mosque for afternoon prayer and then parted ways, never to meet in person again.

Chapter 3
The Good Doctor?

Chicago, Illinois

Sheikh Ibrahim Eliamam had immigrated to the US in the late 1980s after fighting in Afghanistan as one of the Mujahedeen that the CIA had trained. He was one of many Saudi Muslims who had traveled to Pakistan to attack the Soviets for the Americans. In return, he had been rewarded with a green card and a pathway to citizenship.

Prior to volunteering to be a Mujahedeen, Ibrahim had gone to King Saud University and been educated as a doctor. He had used his medical training to provide medical services to the Mujahedeen and the local villages they protected. When he arrived in America, he settled in Chicago and went to work at the University of Chicago Medicine as an ER doctor. His experience working as a clinician in a war zone was highly valued since he had enormous experience in combat trauma injuries. Ibrahim also taught several medical courses on gunshot trauma and other battlefield injuries at the teaching hospital.

Ibrahim quickly made a name for himself as one of the best trauma doctors in the city, and his courses at the university were among the most sought after. Ibrahim was not an overtly pious Muslim, though he did actively practice his faith, and he routinely volunteered his limited time at free clinics that served the Muslim community of Chicago.

It was not until the September 11, 2001 attacks that he became more heavily involved in the Islamic community. When it was announced that Osama bin Laden's Al Qaeda organization was responsible for the attacks, he flashed back to a training camp that he had attended in Afghanistan where he had heard bin Laden teach; the memory had remained dormant until Ibrahim had seen his face again on the news.

Following that day of days, he noticed that his colleagues at the hospital viewed him differently, and so did his patients. Despite having assimilated into his adopted home and speaking fluent English, he suddenly felt like an outsider. Everyone looked at him suspiciously, even though he had gone through the hard work of obtaining dual citizenship with the United States and probably knew more about the country's history than most of them did.

One day, while he was attending to a patient at the hospital, he was approached by several FBI agents. They barged into the treatment room of the ER while he was stitching up a patient and barked, "Ibrahim Eliamam, you are under arrest! Step away from the patient!"

He stood there for a second, stunned, not sure if this was some sort of dream. As he came to his senses, he managed to ask, "What are the charges?"

The FBI agent, who was wearing dark sunglasses indoors, pulled out a warrant and announced in an unnecessarily loud voice, "You are under arrest for suspected ties to Al Qaeda!"

Everyone around Ibrahim stood there shocked. Then worry and panic set in. They were all concerned that they might have had a terrorist living and working amongst them all this time. The agents turned him around and cuffed him in a not-very-delicate manner. They marched him out of the ER in front of his fellow colleagues and patients as if they had just arrested Osama bin Laden himself. He saw the looks of shock, anger, and fear on the faces of his peers. One of the nurses that he used to have coffee with spat on him as he walked past her.

Fortunately, Ibrahim was a highly-paid doctor, so he had the financial means to hire a high-powered lawyer, and that was exactly what he did. His attorney wasn't happy that his client had been interrogated for nearly forty-eight hours straight before he was allowed to contact his legal counsel, and he came in with guns blazing, threatening a lawsuit from the ACLU.

After being held for nearly three days in FBI custody, Ibrahim was released, with no charges filed. His lawyer brought him to a café to get some food into his system. Ibrahim didn't wait until they were in a more private place to talk. "What in the world do they have on me?" he probed in between ravenous bites of scrambled eggs.

"Well, the FBI already knew that you had fought with the Mujahedeen in Afghanistan, but they recently learned that you had attended a training camp run by bin Laden. They have no evidence linking you to Al Qaeda, other than being at the same place as the world's most wanted terrorist fifteen years ago…Ibrahim, you need to keep a low profile. Don't do anything to attract additional attention. I would also recommend that you keep my law firm on retainer, in case you need us again."

Unfortunately for Ibrahim, when the FBI had arrested him, they had made a big deal about it at his place of work. Someone at the hospital had also tipped off the *Chicago Tribune*, which had run a story about the FBI detaining a local ER doctor for allegedly having ties to Al Qaeda. An unnamed source at the FBI had leaked that Ibrahim had attended a Mujahedeen training camp run by bin Laden in Afghanistan in the mid-1980s. Most Americans didn't know the difference between the Mujahedeen fighters, who had fought against the Soviet Union, and Al Qaeda, so this was devastating to his reputation.

When Ibrahim went back to the hospital the next day after being released from the FBI, he was stopped by a security guard. "You are not allowed on the property, Sir," he was told.

The following day, he was asked to report to Human Resources. He met with his boss, several people from HR, and the hospital lawyer. He explained to them, "This was just a mix-up. I am not a member of Al Qaeda. The FBI made a mistake. They didn't charge me with any crime. Why else would they release me?"

The damage, however, had been done, and there was no undoing it. One of the HR staff announced, "You are being terminated for failure to show up to work for three consecutive days."

"But, Sir," Ibrahim protested, "that was the amount of time I was held by the FBI without charges."

It didn't matter. He wasn't getting out of that room with his job still intact.

As they walked out, his supervisor pulled him aside and told him privately, "I'm sorry, Ibrahim. Several of the nurses and doctors expressed concerns about working with you.

They don't feel safe, even if you weren't charged by the FBI."

Ibrahim said nothing in response. Instead, he filed a wrongful termination and discrimination suit against the hospital. The matter was settled quietly out of court for ten million dollars.

Afterwards, Ibrahim tried to get hired at nearly a dozen hospitals. Each time, his arrest was discovered during a routine background check and he was passed over. Then the Americans invaded Iraq, and Islamophobia was at its height. He began to spend more time at the Chicago Metro Islamic Center, the one place he felt accepted.

Since he could not practice medicine the way he had in a hospital setting, he spoke with the imam and was granted permission to establish a medical clinic for the local Muslim community of Chicago. Ibrahim donated several hundred thousand dollars of his own money to get the clinic up and running. He also wrote a letter to the Saudi consulate in Chicago and asked if his clinic, "Access Clinic," might be eligible for any grant money.

Within a month, Ibrahim had been invited to the consulate to talk with the Consular. The Saudi representative thought his health center was a great idea to help counter the rise of Islamophobia sweeping across America. The Saudi government agreed to provide Ibrahim with ten million dollars to get the clinic up and running and deliver an additional three million dollars a year in funding. With the seed money and support from the imam and the center, Ibrahim moved forward with establishing the only Islamic medical clinic in the city of Chicago.

****

Ibrahim had focused his talents on treating his patients and building trust within the community, particularly the low-income ghettos of Chicago. He sponsored several other Muslim doctors from the Middle East to work at his clinic as it grew in size and popularity within the community. His free walk-in clinic hours on Mondays and Fridays were a big success in a city where the cost to see a doctor was often outside the financial reach of many. He was happy to be making a difference in people's lives.

Life was moving on, and he was felt he was returning to some sort of normal, at least until the 2003 invasion of Iraq. Like many Muslims, Ibrahim was skeptical about the Americans' intentions. Then, when the news stories came out about what the American soldiers had done to Iraqi prisoners at Abu Ghraib, Ibrahim became more politically involved. He began to listen to more radical imams' teachings online, and made several pilgrimages to the Haj, where he resolved to dedicate his life to the advancement of Islam, even if that meant through jihad. It was during one of his yearly visits that he was invited to meet with one of the lower-level princes in the Saudi royal family.

Ibrahim had been a bit bewildered that he had attracted the attention of royalty, but he was very grateful for the invitation. When he arrived, he was overwhelmed by the utter opulence of his surroundings.

And this is supposed to be one of the princes lower down on the totem pole? he marveled.

The prince extended his hand immediately in welcome. "It's very good to meet you in person, Ibrahim," the mysterious man announced. "I've heard of the great work that you are doing in Chicago. You have become a pillar of the community, even providing free medical services to poor and struggling Muslims."

"Thank you, Your Royal Highness," Ibrahim responded. "The honor is all mine, however."

The prince asked, "Ibrahim, hypothetically, if a person had been wounded while waging jihad, would you provide the man medical treatment, or turn him in to the police?"

Ibrahim replied, "I am a doctor, and I would follow the Hippocratic Oath. I would not turn him into the police."

This answer satisfied the young prince, who said, "The Saudi government may, from time to time, send a patient to America to receive medical treatment. We will direct the individual to your clinic to be treated by you."

Ibrahim nodded in agreement. The prince continued, "Once the patients recover, we will have them request asylum based on their converting to Christianity while in America. Each one will need to claim that if he returned to Saudi Arabia, he would be killed."

Ibrahim looked confused, as if he were about to ask a question. The prince signaled for him to wait. Leaning in closer, the prince continued, "We're going to begin to place sleeper cells in the US. Your clinic will be the conduit. We want you to be the leader for the American Midwest region." He slowly sat back in his chair to gauge Ibrahim's response.

At first, Ibrahim didn't know if he was being tricked into agreeing to work with Islamic extremists, or if he was being offered the opportunity he so longed for—the chance to strike at the American infidels, the same infidels that had taken away his livelihood with false allegations—the same brutes that had tortured his fellow Muslims and carried out indiscriminate drone strikes.

Could this Saudi royal really be working with Al Qaeda? he wondered.

No one said anything for a couple of minutes. Finally, Ibrahim nodded in agreement. The prince smiled and clasped his hands together with Ibrahim's as he leaned forward. "I am excited to be working with you, Ibrahim. Your imam, Imam Abdullah, said you would be a great warrior for Allah. From time to time, you will be asked to attend meetings at the Saudi embassy. It will be at those meetings that I, personally, will brief you on any missions you may receive. In the meantime, you will continue with your work, and we will continue to fund your clinic."

The following day, Ibrahim flew back to Chicago a changed man—a man with a new purpose and mission, a new jihad.

Over the following three years, nearly two dozen children and their families were flown to Chicago and treated at his clinic. Eighteen of the nineteen families were successful in obtaining religious or political asylum and began their new lives undercover in America.

Chapter 4

The Knights Meet

Dubai, United Arab Emirates
Burj Al Arab Jumeirah Hotel

There was a sandstorm forming off in the horizon. Maktoum bin Rashid observed the coming tempest from the floor-to-ceiling panoramic glass window of his presidential suite. At $37,000 a night, this seven-star hotel had amazing views of Dubai from any vantage point. Maktoum bin Rashid, also known as Sheikh Maktoum, was meeting a close friend of his to discuss some business opportunities and push him to move forward with what was perhaps their most radical agenda to date. The war on terrorism had made their group incredibly wealthy, but the Islamic State had given them something unique, an opportunity to bring the Islamic war to the streets of Europe and America.

He heard the beep of the electronic card entry for the room and turned around. As expected, his long-time friend, Prince Nawaf bin Abdullah, came around the other side of the door. He greeted Maktoum warmly with a hug and a kiss to each cheek. "Sheikh Maktoum, *Asalaam Alaikum*," he said.

"*Alaikum asalaam*, my friend," Maktoum replied, motioning for his friend to sit down.

The two comrades talked socially for a short while before getting down to business. When it was time to change the conversation, Maktoum began, "The situation in Syria presents an opportunity for us, Nawaf. As the violence of the Islamic State continues to get worse, more and more refugees are going to start fleeing the country."

Prince Nawaf nodded. "Yes, but that creates a potential problem for all of us as well."

"I agree, but just look for the bright side," Maktoum replied. "When we founded our clandestine organization, we agreed we would do whatever was necessary to spread Islam across the world and to make it the dominant religion. We've funded tens of thousands of madrasas across the world and made hundreds of millions of dollars in political donations around the world. The refugee crisis that continues to get worse in Syria gives us the opportunity to relocate millions of devoted Muslims to Europe and America. It also gives us the perfect cover to infiltrate hundreds if not thousands of Mujahedeen into the West." Maktoum spoke as if he was talking about a corporate merger.

Prince Nawaf's eyes drifted briefly toward the window. A wall of sand moved ever closer to the city. "You always did have a head for these things, Maktoum. However, I caution you about being overly zealous." He motioned toward the windowpane. "You see that sandstorm?"

Maktoum nodded.

Prince bin Abdullah continued, "That storm is like us. We need to move slowly and steadily, like an unstoppable force that will slowly envelop everything it encounters. Islam is already the dominant religion in the world. Through our proxy, the Center for Advancing Global Islamic Relations, and the political donations we continue to make to the American and European political parties, it won't be long until we envelop the West."

"I concur, but now is the time to make our move," Sheikh Maktoum countered. "We have a receptive American president who will not openly challenge us, and a willing proxy that can be manipulated into doing our bidding. What I need your help with is identifying an intermediary who can be the go-between for the Knights, ISIS, and our various contacts in Europe and America. Someone who has exceptional intelligence training, a person who can be trusted."

The prince furrowed his brow. "What do you want the end state of this next venture to be? I mean, aside from further enriching the Knights."

"What we have all agreed upon—to further the spread of Islam through any means necessary," Maktoum responded. He finished off the brandy in his glass and began to pour himself another one. Neither of them were strict Salafist Muslims; they took full advantage of the philosophy that they had been taught, that the Quran allowed them to drink alcohol or do whatever else was necessary to fit in with their enemies.

"If you want my help on this, then I need more details. Be specific," Nawaf said, reaching for his own glass of brandy.

Maktoum pulled out a folder and began to organize several pieces of paper. He had listed primary objectives, secondary objectives, and a separate column with the types of companies and investment instruments they should finance.

"Stage one: escalate the destabilization of Syria, Libya and the rest of North Africa. This will cause massive waves of refugees to flood into Europe. Our psychological operations group will develop a media campaign that will focus on the human suffering of the refugees. A comprehensive media effort to expose the travesties of the humanitarian crisis will be pushed throughout every group and affiliate we have in Europe and America."

Maktoum pulled out another paper with a map on it before he continued, "The challenge with getting the refugees to America is geography. Our plan to overcome this is twofold. The first is that, in Canada, we're going to make a push for them to establish a refugee program. A similar platform will be driven forward in America via CAGIR. These refugee programs will be our conduit for moving the ISIS fighters into America. Of course, they must be under strict orders to keep a low profile and stay under the radar until they're activated."

The prince responded, "OK, so America will take time. I agree that that's the best approach. What about Europe? What are the plans for them?"

"Europe is easier—we already have a strong presence there. With the influx of refugees, our people are going to start using the cover of this mass migration crisis to stir up antirefugee and, more importantly, anti-Islamic sentiment. We'll start small at first and then begin to initiate actual terrorist attacks. By the time the strikes start to take place, millions of refugees will have already made their way into the EU. When the EU governments begin to realize that they have a terrorist problem, I will ensure that our partners at the UN put forward a strong resolution to condemn them over their anti-Muslim attitudes. We'll begin to hold demonstrations and rallies all across Europe."

Nawaf laughed and then reaching for his own glass of brandy. "You are devious, my friend—truly a mastermind."

Smiling and shrugging off the compliment, Maktoum responded, "I'm merely the money man. I create long-term opportunities for us to make substantial profits, which we in turn reinvest into the spread of Islam." He paused for a moment as he rearranged his folder, and then changed the topic. "Nawaf, do you know how the Chinese defeated the Mongol empire?"

"No, but I'm sure you are about to tell me," Prince bin Abdullah smirked.

"Through assimilation," Maktoum explained. "The Chinese couldn't beat the Mongols militarily, just as us Muslims can't beat the West strictly through brute force. What the Chinese did was intermarry into their culture, integrating their culture and customs into their education system and government. It took multiple generations, but one day, the Mongols were no longer Mongols; they were Chinese. That is how we are going to beat the West. The refugee crisis in the Middle East and North Africa is going to be our means of accomplishing this mission."

Nawaf stroked his beard in thought. "Tell me more about the plan."

Maktoum pulled out a map of the US that had several cities circled on it. "Once we have our people in place, we will awaken our sleeper cells. Prior to each attack they carry out, strategic investments will be made that'll enable us to capitalize on that event. The first wave of assaults will take place in Chicago. That's how we'll initiate the intensified culture war between Islam and the West in America. I anticipate this phase of our plan will last about six months. We'll leverage ISIS to turn Chicago into a war zone, and while that's happening, we'll make a fortune shorting the impacted segments of the US market."

"How are we going to keep the suspicion away from our group as we start to post substantial profits?" asked Prince Nawaf.

Pulling out a separate paper with a list of companies, Sheikh Maktoum replied, "I have dozens of shell companies established in various offshore locations. Each has a substantial amount of cash already available on their balance sheets. Prior to the attacks, those entities will make the shorts and stock purchases. Once the profits have been made, they will sell off their positions and then transfer the cash into Bitcoin. The Bitcoin will then move to other offshore investment companies. We'll repeat the process over and over. Using Bitcoin and then closing the shell companies after they have made their transfers will not only cover our tracks; it will make it virtually impossible for anyone else to be able to connect the dots. Bitcoin is impossible to track and will provide us the anonymity we seek."

Maktoum spent some time walking Nawaf through how Bitcoin worked and how they could leverage the dark net as a means of moving money from one company to another, bypassing the traditional banking system.

With one corner of his mouth turned up in a mischievous smile, the prince replied, "Maktoum, Maktoum…ever the strategist. I like the idea, but it sounds complicated. We are also going to need to establish a few new layers of intermediaries between us, the shell companies, and ISIS. We can use ISIS as our proxy for this, but we will need multiple levels of go-betweens to ensure our plan can never be traced back to us or the kingdoms of Saudi Arabia and the UAE." He paused for a moment, thinking, then declared, "I have an operative we can use. I've used him for some complicated missions in the past."

"Can he be trusted with something like this?" asked Maktoum, a bit unsure.

A broad smile swept across Prince Nawaf's face. "Yes, he can be depended upon. He was the man our government used to place those WMDs in Iraq in 2002 as a false flag. Through that ruse, we managed to fool that idiot Ahmed Chalabi into believing that Saddam had an active and flourishing WMD program, and he in turn made a very strong case to the West."

Sheikh Maktoum chuckled as he lit a cigarette. "That was probably our greatest coup ever, getting theWestern intelligence agencies to believe that gullible fool. To think all we had to do was place some stolen chemical warheads in an abandoned military base, and they fell for it." He took a long drag off his cigarette. "It'll be just like 9/11, my friend. We'll make a fortune, and the Islamic cause will be furthered."

The two of them talked for several more hours as they began to establish their plan of action. This next initiative would probably last ten years or more. It was a high-risk proposition but would yield an incredibly great reward if they were successful.

They ordered room service and continued their conversation. After they had finished their meal, they concluded their meeting, agreeing that they would need to bring in the others and obtain a consensus before they moved forward.

****

Throughout history, the world has been rife with secret organizations and cabals vying for control. Over time, many learned about the Freemasons, the Illuminati, and the Rothschilds' New World Order, but few knew about the Knights of Islam. They were the modern Islamic version of the Illuminati, bent not on military or financial domination but rather religious domination. Their end goal was to see Islam as the religion of the world, eventually eliminating all others.

In the early 1980s, Sheikh Maktoum had formed this secret society. The members of the group were carefully selected and only admitted once they had completed a comprehensive background check and been sworn to secrecy on threat of death. Sheikh Maktoum and his four closest friends tightly controlled the leadership of the organization, and they were all members of either the Saudi or United Arab Emirates royal families. They were men of great wealth, with significant connections and influence in the Middle East.

These five men had developed their friendships during their teen years while at boarding school in Switzerland. They had continued those connections as they went their separate ways to attend various universities. Several years after completing his education, Maktoum formally established the clandestine organization as a private equity and investment firm, with the secret aim of promoting Wahhabi Islam within Europe and America.

When Maktoum's younger brother, Khalil bin Rashid, graduated from Harvard in 1985, he went to work for Goldman Sachs. Since Khalil was a member of the UAE's royal family, Goldman Sachs wanted to curry favor with their father, Sheikh Rashid bin Saeed, a managing partner of the UAE's sovereign wealth fund. Khalil was moved up quickly and began to work in the mergers and acquisitions or M & A group within Goldman.

This position gave him insider access to the M & A deals Goldman was working on, and familiarity with the fine inner workings of the companies who were pursuing mergers. Despite the penalty for sharing insider information, Khalil routinely divulged his knowledge to his father, who would have the UAE wealth fund immediately invest in the best companies. His brother Maktoum, who had started Gulf States International or GSI, would also get in on the action.

In exchange for looking the other way as to what Khalil was doing, Goldman was privy to opportunities within the UAE and Saudi Arabia, which were booming with infrastructure and construction projects. The UAE and Saudi Arabia also held a large portion of the nation's sovereign wealth fund with Goldman Sachs, making them one of the largest investors in the bank.

For nearly twenty years, this proved to be a very fruitful relationship for all parties. Goldman Sachs made a fortune investing in the Middle East, and the UAE sovereign wealth fund became one of the largest private funds in the world. The UAE was also one of Goldman's largest clients. Maktoum's GSI also garnered an enormous amount of wealth, and with wealth came power.

The Knights of Islam met quarterly to discuss the direction of the GSI and their organization. They were always looking for ways to integrate Islam into Western democracies and influence legislation wherever possible. As GSI's investment fund grew, largely based on insider information, they also began to invest heavily in education, believing that the schooling system was the best way to influence future generations. Their investments largely centered around the Middle East, North Africa and Europe. Through various Islamic charity organizations, they helped to establish thousands of Islamic centers across Europe and slowly in the United States. This was their way of spreading Islam, through peace and education—at least until the 1991 Persian Gulf War.

Following that conflict, Sheikh Maktoum and the leadership of the Knights agreed that Saudi Arabia should have relied on the Mujahedeen to defend the kingdom, not the godless Americans. This was a sentiment widely held by those living in the Gulf States, who now saw the Americans establishing permanent bases in their countries, bringing their immoral culture, religion and influence on the youth of their nations. Yet they tolerated the Americans because they also provided a bulwark against what they saw as a defiant Persian government, one that was actively working against the Sunni governments of the Middle East.

It was during a seminal moment at one of their annual leadership meetings that the direction of the organization forever changed. In 1992, they were joined by a relatively unknown but charismatic Saudi cleric, a man named Osama bin Laden.

"I was trained by the American CIA during the 1980s to be a Mujahedeen fighter in Afghanistan when the Soviet Union invaded," Osama began. "Now I have used those skills to form a new organization named Al Qaeda. I have been blessed by Allah with a large and active network of former Mujahedeen fighters, all of whom can be relied upon to defend Islam."

Sheikh Maktoum was intrigued but unsure of the greater picture. "How do you see our organization partnering with you?" he inquired.

Bin Laden replied, "Well, since you ask, I need money to accomplish our goals. I also need a means to move money from one location to another without the West—particularly the Americans—tracking the movement of the funds."

The men discussed the situation at length and eventually agreed that GSI would provide some funding and facilitate the creation of various front companies to hide the movement of money. However, they agreed that a go-between would be necessary, and that GSI and the Knights of Islam should never meet directly with Osama bin Laden again.

Prince Nawaf bin Abdullah was a rising star in the Al-Mabahith Al-'Amma, the Saudi version of the American FBI and CIA. He arranged for a spy within the Al-Mabahith Al-'Amma to act as their official go-between. While Sheikh Maktoum and the other leaders of the Knights agreed that they couldn't *publicly* support this new organization, they would invest in them financially, just like they would any other business. From that point forward, they became a secret financial backer of Al Qaeda and its many affiliates.

As the Knights of Islam began to look for ways to leverage their wealth to advance Islam around the globe, they also sought to increase their influence in America and Europe. They learned to use Western laws to help support their cause. In the early '90s, the group financed the creation of the Center for Advancing Global Islamic Relations or CAGIR, which officially opened for operations in 1994. They also acquired several other organizations in the US and Europe and began to use those entities to make substantial political donations to candidates who would push their agenda. Over the next six years, CAGIR and their other proxies began to donate tens of millions of dollars in the US to both Republican and Democratic candidates, who in turn pushed for laws and agendas that benefited Islam and their corporate positions.

Then, in 1999, as Osama bin Laden's plot to destroy the World Trade Center in America took shape, Sheikh Maktoum began to move money into specific defense stocks and antiterrorism technologies. Knowing that an impending attack was going to happen, they were able to position nearly $6.3 billion to capitalize on what they knew would surely be a shock to the markets.

When the attacks on September 11, 2001, happened, GSI had shorted all the airline stocks, generating a 5300% profit and turning sixty million dollars into over $3,250,000,000 overnight. GSI was now flush with cash, which they used to purchase defense stocks and other staple stocks that would generate long-term cash flow. Their investment in Al Qaeda would eventually lead them to turn a seven-billion-dollar investment firm into a portfolio of nearly twenty billion dollars, all in the short span of five years.

Chapter 5

New Boss, New Mission

McClean, Virginia
Central Intelligence Agency

Following his successful posting in Turkey, Michael Stone was recalled to Langley. He'd spent the last five years living abroad, and his mentor and supervisor felt it was time for him to fulfill his obligatory tour at the flagpole. He'd spent the last six years hunting down terrorists as a paramilitary operations officer, and he'd loved every minute of it. However, his mentor and supervisor, Trevor Cole, saw something in him—a bright future in senior management.

Trevor was ambitious to become the next director of the CIA, but in order to get there, he'd have to build out his own trusted cadre within the leadership. He had made it a mission to find and groom exceptional operators and then position them to advance through the ranks of the Agency to help transform it from within.

Trevor needed people who had immense operational experience in the field if they were going to replace the bureaucratic deadweight of the seventh floor, but Mike would never be considered for those positions if he didn't agree to some stateside assignments at headquarters or at least an interagency posting. His successes in the field would only get him so far. Now he needed to learn how to network his way into the more powerful positions where his expertise could truly be leveraged for the good of the Agency.

As he began his reintegration to life in the United States, Mike quickly found that he was a virtual stranger to his own country and to the normality of American life. The thought of going to work at a nine-to-five job and then hitting up the gym and the grocery store over and over was a bit overwhelming for him after an action-packed adrenaline-filled schedule that was never the same from day-to-day.

To try and compensate for what he knew was going to be a rough transition, Mike and his mentor decided it would be best for him to take a month off when he got back to the States. He wanted to travel across the country, see old friends, and spend some time with family, something he had neglected while living abroad. That connection to other human beings was just what he needed to reset mentally for his next assignment.

Despite the good that his time with family and friends did for his soul, the slowing of pace made Mike acutely aware of the giant hole that still lurked in his life. During his time in Turkey and elsewhere in the Middle East, he hadn't had the time to really develop any romantic relationships—his emotions were still a little raw from the loss of his daughter and his subsequent divorce. Despite both tragedies having taken place more than a decade earlier, he had never emotionally recovered the simultaneous losses. Instead, he poured everything he had into his work and allowed it to fully consume him.

****

Once he'd returned to D.C., it was time for Mike to meet with Trevor at Langley to talk over his next assignment. On the way to his 0900 meeting, he stopped at Starbucks to make sure he was properly caffeinated. Ever since their first mission in South America, Trevor had taken a liking to him. Trevor's son had been a part of the Army Ranger unit that had been stationed in Mogadishu, Somalia, during what has commonly been referred to as the "Blackhawk Down" mission, and he had died that fateful day. For some odd reason, Mike reminded him of his son as he had also come to the Agency from a Special Forces background.

Approaching Trevor's door, Mike knocked twice on the frame, announcing his presence.

His boss's face lit up with a smile when he saw him. "Come on in, Mike," he beckoned, waving him to a chair. "It's good to see you. How'd the time off go?"

"Well, you were right," Mike began. "I needed the time to unwind. It was nice to see my parents. I should've tried to see them more these past few years. My dad has really aged—I guess it kind of caught me off guard. You know, you always believe that they'll be there, when in reality, none of us really know how long we have."

Trevor nodded. "That's true, Mike. I'm glad you were able to spend some time with your parents," he said. Pausing for a second, Trevor pulled a bronze coin out of his pocket and held it up. "How are you holding out in regard to this?"

Mike snorted at the question and shook his head. In addition to being his supervisor, Trevor was also his AA sponsor. The sight of his twenty-year sobriety coin brought back a flood of memories.

A couple years after joining the Agency, Mike had been out on a mission and out of contact with his family when his daughter had suddenly become very ill. Her bone marrow had shut down, and she had been in desperate need of a transplant. Unfortunately, his wife and other family members were not a match, and her aplastic anemia had been so advanced that without a donor, she'd died before Mike had even returned from his mission. His wife had been torn with grief and hadn't been shy about blaming Mike for not being there. She always wondered if their daughter would have survived if he had been home. Maybe he would have been a match.

After the tragic loss of his daughter, Mike blamed himself and quickly became a functional alcoholic to cope with the pain. That was the last straw for his ex-wife, who split up with him shortly afterwards.

Despite the dissolution of his marriage, Mike had managed to hide his dirty secret at work until one day when he and Trevor were on assignment together in South America. The timeframe that he and Trevor were supposed to meet up with an asset got moved up by fifteen hours, and when Trevor saw him, he quickly ascertained that while he wasn't outright drunk, he was definitely buzzed.

The following day, Trevor sat him down. "Look, I'm going to give you two choices," he'd said. "Either join AA and I'll be your sponsor, or I'll see to it that you never finish your probation period with the Agency."

Mike hadn't said anything at first. He was a bit stunned to be called out, and shocked that Trevor was a part of AA.

"Mike, I see what you're going through. After my son died, I took it pretty hard too. I also turned to the drink, and it nearly cost me my own career. A man I respected gave me the same option—join AA or he'd make sure I washed out. It saved my life. I'd like to think you're worth saving, too."

Mike recognized that he needed help, and despite any misgivings he'd had, he'd joined the program and worked the steps. It had been a long journey.

Mike sighed as he finished his daydream of memories. "I'm still sober, if that's what you're asking, Trevor. It's been tough, and man do I crave it at times, but I've stayed on the path. Not a single drink since I started the program. Scout's honor," he added, holding up two fingers with a grin on his face.

Trevor snickered. "I can see you've picked up smoking instead," he retorted.

"Come on, Trevor. You can't expect me to give up one vice without picking up another. Besides, it's my coping mechanism. When I feel the urge to drink, I reach for a cigarette instead. It's kept me from breaking sobriety on many occasions, and it still allows me to hang out with the teams."

"Fair enough," Trevor replied. "Speaking of the teams—you think you're going to be able to handle a job that doesn't directly involve killing people? If you can't, I need to know. This is a red-hot position I've managed to get you, but I can't have you screwing it up for me. I'm putting my neck on the line to get you this position," Trevor said. He leaned forward, his eyes narrowing.

Sensing the change in tenor, Mike didn't hesitate. "I'm ready for this. The fieldwork has been the most thrilling thing I've done since I left the Unit, but I'm ready to start looking at the long-term picture. As you've said, we need more field officers and less bureaucrats on the seventh floor. I'm just glad you think I have that kind of potential."

Trevor seemed pleased with that answer. "Look, this next assignment I have for you is a tricky one. It's a multifold opportunity. First, it's a deputy director position with an interagency partner, so it's a true joint billet. It'll get you noticed and allow you to do some good networking. Second, I don't trust the current director or the program and neither do a lot of people on the seventh floor, so we want you to be our eyes and ears. You think you can handle that?"

Mike raised an eyebrow. "So, a mission inside a mission, eh? What's the job and what agency?" he asked.

"Oh, you're going to love this," Trevor said with a smile as he handed him a folder with his new assignment. "I'm sending you to the National Counterterrorism Center to take over as the new deputy director of the floundering Immigration and Refugee Vetting Division. You'll have a week to get prepped and do your research before you report to the NCTC. They know you're coming, but they have no idea you'll be spying on them.

"As far as your new boss is concerned, you're going to be the Agency's liaison officer and fill in as her new deputy while you do your obligatory interagency posting, so you can get your next promotion. While the director will know what agency you work for, everyone else will be told you're transferring over from Homeland Security. Technically, we're not allowed to operate on US soil. However, since this group you'll be working with only deals with foreign nationals, you're still technically operating within our charter," Trevor explained.

There was a pause for a moment as Mike read through some of the initial information in the packet. He wasn't exactly sure how to take this news. This was definitely going to be outside his wheelhouse. On the one hand, this was a very important position. The NCTC had been developed in August of 2004 by then-president George W. Bush and was created to be a truly joint counterterrorism center that integrated members from nearly every government and intelligence agency under one roof. They reported directly to the Director of National Intelligence and to the President. Over the years, the NCTC had developed into the lead agency: assessing, preventing, and countering terrorist threats against the nation. The division that he would be working in had the crucial task of screening every visitor that entered the United States to ensure that no one posed a security risk to the nation. On the other hand, despite the significance of the responsibility, Michael pictured himself chained to a desk with mounds of paperwork strewn in front of him. It was not his ideal position, considering he'd spent most of his adult life as an operator.

"Trevor," he began cautiously, "you know that I'm a team player and I will do whatever needs to be done, but are you sure this is where you want me? Sounds like a journey down bureaucratic red tape lane."

Trevor chuckled. "I figured you might say something like that. Look, you are a true spy. You've spent twelve out of the last fourteen years abroad, obtaining as much operational and field experience as possible. I know you'd rather be running a task force or be a station chief, but if you want to be promoted, this is what needs to happen."

Stone held up his hands in mock surrender. "I get it. I need to learn the bureaucratic side of the business better. But what specifically do you want me to look for? You obviously want me there for a reason, so what is it?"

"To be honest, we're not one hundred percent sure what's going over there. Some folks who are getting greenlighted for entry into the country were previously flagged by us as questionable, yet our recommendations have been overruled on a number of occasions. Something just isn't adding up."

"Hmm…all right," Mike countered. "I'll play active observer for a while and see what's what. Just don't leave me chained to a desk any longer than necessary, OK?"

He and Trevor both grinned. "I wasn't planning on it," Trevor said with a smile.

****

McClean, Virginia
National Counterterrorism Center
Immigration and Refugee Vetting Division

Pulling up to the secured parking garage with his silver Audi S5 coupe, Mike held his ID and credentials out for the security guard to examine. The guard gave them a quick once-over as he pulled a clipboard out to check his name against the roster of authorized personnel.

The man looked up from his list. "You're new, aren't you?"

Mike nodded. "First day, actually."

Smiling, the guard handed him his ID and credentials back. "Welcome to NCTC. Please pull ahead," he said. He waved him through and signaled for the next vehicle behind him to pull forward.

Mike parked and got out. Walking up to the building, Mike had to admit that the outside sure looked a lot nicer than the exterior of the George Bush Center for Intelligence building at Langley. Even the new CIA building didn't look quite this nice from the outside.

Mike walked through the glass turnstile doors and made his way over to the front desk. He showed his ID and credentials again, and the clerk quickly began the process of adding his ID's PKI and RFID code into their system. This would allow him to pass effortlessly through security each day and give him his access to his designated workspaces. With the initial formalities of registration completed, Mike was given a quick description of where his department was located, and off he went.

After getting lost once and being guided to the right location, Mike finally made it to his new home. Scanning the bullpen, he saw dozens of desks laid out in the center of the open-floorplan room, with offices and conference rooms set up along the edges. Looking for a corner office, Mike headed in that direction, assuming his new boss would probably have the largest office with the best view possible.

As he approached the office, he saw the name placard on the outside, which read, "Director Mallory Harper."

Bingo, he thought.

Approaching the open door, Mike knocked on the door frame. At that moment, he saw his boss for the first time. She was a middle-aged woman with striking red hair and piercing green eyes.

Mike had been told that his new boss had been a senior advisor to Senator Diane Feinstein. She had practically run her intelligence committee staff prior to her political appointment to this position. Apparently, Mallory had worked with the intelligence community on behalf of the senator for nearly twelve years, despite having no actual intelligence training or experience. Somehow, she'd managed to pull it off—she *was* extremely bright and well connected.

Mallory looked up from what she was doing and signaled for him to come in and take a seat across from her. She finalized an email and then looked warmly at him and smiled.

"Hello, Mr. Stone, it's a pleasure to meet you," she said. She extended her hand to shake his. "Or would you like me to just call you Michael?"

He shook her hand and said, "I'm equally glad to meet you, Ma'am. Mr. Stone sounds a bit too formal for me—let's stick with Mike." Then he cut right to the chase. "So, how may I be of assistance to your department? What are my objectives?" he asked.

She smiled at his directness. "You are all business, aren't you? I was told that about you." She sat back and then opened a folder that had been on the left side of her desk and began to read from it.

"I've been told by the Director of National Intelligence that you're to be my official CIA liaison officer while you fill in as my deputy. Officially, in this office, you work for Homeland Security as far as anyone else is concerned. Unofficially, you and I and the DNI are the only ones that know who you really work for. Let's try to keep it that way, shall we?" Her tone of voice indicated that she was not entirely thrilled with having a CIA officer assigned as her deputy.

Her gaze returned to the folder in front of her. "Your file has a lot of redacted pages in it, but it says here that you were in the Army for eight years, First Special Forces Battalion, detachment Delta. You separated from the military as a major after being wounded in Afghanistan in early 2002, and then you were recruited by the Agency while attending graduate school at the University of Oxford. You were then placed in the National Clandestine Service. You've had overseas assignments across the Middle East and, most recently, worked on an anti-ISIS task force." As she read, she kept looking up at him, trying to size him up.

She paused. "So, let me be frank, Mike—are you a cowboy?" she asked. "Can I rely on you to carry out my orders, and thus those of the Director and the President, or do I need to keep you on a short leash?" Her voice suddenly had a sternness to it that Mike hadn't expected.

Realizing she might be a bit more of an iron fist than he had first assessed, he immediately played the political game until he learned more about her. "Ma'am, I am an intelligence professional. I implement the strategies and plans given to me by those in charge," he calmly replied, hoping this answer might satisfy her.

It seemed to do the trick. She smiled and responded, "I'm glad to hear that. Your predecessor had a problem following orders, and as you can see, he's no longer here with us."

He shuddered ever so slightly. He didn't want to get on her bad side. He might hate the idea of working an office job at the flagpole, but he certainly didn't want to get persona non grata status from an assignment.

She turned her monitor so they both could see it. "Our department was formed three years ago within the NCTC to work directly on a program that the President and National Senior Advisor trust me to handle. The objective is simple— we're supposed to assess roughly three dozen cities across the country for suitability of the President's new refugee resettlement program. We are also responsible for the intelligence screening and vetting of the refugees that have already passed a preliminary screening from the State Department. It's our job to identify those that pose a risk and weed them out from the rest of the refugees and asylum seekers. This is a major program for the President, and thus it's our department's job to make sure it all goes smoothly.

"On top of all this, we still coordinate with TSA and Homeland to screen all travelers entering the country. So, as you can see, we have a huge mission with a lot of working parts to it, which is why I need a strong deputy who can help me manage this beast."

She sighed before she continued. "What I need from you is for you to work with the local communities and law enforcement in these cities to get them all on board. We've already settled tens of thousands of refugees into many of these cities, but we have some that are doing everything they can to stop us. The governor of Texas, for example, has been an outspoken critic and has railroaded us at every turn. In comparison, we have the mayors of Chicago, Detroit, and San Francisco all offering to take in more refugees." She was clearly annoyed at those who weren't adhering to the President's directive to accept refugees and asylum seekers from the Middle East and the Syrian conflict.

Having just spent the last three years leading the counter-ISIS task force in the Middle East, Mike knew more than most that these refugees and asylum seekers posed a serious security risk if not properly vetted. As Mallory continued to explain the department's mission and what she wanted him to handle, he began to understand why his boss had sent him here. The Agency was concerned that the President or those around him might not fully understand or appreciate the tenacity of America's enemies to use this program as a means of infiltrating the country.

Stone leaned forward, showing that he was paying attention. "What do you want me specifically to do?" he asked, ever the professional. He'd do what he was directed to do to the best of his ability, regardless of his own opinions.

Mallory seemed excited that he appeared eager to help. She explained, "I want you to travel to Detroit, Chicago, and San Francisco. Meet with the mayors' offices there, and the local police and FBI offices. Find out what's working in those cities with the refugee program and see if maybe we can replicate their process elsewhere.

"Then I want you to try to convince the governor of Texas and the other officials that are not playing ball to get with the program. Remind them that this is a presidential directive and they must comply. Take anyone from the office you would like with you, but I'd like a report by the end of the month on what's working and what's not, and recommendations to get the rest of these other cities to comply. Starting in January, we're going to accelerate the program, so our office needs to be ready."

Mike interrupted, "—You said accelerate the program. Can you elaborate?"

Mallory scowled. "I was still speaking, Mike. Please don't interrupt me. To answer your question—starting in January, we're going to move from accepting three thousand refugees and asylum seekers a month to accepting twelve thousand. I need to know where we can send most of them without having a negative impact on public safety."

Mike waited a second to make sure he didn't interrupt again, then he asked, "Perhaps I'm missing something. Why is the NCTC involved in this type of resettlement work? This is clearly a State Department or Homeland Security mission. If anything, we should be monitoring these individuals who are being resettled here."

Appearing slightly annoyed at the question, Mallory replied, "NCTC is involved because we're the ones doing the intelligence vetting for the State Department, not the FBI. We're also certifying that these individuals don't pose a threat and doing what we can to assist the cities and local law enforcement in taking these people in. This is also why your official cover is with Homeland Security. You're our Homeland Security special agent officially assigned to be my deputy and help institute and streamline this initiative."

They talked for another hour about the program's objectives, and more specifically, what she wanted him to do. She said there were several people in her department that were against the initiative. She explained that they would routinely flag large numbers of people as dangerous, compared to those who were on board with the program. She wanted to know why these individuals seemed to be bent on flagging far more individuals than those who were supportive of the plan and see if there was some sort of bias going on. Mike told her that he would look into it and see if they were being flagged for legitimate reasons, or if there was something more at play.

Chapter 6
The Windy City

Chicago, Illinois
Mayor's Office

Alexander Grant had been the mayor of Chicago for the past five years. He had been a close friend of the President and had helped to engineer his decisive win in 2008. The Commander-in-Chief had personally helped him with the mayoral race in 2010, so he owed him a debt of gratitude. One of the favors the President had called in was helping his administration with the resettling of refugees from Syria and the Middle East. Chicago, like other major cities in the country, was doing their part to help relocate the people of this war-torn region, offering them a new start—a chance at a better life for them and their families. Of course, there were those who fought this program tooth and nail, saying they were dangerous and could not be properly vetted, but in all reality, the refugees just wanted to escape and look for a better life.

Jorge Montoya, the mayor's senior aide, had walked into Grant's office to place a couple of documents on the mayor's desk, along with the agenda for the refugee resettlement meeting. Mayor Grant walked in just as he was finishing his arrangement of those papers, and asked, "Jorge, are things set for the meeting with the people from D.C.?"

He turned around to look at his boss and responded, "Yes, Mr. Mayor. They should be arriving shortly."

The mayor smiled. Jorge was extremely competent. As an organizational and IT whiz, he almost didn't even need to ask any questions; he could trust that Jorge had it handled. Plus, it didn't hurt anything that he was an openly gay Latino, so that scored him points with the Hispanic and LGBTQ communities as well.

****

The taxicab deftly made his way through the morning rush-hour traffic, weaving through any gaps to steadily move ahead of the nearby competition. Michael Stone and his FBI counterpart, Special Agent Jim Leary, held on for dear life as their driver routinely cut one person off after another. Eventually, the cab screeched to a halt in front of city hall. Mike paid the driver, making sure to get his receipt for the inevitable travel voucher that would have to be filled out at the end of the trip.

Stretching as he unfolded his large frame from the vehicle, Jim looked at Mike with an ashen face. Once he'd closed the door, he muttered, "I hate driving in cabs. I swear they'll be the death of me one of these days."

Mike chuckled. "Yeah, that guy was in a bit of a hurry," he replied. The taxi had already sped off to look for his next fare.

"You ever been to Chicago before, Jim?" asked Mike, changing the topic.

Jim shook his head. "Surprisingly, no. My first assignment out of Quantico was to the New York field office. I spent eight years working white-collar crimes before transferring to the counterterrorism division in D.C. For whatever reason, Chicago was a quiet city when it came to terrorism. How about you?"

"Yeah. I grew up in the area, actually. I still have some cousins that live out in the suburbs," Mike replied. The two of them made their way toward the mayor's office.

Ten minutes later, Mike and Jim walked into Grant's office. Alexander Grant gave them a quick look over as they walked in.

Mike kept himself from chuckling as he surmised the internal conversation of the mayor. *One white guy, average height and build, and a muscular African American, both in their thirties. Definitely CIA.*

Stepping forward, Alexander extended his hand as they approached him. "I'm Alexander Grant. I hope your trip into the city went well," he said good-naturedly. He guided them to the chairs around the table.

"It's good to meet you, Mr. Mayor. I'm Michael Stone, and this is Special Agent Jim Leary. We're from the National Counterterrorism Center's refugee resettlement program office. Director Harper sends her regards," Mike said as he introduced the two of them.

"That's nice of Mallory. How is she doing?" asked the mayor.

"She's doing good. She's very pleased with the help your team has provided."

"Mallory and I worked together during the President's first term, back when she was still with Feinstein's office. Good people," the mayor added.

Once Mike and Jim had sat down, Mayor Grant announced, "My Chief of Police should be here shortly, along with my deputy, who is largely responsible for handling the refugee program."

Mike smiled and nodded. "That sounds great. They're probably the folks we need to talk with most. Do you have any coffee available, by chance?" he asked, hoping to get a cup before the meeting started.

Jorge Montoya was quick to respond, "Yes, of course. Let me get you gentlemen some java before everyone arrives." Then he quickly dashed off to get the group some coffee.

The mayor and Mike talked for a few minutes, until the Chief of Police and his deputy walked in. Everyone at the table stood, shook hands, and exchanged greetings.

Once all parties had been seated, Alexander began the introduction. "Mr. Stone, Agent Leary, this is Chief George Monroe. He can answer your questions about the public safety and crime stats concerning the refugee resettlements. Next to George is Melissa Mauly, one of my deputy mayors. She's specifically running the refugee resettlement program for the city. She helps identify where we're going to place new refugees as they arrive and helps them get settled in, find jobs, and locate any other immediate services they may need to make their transition as smooth as possible."

Mike smiled. He was glad to have what appeared to be all the key players in the room needed to give him a thorough briefing of the Chicago program. "Thank you all for your time. I appreciate you agreeing to this short-notice meeting so we can discuss the program and how Chicago is leading the way for the rest of the country."

The mayor clearly beamed at the idea that Chicago was a shining example for the nation. Everyone else in the meeting seemed quite pleased as well.

Gesturing toward the other agent with him, Mike continued, "This is Special Agent Jim Leary. He works with me at the National Counterterrorism Center. As you know, my name is Michael Stone. I am the deputy director for the refugee and asylum vetting program at the NCTC. I've been asked by our director, Mallory Harper, to meet with you and specifically ask how things with your program are going so we can work with other cities to try and use your program as a template, and to discuss with you an increase in the number of refugees we are going to need you to start accepting in January."

The mayor broke in, saying, "It would be an honor to share our program with the other cities of our great nation. We've spent a lot of time and resources ironing out the kinks in our system to get it to where it is today."

"I don't mean to interrupt," said Melissa Mauly, "but what specifically do you want to know?"

"OK, straight to it. We'd like to know what the process is from greeting the newly arrived refugees to how you get them integrated into the community," Mike said as he indicated for his colleague to begin taking some notes and record the conversation.

Grinning, Melissa began, "Well, when the refugee has been identified as coming to Chicago, we get a dossier that outlines some of their skills, English language proficiency level, and any family members that may be traveling with them from the State Department. Once they arrive, we take them to a temporary lodging facility. We typically have them stay at one of four designated hotels near O'Hare for about a week. This allows us time to get them placed into a permanent home. The city receives a federal block grant of $25,000 per refugee to assist them in getting established and integrated into the community."

Stone nodded, and Mauly continued, "We arrange an apartment for them to move into and provide them with the first six months' rent, paid in advance. Whether they have family or not will determine how large of an apartment we find them. We typically secure fully furnished apartments, so they don't need to buy furniture right away. Then we arrange for them to have two hours of English lessons a day if they aren't already fluent. We also evaluate their skills and then work with local employers to get them jobs."

Melissa stopped just long enough to take a sip of her coffee before she went on. "Once the refugee has secured a job and is taking their language courses, we provide them with a $2,000 a- month stipend for the first six months. We also work with them to ensure that they can get a checking account established and know how to use a debit card. After six months, most refugees have established themselves with a job and have some money in savings. At that point, they begin to take over the rent of their apartment and are essentially on their own. We check in with them every quarter after the first six months and provide additional assistance if needed." She was clearly very proud of the program she had developed.

Mike smiled and commended her. "I must say, your plan is significantly better than the other cities we have reviewed. I can see why Director Harper believes the Chicago plan is the way to go." He was doing his best to stroke their egos so he could gain their trust and establish a rapport with them. His CIA training on recruiting assets could be put to other uses as well.

Mike then turned to Chief Monroe before he changed topics. "I'd like to talk next about the crime stats. Have any of the refugees gotten themselves into any trouble with the police? Have any of them been victims of hate crimes or anything else that would attract police attention?"

Chief Monroe cleared his throat and began to walk the group through the crime statistics he had written down on a talking points sheet in front of him. By and large, the immigrants were doing a good job of not attracting police attention. Likewise, there weren't any noticeable increases in crimes against the refugees either.

"The only thing I would point out as a difference between the refugees we've been taking in and those that are headed to the other cities is that we tend to get a higher proportion of single young men. They're mostly from Syria, Iraq, Afghanistan and Pakistan. I'm not sure if there's anything to it, but for every three families we receive, we receive a single male between twenty and thirty-two years old. These single men are also exclusively Muslim, whereas nearly half of the families we receive are non-Muslims." As the chief finished speaking, he seemed to second-guess that last sentence, hoping it didn't sound too Islamophobic.

The mayor and Melissa seemed a bit tweaked by the chief's comments but held their tongues. Mike was unfazed. "Thank you for the information, Chief Monroe. I'm not sure there's a rhyme or reason why Chicago is receiving more single male Muslims than other cities, but I can look into it."

The group talked for another thirty minutes with the mayor, and then spent an additional hour talking with

Melissa and Chief Monroe. By the time they left, the officials in Chicago walked out of the room feeling on top of the world over the compliments Mike made sure to keep giving.

At the end of the meeting, Mike and Jim finally had something of interest to dig into. It was odd that of all the cities, Chicago and Baltimore had a much higher percentage of single Muslim males, all between the ages of twenty and thirty-two. The groups from Chicago almost all came from Syria and Pakistan, whereas the young men going to Baltimore appeared to be refugees from Iraq and Afghanistan. Mike's curiosity was piqued.

Chapter 7
Under Their Noses

McClean, Virginia
National Counterterrorism Center

After meeting with the mayors and police chiefs of twenty-three different cities, Mike and Jim had identified what was working in the program and what was not. Some cities' programs were better than others. Chicago was a great case study of how an effective refugee resettlement program could be run. Others, like the ones in Ohio, Michigan, and Texas, were not.

As Mike walked into the open room that was the nerve center of their little department, he quickly located Special Agent Leary. "Jim, I'm glad I found you before you got buried in something else," Mike began. "I'd like you to work with a couple of the analysts and see what you can dig up on the groups of single military-age males that appear to be settling in Chicago and Baltimore. The more I investigate it myself, the more I think there's something fishy about the situation. Chief Monroe was right; there should have been more families interspersed in Chicago and Baltimore."

Jim nodded. "I agree, Mike. I'll grab a couple of analysts and we'll see what we can find on them. We'll get back to you by the end of the week." He was glad he wasn't the only one suspicious about the situation.

After grabbing a cup of coffee, Mike went back to his office to write up his report. He'd been writing bits and pieces of it after each city meeting, but now it was time to consolidate it and make his recommendations to his boss. Mike still wasn't sure about Mallory Harper. She was an ardently loyal supporter of the current president and was really pushing this refugee program, but something was off. He just couldn't quite put his finger on it. He didn't have a problem with bringing in refugees, but he was definitely concerned they were letting in the wrong people.

Am I overthinking this? he wondered.

After lunch, Mike walked toward one of the screeners who Director Harper had said was flagging far more people than her colleagues as threats. He wanted to find out from her what she was finding that others were not.

Approaching her desk, he noticed the plethora of University of Texas memorabilia. He rapped his knuckles softly on the desk to get her attention. She looked up at him, almost caught off guard at how silently he'd snuck up on her.

"Hello, Julie," Mike began. "We haven't really had a lot of time to talk and get to know each other since I joined the team. Director Harper has had me traveling a bit, but I wanted to say hi and pick your brain a bit on something." He sported a warm, inviting smile.

"Hi, Mike. Sure thing—what did you want to ask me about?" she asked tentatively. She was probably hoping she wasn't in any more trouble with Director Harper.

Mike took a seat at the chair next to her desk. "I know Director Harper hasn't been happy with the number of people you've been flagging as potential risks, but I'd like to talk with you about it and find out your side of the story. What do you think you're seeing that the others aren't?" he asked quizzically.

Julie sighed. She had a look on her face as if she'd just been called into the principal's office at school. Meekly, she answered, "OK. Most of the individuals I've been marking as potential risks are the single Muslim men that have been requesting to be settled in Chicago and Baltimore."

When Julie mentioned Baltimore and Chicago, he raised an eyebrow, then encouraged her to continue.

"For one, most of these men's applications originate from two camps. Nearly all the applications for Chicago came from a camp in Harran, Turkey. This is only about 130 kilometers from Ar Raqqa, Syria, which is the location of the ISIS official headquarters. Most of the men applying to Baltimore come from the camp near Gaziantep, Turkey. Each of these camps have been previously identified as ISIS recruitment stations and have been the birthplace of a lot of extremist activity."

Mike listened and then looked at several dossiers she showed him of people she had flagged. He sat back in his chair and thought about what this all meant, wondering if any of it correlated with what he had found when he was running the counter-ISIS team in Turkey.

Mike knew what she was implying but wanted to hear her say it for himself. "So, Julie, if I'm connecting the dots correctly, you believe some of these men may be ISIS fighters that are trying to infiltrate into the US, correct?"

Julie looked around the room to see if anyone else was listening to their conversation. In a lowered voice, she said, "I do. I think ISIS has managed to infiltrate several hundred of its members to these cities over the past three years that this program has been running. I tried to bring this conclusion to Director Harper, but she quickly shut me down. She said I was looking for ways not to support the President's initiative. Honestly, though, my only objective is to protect our country. I don't care about politics."

Mike remembered that his own group in Turkey had suspected this and knew those camps were trouble. One of the ISIS operatives they'd interrogated had said they had already infiltrated hundreds of ISIS fighters into America. Of course, with no proof, this was just another unsubstantiated claim.

Mike looked Julie in the eyes and quietly replied, "I believe you."

Julie looked surprised and then relieved.

He explained, "Before coming to the NCTC, I worked in Homeland's Office of Intelligence and Analysis. I'm familiar with the camps you're referencing. I'm also aware of this idea of using the refugee program as a means of infiltrating ISIS fighters into America. They had already used it successfully to infiltrate Europe."

He paused for a second, considering his options, then continued, "To ease your problem with Director Harper, I'm going to tell her that you are going to work directly for me so I can 'keep an eye on you,' but in reality, I want you to work with Agent Leary on digging into the history of these refugees who've already settled into Chicago and Baltimore. I want to know more about them and see if we can't identify some potential problem children."

Mike needed to keep this activity on the down-low. He knew Director Harper wouldn't agree. Having Julie work on the research was a win-win because he already knew that she agreed with his viewpoint, and she was equally motivated not to stir up any more trouble.

****

A week had quietly gone by with Agent Leary and Julie doing some digging on the refugees from Chicago. Then, they found something worth immediate attention.

Jim knocked on Mike's office door frame. "Mike, we have something we'd like to show you. This is big."

"Sure thing," Mike replied. "Come in and close the door. What have you guys found?"

Julie nodded for Jim to break the news. "Well, one of the guys who settled in Baltimore about a year ago is definitely a problem. His biographical information didn't show any matches, so it's easy to see how it could have been missed. We ran his biometrics against the FBI and DHS databases, and again, we got no matches. However, when we ran his biometrics against the DoD biometric database, we got a hit."

Mike's eyes lit up. "What type of hit was it?"

Jim continued, "His prints matched to several latent fingerprints that were recovered from an IED in Iraq in 2007 and to a weapon and computer that were recovered during a targeted raid in Yemen in 2013."

Mike let out a soft whistle. This was an incredible find. This guy should never have been allowed in the US as a part of the refugee program. "Who conducted the screening of this individual?" asked Mike. He was going to want to talk with this analyst to find out why they hadn't found this information on their own.

Julie piped in. "It was done by Constance Pool, one of Director Harper's people that transferred here from the Senate Intelligence Committee she used to head."

"Interesting...OK, here's what I want you guys to do. Start working up this guy's profile. Pull up all the data you can on him. See what you can find from his time in Iraq, and what possible connection he could have had in Yemen. I also want to know exactly what this guy has been up to since he arrived here in the US. It would be best if you could pull this together by the end of tomorrow," Mike said, knowing that he was tasking them with a lot of information to gather.

He continued, "I'm going to brief this to Director Harper on Friday morning, during our leadership meeting. I'll ask for permission for us to get a wiretap up on this guy and start monitoring all his electronic communications. I'm also going to see if we can assign someone from the Baltimore field office to monitor him as well."

Julie spoke up, asking, "What are you going to do if she says no?"

Mike thought about that for a moment before responding, "Well, if she wants to play that game, I'll talk to a few friends at Homeland and see what I can make happen," he said with a slight chuckle.

Jim asserted, "You'd better be careful, my friend. If Director Harper ever catches wind that you went around her to another agency, she'll chew you up and spit you out."

Mike just smiled. "I guess we'll just have to make sure we don't get caught, then."

Later that evening, Mike compiled a short message about what they had found and sent it over to Trevor at Langley. They had their first bread crumb of proof something amiss was going on.

****

Over the next twenty-four hours, Julie and Jim worked to put together as comprehensive a dossier on the target as possible. They presented the document to Mike an hour before his morning meeting with Mallory. As Mike perused the dossier, he was impressed with what his small team had found in such a short time.

The target was a man named Khalid Mohammed al-Baghdadi. He had apparently matched to three separate IED attacks: one in 2004, another in 2006, and a third in 2007. Khalid was born in Baghdad, Iraq, in 1982 to a wealthy Sunni family. His father had worked in the Ministry of Defense prior to the fall of the Saddam regime. Official documents showed that Khalid had obtained an engineering degree from the University of Baghdad before he joined the Iraqi Intelligence Service. From the government documents seized in 2003, Khalid was assigned to a counterintelligence program and had specialized experience in counterinsurgency operations. Prior to the 2003 war, he had been working in the Kurdish areas. When the war broke out, he was transferred to Baghdad. That was the last official report before the government fell.

As he continued reading, he reflected. He could see why this guy had been hard to track—he'd been trained on how not to be found. But something bothered him. *Why would his fingerprints have been found on an IED?* he wondered.

Mike looked up at Jim and Julie, who were still in the room, waiting for feedback. "This is great work, you guys. What I'd like you research further is the IED attacks where his fingerprints were found. What kind of IED attacks were they? Were they simple devices, or something more specialized and complex? This guy appears to be too smart to be the one placing IEDs on the side of roads, and I'm not certain he had the training necessary to build them. I could be wrong, but I'd like you guys to look into the details of the attacks for further clues, OK?"

They nodded in agreement as they scribbled a few notes.

He closed the dossier and grabbed his notepad. "I've got to run to the meeting now, but see if you can find that information for me ASAP." Julie and Jim nodded, and Mike headed out of his office and knocked on Mallory's door.

"Boss, I know you're busy, but I've got something I should brief you on before we have this leadership meeting," he asserted.

"Mike, I'm really busy right now. Just brief it in the meeting, OK?" she urged.

"I think you're going to want to hear it beforehand," he emphasized.

"No, I really don't have time. I'm sure it will be fine, just brief the group," she said. Then she frantically began to type something on her computer.

Mike decided not to push it any further. He replied, "All right, Boss," then headed back to his desk. He printed some documents and then made his way toward the conference room where the leadership meeting took place every Friday.

As Mike walked in, everyone was still mingling and talking about what they were going to do that weekend. Most of the group was gaggled around the doughnuts and coffee that had been delivered to the room a few minutes before he arrived. As everyone was grabbing their morning java, Mike took his seat next to where Director Harper would be sitting.
****

Mallory walked into the conference room, ready to begin what she probably thought would be another mundane Friday update meeting. She'd finished reviewing Mike's field report, and she had to admit, she was impressed. He was immaculately detailed in his assessment and had identified several specific aspects of the refugee programs that had been implemented that had worked well and had also outlined those that had not. He also put together what she thought was an exceptional recommendation for a refugee resettlement program that could be replicated across the country.

She had initially been mad at Mike for missing her deadline and asking for an extra day to complete the report, but once she received it, she was pleasantly surprised. She felt as if she'd finally found a solid Number Two, one who understood the President's refugee agenda and would work to see it implemented.

As Mallory took her seat, she smiled at Mike and signaled for everyone to begin their updates. Each department head gave their weekly recap of what their department had been working on, along with any significant activities that had come up.

As the meeting neared its conclusion, Director Harper noticed that Mike hadn't spoken yet and had a file in front of him that was labeled "Eyes Only." She tapped the table in front of him. "Mike, I think it's your turn. You have something to share with the group?" she asked.

He seemed hesitant. "I can, but I believe this might be better discussed privately," he contended.

"Nonsense," she said encouragingly. "We're all one team. Go ahead, Mike. We'll tackle whatever it is as a group."

Taking a deep breath before he began, Agent Stone began to pass out a summary to each department head and to Director Harper.

As they reviewed the summary, he began to brief them on what he'd found. He explained how he had a hunch something just wasn't right with the disproportionate number of single males being resettled in Chicago and Baltimore. He then ran their biometrics against the DoD terrorist watch lists and the DoD latent fingerprint databases, just in case they found a match.

Unfortunately for Director Harper, Mike's thorough investigation had actually identified one person who, in all honesty, should never have been allowed into the refugee program or permitted to enter the US. As everyone looked over the summary, several people had questions. Mallory just sat silently, letting everyone else talk while she pondered what to do about the information Mike had just unearthed.

Several department heads were asking questions all at the same time. "Who did the vetting of this individual? Why was he not flagged?" Another department head added, "We need to find this person and figure out what he's been doing since he arrived here. This is a huge screwup if this guy has done something."

Director Harper cleared her throat, indicating she wanted everyone to be quiet for a minute. As she surveyed the faces in the room, she then turned to her side and said, "Mike, this is an incredible find. We should have a talk with the person who conducted this man's screening. This should have been found during that process. That said, we obviously can't let this refugee continue to freely walk around in

Baltimore. We need to figure out what he's been up to, who he's been meeting with, and what he's been doing in Baltimore the past thirteen months since he's been here."

Looking toward her FBI and US marshal representatives, she continued, "I would like your organizations to work together and get this person apprehended immediately. We need to keep this as hush-hush as possible. I don't want local law enforcement involved, and I don't want this getting out into the press. This is the type of thing that could really embarrass our department and the President. Does everyone understand?" she asked in a very stern voice.

Everyone nodded. The meeting quickly ended, and Director Harper told Mike to follow her to her office. When they walked into the room, she motioned for him to take a seat. "Please close the door." Then she walked over to the window that faced out into cubicle land and closed the blinds.

She turned to Mike and immediately tore into him. "What was that?" she yelled. "You embarrassed me in front of my division heads! You should have brought this information to me privately, so we could discuss it and what to do with it. Now everyone in the department will know about it in short order!" She seethed, clearly irate at being blindsided. Mike just sat there, silent.

"What do you have to say for yourself?" she demanded, in a slightly lower voice than her previous yelling.

Clearing his throat, Mike calmly responded, "Director Harper, you're right. I should have brought this to you first. I did try to talk to you privately before the meeting, but you were clearly preoccupied with something important and told me to just brief it during the meeting, which I did. That said, the leadership meeting wasn't the worst place to bring this up, since we are going to need assistance from the FBI and NSA to find out what this guy has been up to electronically, and the marshals have the manpower to place a tail on this guy or apprehend him when the time comes."

If Mallory Harper's eyes could have killed, Mike would've dropped to the floor right then and there. "You don't understand," she insisted. "This program is already under enough scrutiny by congressional leaders. If they caught wind of this, they would demand to hold hearings. It would be a witch hunt and an embarrassment to the administration, especially since we're about to ramp up the number of refugees we are going to take in. With this being an election year, we don't need to give the GOP any additional cannon fodder to use on the campaign trail." She gradually calmed down as she spoke.

Mike sighed before he responded, "I see your point. I wasn't aware that this program was already under a tight microscope by Congress; this is only my second month here. I do still believe bringing this forward now is a good thing. Can you imagine if we hadn't found this guy and he'd somehow pulled off a terrorist attack during the campaign? That would be gold for the GOP."

He continued, "Look at it from this perspective. *If* this guy has been up to something nefarious, then you'll get to look like the hero for finding out before he did something terrible."

Mallory's shoulders slumped in resignation. "Well, I suppose we could spin it that way. In either case, what's done is done. You found something that could be damaging to this office, so we need to act on it. Who was the analyst who signed off on the vetting package?" she asked, wanting to get this problem nipped in the bud quickly.

Mike pulled a piece of paper from the folder he had brought with him to the meeting and handed it to Mallory. "It was Constance Pool. The file had originally been flagged by George Lee before Constance overrode his objection and approved it." Mike was pulling no punches in his response.

Mallory sat back for a second, lost in thought. Constance had been one of the people she had brought over from Senator Feinstein's staff. She was a real team player, which was why Mallory had named her as one of the team leaders to oversee several contractor analysts and some of the junior government employees.

"Are you sure?" asked Mallory, hoping that maybe Mike was wrong.

"Yes," he answered in a very matter-of-fact tone. "Julie Wells verified it before handing me the information."

Great, she thought. *Wells—another person who would do anything to sabotage this program*. She let out one long, slow breath.

"Send her to my office on your way out. I will talk with her," she said. Her voice betrayed her sense of defeat.

As Mike was getting up, he asked, "What do you plan on doing with her?"

Mallory snorted before responding, "I'm going to have to suspend her and revoke her clearance with the NCTC. It'll be up to HR as to where she goes next or if she'll be terminated." Mallory was irritated by the question. She didn't like the insinuation that she might try to sweep this under the rug.

After Mike left Director Harper's office, a lightbulb went off in her head as she connected the dots in her memory. She picked up her secured Blackberry and sent a quick text message to the National Security Advisor, Leah Bishop. "We need to talk ASAP. We may have a problem."

A couple of minutes later, she received a response. "Meet me at the Lincoln Memorial in two hours."

****

Exactly two hours later, Leah was sitting on a bench facing one way while Mallory sat nearby facing the opposite direction. Both had their cell phones out as if they were talking to someone, while in reality, they were talking to each other.

"What's the problem that required me to have to meet you?" Leah asked, a bit annoyed at having to take time out of her day.

Mallory replied, "You remember that name you gave me at Senator Warren's cocktail party two years ago? The one where that waiter spilled an entire glass of wine on your husband? You asked me to expedite his vetting and get him approved through the refugee program."

Leah thought for a minute, and then she remembered. The name had been given to her by Nihad Nassimi, the

National Director for CAGIR. He had said "friends of the administration" would be very appreciative for any assistance in speeding up his vetting, to the tune of half a million dollars to her husband's congressional reelection campaign SuperPAC in New York. At the time, it hadn't seemed like a big deal.

Leah replied, "Yes, now I remember. I'm not sure I recall the man's name, but I do remember the conversation. My husband was pissed off at that waiter; he had to leave early, and he still had a couple of people to talk to about campaign donations."

"Well, there's a problem with him," blurted Mallory.

Leah interrupted, "—What do you mean, 'problem,' exactly?"

"My new deputy—he did some digging into some of the people we had cleared. This particular guy is linked to three separate IED attacks in Iraq, and his biometrics were found on some computers and documents of a Special Forces raid conducted in Yemen six months prior to us approving his refugee application," Mallory said.

There was an awkward pause. Leah thought for a minute. *My God, this is a huge problem. If this gets out, I'm toast, and the President is going to crucify me.*

"Who else knows about this information?" she asked tepidly.

"Right now, it's just my division leaders and a few people in my department. By Monday, I suspect just about everyone in my department is going to know about it, though," Mallory said, seemingly resigned to her fate.

Thinking quickly, Leah replied, "OK, here's what we're going to do. I'm going to have the Justice Department issue a gag order on this information before the end of the day. We will say the matter is now being handled by the National Security Council while 'we' investigate how this happened. If anyone leaks this information, then they will face immediate prosecution." As Leah spoke, the confidence in her voice grew.

Yes, I can regain control of this situation with Mallory, she thought.

Mallory nodded. "There's one other question I need to ask before we go our separate ways. What do you want me to do about the other twenty-two names you gave me?" she asked.

That *was* a good question. Leah pondered what to do about them for a minute before responding, "Right now, nothing. We need to contain this situation. Your deputy, he's CIA, right?" she asked.

"Yes, but operating under Homeland Security cover. Apparently, he's really good at his job. He's only been in my department for two months and he found this guy already."

"Hmm…OK, let him know that the NSC is going to review *all* of the people who were placed in Chicago and Baltimore. This will buy us some time to sort things out. In the meantime, send him to the refugee camps in Jordan and Turkey. Tell him you want him to evaluate what they're doing out there and how it could be improved. Tell him this is in preparation for the influx that's about to start. That should keep him busy for the next six or eight weeks while we figure out if any of those other people are potential threats."

Mallory just nodded, then stood up and walked away.

Once Mallory had left, Leah placed her government Blackberry in her handbag and pulled out her personal smartphone. She typed out a cryptic message to Nihad Nassimi, the National Director of CAGIR, saying, "We need to meet ASAP."

A couple of minutes went by and then her phone beeped. Nihad responded, "I can meet at five o'clock at our usual place." She knew his message meant that they would soon be sitting at a bench in the orchid room at the Botanical

Gardens. She went off to try and tie up some other loose ends at the White House before that meeting.

****

Nihad arrived right on time. He quickly found Leah and, by her facial expression, gathered that she was gravely concerned about something.

He walked up to Leah with hand extended and said, "Hello, Ms. Bishop, it's a great honor to see you again."

Leah brushed off his greeting and got right down to business. "Nihad, I don't have much time, so I'll be frank. Two years ago, at a fundraiser for Senator Warren, you gave me the name of a refugee that you said I needed to ensure was accepted into the program and allowed to immigrate here," she said in a hushed tone. As she spoke, she stood up and slowly began walking next to him, steering them so it would appear that they were casually enjoying the flowers.

Nihad had to think for a minute before he could summon up the memory. "Yes, now I remember. I can't recall the man's name, but I do remember the conversation," he said, also in a hushed tone.

Leah stopped walking and looked up at a particularly delicate selection of orchids. "We have a problem. That man has a history of involvement in terrorism. An analyst at

NCTC just discovered this. Who in the world is this guy, and why did you have me clear him to enter the country?" she demanded, still speaking quietly but with quite a bit of an edge to her voice.

Nihad was taken aback. He wasn't used to being talked down to or accused of something, especially by a woman. "I'm afraid I don't know what you're talking about. I was given this name by a person with influence in the Saudi government as a personal favor. I didn't ask questions beyond that," he replied, trying to calm the conversation down.

Leah turned and looked Nihad in the eyes. "There's nothing more I can do; he's going to be arrested. There is evidence linking him to several IED attacks in Iraq against US and Iraqi Forces. I don't know if he will be charged in America or Iraq, but you can rest assured, he will be prosecuted," she said with authority in her voice.

Nihad snorted. *Who does she think she is?* he thought. *I own her. She works for me.*

He looked at Leah with a steely gaze and said, "Remember that $500K we gave to your husband's reelection campaign? That money came with strings. You essentially accepted a bribe, and if you don't think we will use that against you, then you're kidding yourself. You do what you need to with this man to cover yourself, but we're going to continue to give you names, especially with this influx that is going to start in January…and you are going to approve them. Do I make myself clear, Leah?"

She gritted her teeth, then calmed herself and returned her gaze to the flowers. "Nihad, you may think you have me in your pocket, but don't forget my position or who I work for." With that, she turned around and left the Botanical Gardens to return to work at the White House.

Chapter 8
Overworked, Underpaid

Zaatari Refugee Camp, Jordan

The flight from Dulles to Queen Alia International Airport had been extremely long, but it had afforded Mike, Julie and Jim some time to catch up on some much-needed sleep.

When they stepped off the plane, Mike felt like he was returning to a long-lost friend; he'd been to Jordan several times before. For Julie Wells, this was her first time in Jordan, but not the Middle East. For Special Agent Jim Leary, however, this was his first foray abroad—he'd never traveled outside of the United States before.

When the three of them landed in Jordan, they were met by one of the Regional Security Officers from the embassy who helped them navigate their way through customs and ushered them to the vehicle that would chauffeur them. After a short meeting at the embassy, they were driven over to the Zaatari Refugee Camp, where they would meet up with the folks involved in the refugee screening process to begin their assessment for Director Harper.

Despite the fact that he'd been there before, driving into the camp was still a surreal scene for Mike.

Things have gotten worse, Mike thought.

For as far as the eye could see, there were row after row of tents and literally hundreds of thousands of people milling about. Many of the people looked tired, worn out from fleeing their war-torn homes, only to be herded like cattle into these enormous camps. Mike knew that many of the people before him wanted to try and settle in Amman or any other city where they could find work and try to start over. He guessed that many more were hoping that maybe, just maybe, they could be taken in as a refugee by the United States or a European nation.

Once their vehicle had navigated its way through the camp, they eventually came to a series of portable metal trailers enclosed by large fences and guarded by armed security guards. The embassy driver pulled up to the vehicle entrance and presented his ID. A minute later, they were waved through and directed where to park.

Getting out of the vehicle, Mike, Julie and Jim took a moment to stretch as they observed a long line of people being called forward by the guards one at a time to be checked, before being directed to stand in a separate location where they could apply for refugee status. There had to be close to a fifty people sitting at various tables under a large mesh tent, filling out the appropriate paperwork. Once a person had finished filling out the required documents, they were herded over to another tent where they waited to schedule a screening interview and would then return when it was time for their interview.

The scene was almost overwhelming for Julie and Jim as they stood there taking it all in. For Mike, this was just part of the job.

"Over here, guys," Mike said as he motioned for them to follow him to a couple of trailers a little further away from the crowds.

Mike walked up to the metal door, turning the handle to open it up. In seconds, he was buffeted with the cool A/C from inside. This trailer mostly housed the CIA and State Department teams, who were responsible for the vetting and screening of the refugees and asylum seekers from the camps in Jordan.

One of the screeners, who was sitting at a desk with a computer in front of him, looked up at the newcomers. His face lit up, and he quickly walked over to them. "Mike, my old friend, it's good to see you again. What are you doing out here? I thought you were back in D.C. or something?" he asked out of curiosity.

Mike shook hands with a man he knew very well, Billy Logan. He and Billy had worked together in various countries over the years. They had developed a strong bond during those troubling times.

"Hi, Billy. It's good to see you too. Homeland's kept me busy, and yes, I'm back in D.C.," he said with a wink that said to play along. He didn't need one of his old CIA buddies blowing his cover for him. His friend seemed to have caught the drift and effortlessly transitioned to fawning on Julie.

"You going to introduce me to this beautiful woman, or do I have to do it myself?" he chided Mike, taking her hand in his.

Julie blushed at the sudden attention. Such an interaction would have never flown in the corporate world back in the States, but out there in the field, the rules seemed different.

Mike snickered, then ushered away his friend's hands, which had lingered a bit too long. "This is Julie Wells, my top analyst, and this is Special Agent Jim Leary. He's FBI, so don't hold it against him. He's a good guy, and sharp too." Jim exchanged a handshake with Billy.

"Homeland has me working at the NCTC now, and we've been sent here by Director Mallory Harper, who heads up our department, to check on the vetting process and make sure you guys are ready for the ramp up," Mike explained.

"And here I thought you guys were coming here to help us out," Billy replied with a chuckle. He led them over to a table and some chairs, glancing at Julie a few too many times.

The group took a seat at the table and began to talk about what had been going on at the camp recently. They asked about how many applications they typically saw a week, how many people they could vet a day, and so on.

As Billy passed out some cold water bottles from the fridge to everyone, he said, "Right now, we have about 140,000 people at this camp. There are several other camps in Jordan that have similar numbers as well. As you know from your time in Turkey, Mike, we only have twenty-five Agency screeners in Jordan, and about thirty or so in Turkey. State has sent about forty diplomatic security personnel to Jordan and about sixty to Turkey to also aid in the vetting process."

Billy took a swig of water before continuing. "Each screener can conduct about four interviews a day. So, we can conduct roughly 1,300 interviews a week. But keep in mind, each person is being interviewed twice. After the first interview, if the interviewer passes them, then those names go to our analytical cell, which consists of twelve analysts. They then conduct a full intelligence background and then provide that information to the second screener. If they pass the second interview, then their packet is essentially approved. From there, it's just a matter of when the State Department chooses them for refugee status and flies them to the US. Right now, there's a quota of no more than one thousand people a month. We were just told last week that this quota would be raised to five thousand a week. At that rate, they're going to clear out most of these camps faster than we can screen and vet them," Billy said, looking disgruntled.

Julie piped in and said, "It doesn't sound like you think this is a good idea."

"It's not," he responded. "All of the background investigations are coordinated with your office. I'd say about two or three percent of them should have been denied, but we were overridden by NCTC and told to pass them anyway. I personally think we're accepting some bad apples, but I'm not the one in charge, so I have no say in the process."

Stone sat there for a minute before responding, "That seems to be a common thread. People who should have been discarded from the program are being overridden by NCTC. This is only my third month there, but I'm starting to see that these decisions appear to be more politically motivated than driven by security.

"I understand your frustration, Billy, I really do. I'm not sure I can fully correct the problem, but I sure can highlight it. Our group is traveling to the various camps in Jordan and Turkey over the next three weeks to see if you guys are ready to handle the influx. Have you found any ISIS supporters or recruiters within this camp? Or any of the others in Jordan, for that matter?" Mike asked, wanting to know if there was an immediate security concern that they should underscore in his report.

Billy looked at Mike and then stood up. He signaled for everyone else to stay seated as he winked at Julie, giving her his best smile. He walked over to his desk, pulled a folder from it and handed the file to Mike to look over.

"Those are the ISIS recruiters that we've identified in the various camps in Jordan. There are twenty of them in total. One of our sources tells us that they are training people on what to say during the interviews we conduct. You see, we're required to ask a basic set of twenty questions. We have some leeway to ask a few questions of our own, but these interviews are very structured and mechanical. It's not like an interrogation, although I wish it were." Billy watched as Mike thumbed through the file and then handed it over to Agent Leary.

Leary put the folder down once he had also rummaged through it. "So, Billy, you're saying that these ISIS recruiters are prepping them for the interview and your hands are essentially tied?"

"That's exactly what I'm saying," responded Billy, sighing deeply.

The group continued to talk for another hour before their little impromptu meeting broke up. After they'd been given a tour and spoken with several State Department officials, Mike directed everyone to start working on writing up their assessment of the camp. The consensus was they needed more screeners to meet the new quotas, and without them, a lot of people were going to be approved to travel to the US as part of the refugee and asylum program, potentially without any interviews being done at all.

Chapter 9

The Ghost

Dubai, United Arab Emirates

Burj Al Arab Jumeirah Hotel

Nihad Nassimi, the US Director for CAGIR, was sitting at a table that had been reserved by the man he was meeting with. The GOLD ON 27 was an immensely opulent bar at the world's only seven-star hotel in Dubai, the Burj. The man Nihad was meeting always chose this place for them to talk whenever he was summoned to Dubai, which didn't happen often. Though Nihad had never actually seen the man's whole face, he assumed he must be a rich member of the Saudi royal family as he had a distinct Saudi accent when he spoke Arabic, which was seldom. Nihad had only heard his Arabic in passing though, because their conversations had always been in English.

The man was known to those in a small circle as Al Shabah, which translates to "the Ghost." Nihad had only actually met the Ghost in person two other times. Each time, he had appeared in a different disguise. The first time, he had shown up in traditional white Arab garb, and the next time, he was dressed as a Saudi general officer. His eye color was even different each time they met. Nihad was never one for the cloak-and-dagger sort of games. He did, however, understand the need for secrecy and didn't judge the man for using various disguises to hide his true identity.

As the Ghost exited the elevator, he quickly made eye contact with Nihad, who was sitting at their reserved table in the corner. This time, the Ghost was dressed in a fancy $15,000 suit. Nihad estimated that his shoes must have set him back two grand as well. His contacts made his eyes appear vibrant green, and only as he got much closer did Nihad wonder if his facial hair was actually a very expensive professionally done fake beard and mustache. He appeared every bit like one of the numerous rich businessmen staying at the Burj in Dubai for the Middle East Banking Consortium Conference, which attracted nearly 5,500 attendees each year. It was the perfect cover for their meeting.

The Ghost walked up to Nihad and greeted him in English, "Ah, Nihad, it's great to see you again. I hope you like the venue for our meeting," he said in a jovial tone.

Nihad smiled warmly at the man standing before him. He gestured with his hand for the man to sit down as he replied, "Yes, of course. This place is great. I was just perusing the menu; everything looks quite tasty."

The Ghost smiled at his unwitting fool. "I'm glad you like it. They employ some of the best chefs in the world at this hotel," he said as he sat down. They both placed their order and then got down to business.

"Nihad, I appreciate all that you have done for me over the years. The work CAGIR is doing in America to expand Islam to their heathen lands, and the political influence you have been able to develop, is something that has not gone unnoticed or unappreciated," the Ghost said with a smile, stroking Nihad's ego.

"As you know, this is an election year in America. Everyone believes the former Secretary of State will be elected, but we aren't taking any chances. The group of likeminded people I represent are going to be making some large donations to CAGIR, and we expect the contributions to be handed out appropriately," the Ghost said. He slipped Nihad a piece of paper. On it was a list of candidates that they wanted campaign contributions to be made to—it was a long list.

He continued, "In addition, the President is increasing the number of refugees and asylum seekers the US is going to accept, starting tomorrow. We have additional names we would like your help in expediting."

He slid a new piece of paper across the table to Nihad, who picked up the list and began to look at it. "This is a lot of names, more than you requested the last time we met. I'm not sure I can get them all in," he said tentatively, unsure of the request.

The Ghost simply smiled at Nihad and slid an envelope across the table, waiting for Nihad to open it. Nihad's eyes grew a little wider when he saw the cash, then he quickly slipped the envelope into his suit jacket pocket.

"Nihad, you're a clever man. I'm sure you can find a way for these forty-six individuals' applications to get approved. Work your contacts. We've given you more than enough money. You've always delivered solid results in the past—I'm sure you can handle this," the Ghost said with a devilish grin.

Nihad just smiled and nodded. As long as he was being paid, he could make things happen.

"I appreciate your confidence and trust," he said. "I won't let you down."

Chapter 10
Raid Gone Wrong

Baltimore, Maryland

Deputy Marshal Jim Greer walked up to the front of the room as the gathered police, FBI and marshals talked amongst themselves about last night's spectacular NFL football game. The Baltimore Ravens had defeated the New England Patriots in a gripping game that ran into overtime.

"OK, everyone. Let's cut the chatter. It's time to earn our keep," Jim said in a loud enough voice to be heard over the excited din.

The conversation quickly died down. Jim got down to the business of getting everyone ready for that morning's raid. They had been monitoring the residence Mr. Khalid Mohammed al-Baghdadi had been staying in for the past several weeks. During that time, they had identified a few patterns in his daily routine and planned on exploiting them this morning.

"Today is the day we raid Mr. al-Baghdadi's home. We're going to hit this place just like we do any other fugitive arrest. I want local PD to establish the roadblocks and cordon off the neighborhood while the marshals and FBI move in to make the arrest. I spoke with the police chief last night. He's making their SWAT team available, which I've graciously agreed to use."

Some grumblings could be heard from the marshals, who had hoped they'd be the ones to lead the entry into the house. It was a source of pride for them to be the ones to actually take down the suspect and put him in cuffs, but that honor would now fall to the local SWAT team.

"SWAT's going to lead the breach, quickly followed by the marshals, and then the FBI will come in to begin collecting any evidence left behind." Jim saw the looks of disappointment on some of his agents' faces but quickly dismissed them. His job was to make sure his people came home alive each day and they apprehended their suspects.

"It's 0530 hours right now. We hit the house at exactly 0700 hours, so let's suit up and get ready."

****

Khalid Mohammed al-Baghdadi had just finished his morning prayers when he received an urgent text letting him know the police were on their way to his house. He had minutes left to get things ready. Pushing himself off the floor, he reached over and made sure the wires he had attached to the front door were ready. He then moved quickly to the rear door to check that entrance as well.

With his tripwires in place, Khalid grabbed the iconic American rifle, an AR-15, and made sure the thirty-round magazine was properly seated and a round chambered. When the authorities arrived in a few minutes, he'd be ready for them.

A handful of minutes went by when he heard the roar of several vehicle engines approaching his house from down the street. In seconds, he heard the loud screeching of tires as the drivers slammed on their brakes. Next, he heard a few sharp words spoken by someone in authority as several clusters of black-cladded men rushed toward the front porch of his house.

Just as the first person shouted "US Marshals! US Marshals!" Khalid raised the barrel of his AR-15 at the front door and fired several rapid shots at the whoever was about to barge through it. He heard a couple of loud grunts and some stumbling, followed quickly by a barrage of bullets fired right back at him.

Khalid hit the ground and slid behind the couch he had placed near the hallway to act as a barrier should his first tripwire not work. Suddenly, one of the darkly-clothed figures burst through the front door, fully extending the tripwire and triggering the charges he had rigged throughout the house. In the flash of an eye, the entire structure erupted in one gigantic fireball.

Chapter 11

Hearings

Washington, D.C.

Capitol Building

Director Mallory Harper was under intense scrutiny from the Congressional Intelligence Committee and her old employer, the Senate Select Committee on Intelligence, for the failure in detecting Khalid Mohammed al-Baghdadi before he entered the United States. The subsequent raid at his residency on January 3 had turned into a complete nightmare. When the FBI had executed the arrest warrant along with local police, the entire house had blown up, killing four FBI agents and six police officers and injuring nearly a dozen more.

The explosion had also caused the neighboring houses to catch on fire, making the situation even worse. The resulting explosion had invariably destroyed any evidence that might have been in the house, along with other possible leads that could have been helpful. As the FBI, NSA, and DHS began to conduct a detailed electronic exploitation and social media deep dive of Khalid, the FBI unearthed plans to launch a terrorist attack against several metro stations in the

Baltimore area. They also identified three other men who might have been part of the attack. Two of the three men had also been a part of the refugee program and were now at large as the FBI conducted a nationwide manhunt for them.

Because of the explosion, the raid made front page news, and garnered coverage from all the major TV networks. Of course, Fox News was hyping the incident, parading one terrorism expert after another who was denouncing the President's counterterrorism strategy and preaching the danger of the President's refugee program. It didn't help Mallory's cause that three of the five men now being implicated in this potential terrorist attack had all been refugees themselves.

The congressional and Senate intelligence committees wanted to know how these suspects were missed during the vetting process, and more importantly, how NCTC could assure the country that the increase in the number of refugees being accepted wouldn't pose a greater danger to the USA.

Director Harper was beginning to sound very defensive after hours of being grilled. "Senator, I can assure you my staff are doing all they can to ensure the refugees are being properly vetted," she asserted.

Clearing her throat, the ranking Democratic Senator from California asked, "Director Harper, can you enlighten us on what measures your organization has taken to improve security?" This was clearly a softball question to give her a chance to talk about some of the positive things going on in her department.

Mallory's face softened. "Yes, Senator. The effort to screen and process the refugees is a joint effort between the State Department, the FBI, Homeland Security and the intelligence community. Over the past three months, an additional 120 personnel were sent to the refugee camps in Jordan and Turkey to assist in the vetting process. An additional sixty analysts have been provided by various organizations within the intelligence community to assist in the process. I assure you, we are doing everything we can to ensure they are being properly screened."

The grilling went on for several more hours before the verbal pounding shifted from the Senate chambers to the Congressional chambers, where Director Harper reiterated what she had told the Senate.

****

The following week, the FBI had located the remaining terror suspects and taken them into custody. The refugee dust-up had died down as the GOP presidential debates began to take center stage.

With a very bombastic technology billionaire who had thrown his name into the ring over the summer, the primaries became almost a circus show to watch. The billionaire began to eviscerate his fellow Republicans as being bought-and-paid-for cronies of the special interest groups that the American people continued to rail against. He also took specific aim at the refugee and asylum seeker program, citing the recent terror suspects as an example of how Islamic extremists were manipulating the system to infiltrate their people into the country.

Chapter 12
Preparations

Chicago, Illinois

Jamal Sattar al Sayed had managed to receive asylum status just as he had been told he would. It had been an adjustment when he'd first arrived, but he had fully established his cover in the United States. Because of his education and skill level, it hadn't been very hard for him to get a job, and most of his neighbors just thought of him as a polite but quiet guy. Little did they know he was also known in some circles as "The Chemist," and he was a part of a sinister Valentine's Day attack.

His handler had given him specific instructions, so in his spare time, Jamal had been doing a lot of tourism of the city. He did his best not to draw any attention to himself, but most of the places where he spent his time had so many visitors from all over the world that one more man looking around and snapping pictures was just normal background activity. At Union Station, he spent a lot of time examining the supports holding up the platforms near the tracks, especially around platform nine-eleven. He gathered information on the types of material that were used, and then used his Privoxy to obtain other schematics of the structure online. After thorough calculations, he determined that he could destroy the foundation of the Riverside Plaza with about ninety pounds of high explosives and a shape charge. The rest would be up to gravity.

With that in mind, he bought a large rolling suitcase and began to design a bomb that could do the job and fit inside the suitcase. It would be imperative that the suitcase be laid down correctly next to the column for the shape charge to work. Each projectile would cut through one after another of the support structures under the station along platform nine-eleven. Then the explosive core of the bomb would destroy the ceiling above, which would, in theory, weaken the foundation enough to allow for part of the first floor of the Riverside Plaza to collapse on to the tracks below. From there, the laws of physics would go to work and the rest of the structure didn't stand a chance.

Jamal had been told he needed to build two additional bombs to be used that day as well, to increase the spirit of chaos and confusion. Once the initial bomb went off, two additional attackers were going to drive their utility van to the corner of South Wacker Drive and West Adams Street, as if they were there to conduct a cable repair. This would place the vehicle at the base of the Willis Tower for the second attack.

Jamal had spent considerable time designing the bomb for this vehicle. He had removed everything from the stolen van and loaded the interior walls with nearly 50,000 ball bearings and 8,000 pounds of high explosives. The bomb for this vehicle was being designed to essentially act like a large Claymore antipersonnel mine, the type the US military uses—only this one was a vehicle. The goal of this bomb was not to take down the Willis Tower, but to maim and kill as many people around it as possible. The size of the explosion would, of course, cause significant damage to the surrounding buildings, but it wouldn't be enough to bring down the structures. The bomb would be detonated via a timer, set to go off approximately forty minutes after the first one. If that failed, it could also be detonated via remote control.

Once the first bomb went off, the two attackers in the van would wait a couple of minutes to allow more people to spill out of the various buildings around them. After they had managed to place their van using their cable repair cover, they would then change into their tactical gear and proceed to walk down Wacker Drive, shooting anyone and everyone they came across, causing as much chaos as possible.

Jamal reviewed the plans for the third bomb one more time. He was quite pleased by how well the entire plan seemed to have been orchestrated by the leadership within his organization. He also took great pride in knowing that his devices would play a huge role in the choreography of the day's events.

Even if no one knows that I participated, except under the name "The Chemist," I will still have my revenge for the killing of my family, he thought.

Chapter 13
The Gathering

Deir ez -Zo, Syria
ISIS-Controlled Territory

Fahd al Saud had spent the past two years fighting with ISIS in Syria and Iraq and had proven himself to be a man who could be trusted and handle himself well under pressure. When he returned from the front lines for some R & R, one of the leaders in his group had told him some of the higher-ups wanted to speak with him. At first, he wasn't sure what to make of that, but he knew he hadn't done anything wrong so he was confident it must be something good.

Walking into one of the buildings that was acting as a headquarters of sorts, Fahd was led to a room in the back where several men were seated, waiting for him. Signaling for him to take a seat, one of the men eyed him carefully, as if he wasn't sure what to make of Fahd. He asked, "Have you ever traveled to America?"

Fahd replied, "I have. I studied in America for a year as an exchange student when I was in high school. My father thought it would be good experience for me." He spoke without hesitation, lest they think he was some sort of American spy.

The three men nodded as they talked in hushed tones to each other. The man who had asked him the first question softened his expression a bit. "Excellent." It seemed as if he had already known the answer.

If this was a test of my truthfulness, then I just passed, Fahd thought.

"We have a special mission for you," said one of the other men as he pulled some papers out of a folder.

The man placed a set travel documents for Fahd that appeared to be newly issued. A fresh Saudi Arabia passport with the appropriate accompanying papers to show that Fahd was traveling to visit the University of Chicago as a prospective student. An invitation letter from the engineering department and a professor were neatly printed on the university's letterhead.

"Because of your faithfulness to the cause and your devotion to Islam, you have been chosen to be a part of a great mission—one that will rely on your past experiences of living and traveling in America. It's a mission that no one but you is capable of fulfilling," the man said. He obviously sought to puff Fahd up in front of his fellow ISIS fighters.

His leader added, "This is a great honor, Fahd. I'm proud to have such a man as you to take part of my humbled command. Not all of us have the skills to perform such an important task as this. Allah has blessed us with someone such as yourself."

Fahd felt his cheeks reddening from the praises being heaped upon him. A chance to travel to America, a journey into the belly of the beast—this was a high calling. He also had the sickening feeling that this was going to be a martyrdom mission, something he had hoped he would be able to avoid. He had no problem dying for the cause of Islam; he just wanted his death to have significance.

The stranger who appeared to be the one in charge resumed his instructions. "You will be traveling to the city of Chicago on a tourist visa to visit the university. Once you arrive and make it through customs, a man will meet you at the baggage claim. He'll be holding a sign up with your name on it. You will be provided a coded message to use when you approach him. He'll recite a message back to you. If the message matches what you'll have been given before you leave for America, then you are to travel with him.

"Our friend will take you to a safe house, where you'll be able to spend the night and rest. The following day, you will be shown a suitcase bomb and given instructions on how to use it. You will then take a trip to Union Station, the main train station and the central Metra hub."

Pausing for a second, he looked Fahd in the eyes. "This is important, Fahd. When you are out in public in America, you will need to be discreet. You should not attract attention, but it is essential that you know the route and exactly what to do beforehand."

Fahd nodded in acknowledgement.

His leader put his hands on Fahd's shoulders. "You have shown yourself to be a worthy fighter, and a loyal soldier in the jihad. You are going to be the first martyr in a great attack against the infidel, America. It is a great honor."

Fahd smiled softly. He was very excited to be chosen, but he didn't take the responsibility lightly.

"We are going to arrange for you to travel back to Saudi first," instructed his leader, handing him a piece of paper.

"When you arrive in Jeddah, go to this mosque to speak with the imam there. Recite to him Quran 4:95: 'Not equal are those believers who sit at home and receive no hurt, and those who strive and fight in the cause of Allah with their goods and their persons. Allah hath granted a grade higher to those who strive and fight with their goods and persons than to those who sit at home. Unto all in faith hath Allah promised good: But those who strive and fight hath He distinguished above those who sit at home by a special reward.' Then the imam will give you some money and your plane ticket to fly to Chicago."

It took Fahd nearly three weeks to travel the various smuggling routes from ISIS-controlled Syria back into Saudi Arabia. Once back in the kingdom, he made his way to Jeddah and to the mosque. Fahd spent two days staying with the imam there before he was given his plane ticket and final travel arrangements were made. The day he traveled to the airport, the imam gave him the final code word to use with the man who would meet him in Chicago.

When Fahd arrived at the airport, he made it through customs and the boarding process with ease. Once on the plane, however, he made sure to have a couple of stiff drinks. While his ISIS friends would frown upon his indulgences, he felt he needed something to help calm his nerves.

The flight from Jeddah to Chicago was uneventful but long. The five-hour layover in Dubai was probably the hardest part for him. It was too short of a layover to get a hotel room, but just long enough that he couldn't really sleep in the waiting area without the constant fear that he'd somehow miss his flight.

Wandering through the expansive terminals, Fahd saw people from all countries and walks of life moving about the airport. Some traveled with a companion, while many others appeared to be solo travelers like himself. Not wanting to leave the passport-controlled part of the airport, Fahd settled on eating some food at a restaurant called Hatam. The skypark plaza allowed him to observe people while he enjoyed the traditional Iranian cuisine and killed a few hours waiting for his next flight.

Once it came time for him to board his final leg to Chicago, Fahd settled into the economy plus seat as he prepared for his final flight. Looking around the plane, he realized this was perhaps the nicest plane he had ever flown on. Etihad Airways really knew how to cater to all its passengers, not just those who flew first class.

When his flight landed in Chicago, Fahd grabbed his small carry-on bag, a small Samsonite that held three sets of clothes. His trip only called for him to be at the university three nights, so it would have looked suspicious if he was traveling with more clothes than what was needed for this short four-day trip. As he walked off the plane and onto the jetty that would lead them to the terminal, he shivered slightly. It was February in Chicago and unlike Saudi Arabia, Chicago was brutally cold in February. He walked briskly to get inside the terminal where it was heated.

Once off the jetty, Fahd removed a medium-sized jacket from his carry-on luggage and proceeded to put it on. He hoped the long-sleeved shirt and this coat would be enough to handle the winter weather, but he was having his doubts as he looked around and saw all manner of people wearing much thicker, heavier winter coats. Slowly, he made his way through the terminal, following the signs to baggage claim and the passport control section.

He saw two lines of people were forming. Signs above the lines read "US Persons and Green Card Holders" and "All Others." Most of the travelers approaching the segmented lines headed toward the "All Others" lane. Fahd got in line and followed suit. Slowly, he made his way to the Customs and Border Patrol officer.

"Passport please," asked the CBP officer, all businesslike.

Fahd handed the man his passport. The CBP officer took the document and flipped it open. He took a look at the photo and then compared it to the man standing in front of him. He then held the document open as he placed it under a special light briefly, and then it went facedown on a scanner. His information immediately started to populate the digital file being created of his entry into America.

"What's the purpose of your visit?"

"I'm visiting the University of Chicago as a prospective student," Fahd said confidently, just as he had rehearsed many times before.

"That's a good school. What are you looking to study?" the officer asked as he motioned for Fahd to begin placing his fingers on the Guardian R biometric scanner.

"I'm looking at their engineering department. I'm trying to narrow it down between Chicago and potentially Texas A&M," Fahd replied. He followed the electronic prompts as his finger and thumbprints were captured by the device and added to his newly created electronic dossier.

The CPB officer noticed Fahd had previously traveled to the US four years ago. He quizzed him briefly on his previous travels, but with no red flags showing up, he stamped his passport and handed it back to him.

"Welcome back to America," he concluded. Then he waved the next person forward, probably having already forgotten about Fahd.

When Fahd exited the controlled area, he spotted an African-American man standing in a line with dozens of other people all holding various name placards. Fahd spotted his name and walked up to the man. He leaned in and quietly said his prearranged phrase. The man smiled and said the proper words in return that confirmed his identity. He then motioned for Fahd to follow him back to his car. The two of them made small talk on their way out of the airport, acting as if they had known each other before this moment.

The first thing Fahd noticed when they left the terminal to head to the short-term parking garage was the bitter chill.

Damn, it really is cold outside, he thought.

When they reached the car, Fahd got inside and the two of them drove to a home in the suburbs, where Fahd would spend the night. Instead of meeting up with his next set of contacts the following day as he'd thought he would, he ended up staying with his handler for two days before he was brought to a new location.

When he arrived at the new house, he met several other individuals. He assumed they must be other attackers or part of the team, but until he knew exactly, he'd keep mostly to himself. What he did notice immediately was they were all speaking English fluently, and although Fahd did speak English, he wasn't very comfortable with his language skills.

Two of the men, John Osborn and Zameer Mandi, appeared to have known each other for a little while. Apparently, they were going to be working in a team, because Fahd could hear them discussing their equipment and double-checking their preparations. As time passed, it came closer to the time for evening prayers. They all instinctually began the ritual of washing their hands, feet, and their faces, and soon they were all kneeling, dipping up and down and chanting their prayers in unison. The act brought them together in their common belief and purpose.

John was apparently feeling nostalgic at this point. He turned to Zameer and asked, "So, partner, I know that we all have our own reasons for being here, but how did you come to be in this place with us tonight?"

Zameer sighed. "Well, I grew up in Pakistan. My family lived in the disputed tribal lands near Afghanistan. I wanted to pursue life in the city, away from the rural emptiness. After I completed my schooling, I packed up what little I owned and made my way to Islamabad. Soon, I was enrolled in both English and computer classes. Within a year, I had applied for a job and had begun work at the American embassy."

He held his hand up, wanting to stop any comments on that point. "At the time, I thought that my position would help me to perfect my English. I was even deluded enough to dream of immigrating to America. Then one day, my life took a drastic turn."

They had all poured some tea. He took a sip from his cup and continued, "The rest of my family went to my cousin's wedding in our home village. I was not able to join them because my classes would not give me leave to go home, but this saved me from a horrible fate. An American drone launched a hellfire missile at my family, killing nearly everyone I loved on what was supposed to be a day of celebration.

"The rage I felt at this injustice burned inside of me. I began to spend time in chat rooms online where other people who had lost someone to a drone attack went to share their stories. Some of those men became my friends in real life as well. After about a year, I came to the realization that I needed to attack the Americans. At first, I wanted to carry out some sort of attack against the American embassy where I worked. However, my new friends encouraged me to apply for a student visa and infiltrate the USA.

"One of my friends had connections and told me that I would be contacted once I arrived in the States, so that I could get assistance in obtaining my revenge for the killing of my family members. Eighteen months later, I was accepted to the University of Illinois and, with the help of my new benefactors, I received my student visa. I was set up with a bank account that had funds deposited into it every month; that allowed me to work on my degree and keep up good grades so that I would not have to worry about losing my visa. From then until now, I've just been studying and waiting. Allah has finally brought us to the appointed time."

One of the other men, Mohammed Nabi, responded, "Praise Allah," to which Zameer, Fahd and John all echoed, "Praise Allah."

Mohammed smiled. "Your story is not all that unlike my own, brother, although, I am from Afghanistan. The Americans took my father to a detainment camp before they killed him. I was able to come here to be a part of this great mission because of the refugee program." The other men nodded, and Mohammed was briefly lost in a daydream of memories.

****

Like most young Afghans, Mohammed Nabi had welcomed the Americans coming to his country when he was little. The West brought music, education, and many other things that he enjoyed. However, as he got older, Mohammed grew to hate the Americans. One day, when he was sixteen, his father was taken prisoner by them. They claimed his father had been working with the Taliban. The last Mohammed knew, his father had been detained in an American prison camp. His family had never heard from him again. A year had gone by, and Mohammed still didn't know if his father was going to be released or not. Then one day Mohammed's uncle came to him.

He put his hand on his nephew's shoulder as he told him, "The Afghanistan government has charged your father with terrorism against our nation. He has already been tried, and he was sentenced to death. He will be gone in a month."

The news was hard for Mohammed and the rest of his family to deal with; his mother would not eat for days after he told her the news. The day after the execution, Mohammed's uncle took him aside again and asked, "Nephew, you do know that your father was a senior leader in the Taliban, right?"

Indignant, Mohammed shot back, "No, he wasn't! He was a truck driver, just moving cargo from Pakistan to Afghanistan for the Americans."

His uncle calmly explained, "What your father had been moving was explosives. His work was of great help to the Taliban cause."

Mohammed was shocked. He didn't know what to say, so he just let the news soak in for a moment.

After a minute, his uncle continued, "You know your father was an honorable man, right?"

Mohammed nodded.

"Would you like to take your father's place in the Taliban?" his uncle asked, cautiously.

Mohammed didn't immediately say no. If his father and uncle had both been a part of this organization, that changed his whole view on the Taliban. However, practically, there were some issues.

"Uncle," Mohammed began, "I don't have a truck like my father, and I don't know how to drive one either."

"That's not a problem, nephew. We can arrange for you to obtain your license and teach you how to drive an eighteen-wheeler. We can also give you a truck to drive, one that has special compartments in it. This will allow you to smuggle opium to Pakistan, and explosives and weapons to Afghanistan."

Mohammed hesitated, but only for a moment. He nodded in agreement, and in that instant, his life changed.

For two years, he did as he was told. Then his uncle approached him and said, "I have a man who wants to meet you on your next trip to Pakistan."

"Of course, Uncle," he agreed.

When Mohammed arrived in Pakistan, he was driven to the capital for a special meeting. There he met with what appeared to be a very wealthy Arab. The man used a translator, but he could tell by the way his Arabic sounded that he was probably from one of the Gulf States.

The Arab asked Mohammed, "Would you like to avenge your father's death?"

Mohammed replied, "I believe I am avenging his death by bringing weapons and explosives over the border. These weapons and explosives are used to kill Americans." He spoke with great conviction and pride.

The Arab man asked, "If I were to give you the opportunity to kill many thousands of Americans with a single blow, would you do it?"

Thinking for a moment, Mohammed realized the Arab was asking him if he would become a martyr. "I would, but I have no desire to die young. I have to support my mother and my younger brothers and sisters."

Sitting back in his chair, the Arab took a long drag on his cigarette, holding the smoke in for a while before letting it out. "That's a fair argument. Then, would you be willing to help smuggle fighters into America?"

Mohammed smirked, incredulous at the question. "We are in Pakistan. I only move people and weapons from Pakistan to Afghanistan. How would I possibly move fighters to America, on the other side of the world?"

The Arab frowned and leaned forward. "I would arrange for you to obtain refugee status and go to America. Once you are settled there, I have an established trucking company where you would work for one of my associates. Are you interested in this?" asked the Arab. He hoped that this young man might yet prove to be the answer to his missing link. His previous driver had gotten himself in trouble with the American police and had been sent to jail; he would be deported after he had served his sentence.

Mohammed thought about this for a moment. If he went to America, he could wire American dollars home to support his family. They would be well taken care of, and he wouldn't have to worry about being caught every time he crossed the Afghanistan-Pakistan border.

"I would be interested in this proposition," he replied. "What exactly would I do for this trucking company?" he asked.

"My associate manages the trucking company in Chicago. They move freight from Chicago to other areas in the United States. From time to time, they also move freight from Mexico and Canada to Chicago as well. Because you have experience smuggling explosives across the border, we would use you to move special items as needed. You would also be paid a very good salary, $95,000 USD a year. For all intents and purposes, you would appear to be a normal refugee, just trying to make a new life for yourself."

The Arab began to show Mohammed pictures that told more about the company he would work for, the type of truck he would drive, the special compartments on the truck and how they all worked. Mohammed and the Arab talked for about an hour about the company, his new job and what he would be expected to do.

Then the Arab told him something that gave Mohammed pause. "Your family would need to leave Afghanistan and move to Pakistan. They will be taken care of, but it will need to appear as if your family left Afghanistan because they were being targeted by the Taliban. A credible cover story will be created, and then they will have to live by it."

Once Mohammed was convinced of the necessity of this part of the plan, the Arab moved on. He told him, "You will be given several hours a day of English tutoring and learn about other subjects, such as big rig mechanics and some American history. You will also be schooled on what to say during the refugee application process and what to avoid saying. We have a person working in the American State Department who will shepherd your application through the process and see that it is approved.

"Once in America, you will report to the trucking company and be given a job immediately. Your orders are simple—work hard for the trucking company, don't get in trouble with the police, and don't date any American women. You need to stay single and stay focused on your mission. Don't travel outside the United States, unless it is for work. You are not to attract any suspicion."

Mohammed followed the plan and did as he was told. Almost a year went by. Then one day, he was informed that his refugee application had been approved. He would receive a residency card and work permit to live and work in America. Once he had established himself and held down a job for more than a year, he could begin the process of bringing the rest of his family to America, if he wanted to.

Mohammed couldn't believe the plan the Arab had talked about actually worked. Two weeks later, he arrived in Chicago and was met at the airport by Ibn Abdula, the man who owned and ran the trucking company he would be working for. Ibn Abdula set him up in a small furnished apartment and helped him get on his feet. Then Mohammed drove on several training routes, obtained his trucking license, and began driving on his own.

After some time, Mohammed was contacted once again by the Arab who had brought him to the United States. "I believe you have shown yourself worthy, Mohammed," he began. "You have been very faithful to us in all that we have asked you to do. Now I would like to offer you an even greater honor."

Mohammed swallowed hard. He had a pretty good idea what was about to be asked of him.

Before he could speak, the Arab lifted his hand as if to say, "Wait." Then he pulled out a suitcase full of cash. "I know that you said that you didn't want to become a martyr because you needed to take care of your family, and I have great respect for that. However, if you are willing to make the ultimate sacrifice, your brothers and sisters in the faith will ensure that your family wants for nothing. They will know that you gave your life for the ultimate cause, and they will be cared for in every way."

Mohammed just nodded. There was nothing else to say.
****

Back in the safe house, the men were all still drinking their tea, weighted under the enormity of what lay before them. John, the only black man in the group, took his turn to speak. "It's probably pretty obvious to you just from looking at me that my story is different from yours...but our Great Allah has brought me to this same destiny just the same. I was born here, and I did not know the teachings of the great prophet Mohammed until I was an adult, but now my eyes have been opened and I am ready to become a soldier in the great jihad."

****

John, unlike his Arab partners, had converted to Islam nearly five years ago; it was really a chance occurrence. A woman he had been dating, Miriam Abadi, was a Muslim, and over the months as their relationship grew, his curiosity to understand her religion did as well. Before that time, John hadn't been a religious man and had believed in the words of Karl Marx: "Religion is the opium of the masses."

Then one day, when Miriam's father was talking to him about Islam, it all suddenly clicked. He felt like he had purpose; he felt love and acceptance from a family, something he had never really known while growing up. He converted to Islam and then began to study the Quran faithfully as he was instructed. He began to attend the same mosque as her family and really fell in love with the religion.

John and his fiancée married several months later, and for the first time in his life, he felt complete. His life was moving along smoothly for the next couple of years, until that awful day that changed his life forever. There was a horrific terrorist attack by a man claiming to be a member of ISIS against a gay nightclub in Austin, Texas, that shook America to its core. This was the first time in many years that a mass-casualty terrorist attack had occurred, and it scared people. During the following days, verbal attacks against the Muslim community rose across the country, especially in Texas, until one day, it exploded in Dallas.

John's wife had been attending their mosque for Friday prayers with her family just as she had countless other times. John was at work when a group of men who perfectly fit the stereotype of uneducated Islamophobic rednecks pulled up to the mosque and opened fire on everyone in it. Many were killed in the maelstrom of bullets, including Miriam.

John was devastated by the death of his wife and the senseless violence perpetrated by these ignorant fools. He was a police officer, sworn to protect his community...yet he could not protect his own wife. He changed that day. He went from being an outgoing, humorous guy to one who brooded in silence. Between the benefits that had been offered by the police department and Miriam's employer, he received a large amount of money from his wife's life insurance policies; with the money, he took an extended leave of absence from work and made the pilgrimage to the Kaaba to become closer to Allah in his greatest hour of need.

John spent the entire month of Ramadan in Mecca, asking Allah why he had taken his wife from him and what he could have done differently to have saved her. During that time, he attended a class being taught about jihad—not the minor jihad of war, but the great jihad, of abstaining from worldly temptations to keep oneself pure for Allah. During one of the training sessions, a man who appeared to be quite wealthy approached him.

"I would like to offer you dinner, if you would be interested in talking more about jihad with me. I want to understand what the American concept of jihad is, and how it translates into what the Quran talks about."

John accepted the offer, although he was a bit suspicious about the man's intent. The two men spent many hours over the next few days talking about the great jihad, the loss of John's wife, and how it appeared that the West was in a near-constant war against Islam. During one of their conversations, John mentioned, "I would like to get revenge on the men that killed my wife."

"Why haven't you?" asked his new mysterious friend.

"The men were caught, and they are already serving a prison sentence. They are out of my reach."

John's friend replied, "You should seek revenge against the society that fostered this type of anti-Islamic environment." Then he spoke at length about the Crusades and explained how each religious group came to the rescue of their faith when it was under assault. "You should consider coming to the aid of Islam and those being oppressed in America," he encouraged.

After Miriam's death, John had developed such hatred for those who despised his faith. He blamed them for the killing of his wife. It did not take too much convincing to get John to agree to meet again in the future and talk more about how he could potentially get the revenge that he sought.

John went back to Dallas and his job, though he was now a changed man. He spent a lot of time listening to some of the more radical teachers of Islam on the radio and internet. He read plenty of books, and mostly, he kept to himself.

When his Saudi friend called one day and said he was traveling to Dallas and wanted to meet up, John was more than willing. It was during this meeting that John agreed to be a part of Allah's plan to bring judgment on the American people.

Two years had gone by before John received a message that his time had come, that he was to travel to Chicago and be prepared to carry out Allah's judgment and become a great martyr for Allah and his murdered wife.

****

While each of the men had a different story for how they had arrived at the safe house that night, they were all united in their belief that their plan was righteous. Before the final prayer for the evening, they each took turns standing in front of the ISIS flag, filming their suicide videos. These were to be their last testament of their devotion to Islam and to the cause of liberating their Muslim brothers from the tyranny of the West. Each of them, in their own way, encouraged others to join the struggle—to use their lives to further Islam either through peace, the ballot box, or through the sword. Once their recordings were completed, they collectively participated in the final evening prayer before they tried to get some rest. Some of them weren't able to get very much sleep—not so much because of fear, but because of excitement. They were about to take part in the righteous war, and Allah would have a great reward waiting for them.

Chapter 14
Valentine's Day Attack

Chicago, Illinois
Union Station, Platform Nine-Eleven

It was still dark outside, and the wind howled in from the direction of Lake Michigan. Fahd pulled his scarf tighter across his face as he tried to block the biting wind from hammering his face. He shivered as he did his best to push the incredibly heavy suitcase up the handicap ramp to gain entry into Union Station. Had the suitcase not had wheels, he doubted he would've been strong enough to carry it the distance he needed to.

Once inside the station, he was greeted by the hustle and bustle of the morning commuters. Slowly, Fahd guided his suitcase past the throngs of people as he made his way down to the underground station yard. Looking at the various station numbers, he eventually spotted the track he was looking for. His handler had said he needed to move the suitcase to track nine-eleven, which was roughly in the center of the underground structure.

His instructions were simple: get to the center of the track and look for the chalk mark on the ground and on the support structure next to it. Once he found those marks, he was to stand there with the suitcase and wait until the next train arrived. As they arrived, he was to place the suitcase on its side with the long side of the suitcase running parallel to the length of the tracks. This would place the bidirectional charges in exactly the position they needed to be.

Now that Fahd was situated where he needed to be, he stood there in the morning cold, holding his hands to his mouth. He breathed some heat into his hands in a vain attempt to keep them warm. He thought about this moment, the last few minutes he had left to live. In the next handful of seconds, he would forever change the lives of so many countless thousands of people—people who were heading to work on this Valentine's Day morning, and probably had special lunch or dinner plans with their significant others.

Today would change all of that. Today would be the first time since that fateful day in September of 2001 that America was attacked by someone other than a disorganized lone wolf attacker—*this* attack had been planned and coordinated for more than five years. Fahd's only disappointment was that he wouldn't be alive to watch the chaos that would surely unfold during this day of days.

Suddenly, Fahd al Saud heard the whistle of the Milwaukee West train from Big Timber Road as the double-decker passenger car train slowed to a crawl, pulling all the way up to the front of the station. He looked nervously down at his watch; he was still on time. He searched the cement columns carefully, trying not to attract too much attention. He was looking for a small green X. Once he found the mark, he carefully placed the heavy suitcase he had been given down on its side next to the column.

Fahd calmed his breathing by taking several slow, deep breaths. The train doors opened, and a wave of passengers began to exit the train, filling the platform with rush-hour commuters as people began the start of the new workweek. Fahd opened his eyes, carefully reached down to the suitcase, and pulled the cord with the detonator out from the top exterior pocket of the suitcase. As his fingers closed around the detonator, he gently squeezed the red button, and then his world went black.

****

Tyrone Miller was anxious as the train pulled in to Union Station; they were already running nine minutes late, and he needed to catch his next transfer bus or he was going to be late getting to work. Tyrone and his wife had finally been able to move out of the violence-prone South Side of Chicago two years ago. He had been fortunate; he obtained a scholarship to work on a technology degree, which would ultimately be his ticket out of poverty and the deadly South Side. Now he worked in the IT department for a midsize firm in the Prudential Plaza. He and his wife were finally getting ahead and starting to fulfill that American dream of a house in the burbs and a good job in the city.

As the train pulled into the station and came to a stop, the door opened, and Tyrone was one of the first people out of the train. He sprinted toward the entrance of the station, winding through several curves and hallways in the building. Then suddenly, he heard the loudest explosion of his life. He felt the reverberation of the shock wave through the floor. Then the blast wave hit him, knocking him down to his knees. The last thing Tyrone saw was the pieces of the roof above him starting to fall; then there was nothing.

****

The blast wave from the explosion threw the commuter trains on both tracks nine and eleven apart, shoving them across the other tracks and platform lines like a child's playthings. This added to the immediate human carnage as these platforms were bustling with commuters whose trains had also just arrived. The blast was so powerful that it blew through the ceiling of the underground rail center, sending the growing fireball and debris through the bottom floor of the thirty-five-story Riverside Plaza building located just above.

The explosion, and subsequent implosion of the foundation and structural supports, made the building's weight shift inwards, which caused floors one and two to crumble and collapse into the gaping hole below. The alteration in the structure of the building caused the east face of the edifice to crack and crumble to the ground, exposing most of the interior floors of the east side of the thirty-five-story building. Numerous fires started as burst water pipes and electrical wires began to interact with each other.

Fragments of the explosive force that didn't expand upwards escaped through the underground tunnel connecting the Adams Street entrance with the platforms below. This massive flash of a fireball briefly engulfed many of the pedestrians who were unlucky enough to be crossing this major intersection. Dozens of people were suddenly engulfed in flames as their winter coats, gloves, scarfs and hats easily caught fire.

The attack immediately rocked the downtown heart of Chicago as hundreds of people were thrown around the streets, twisted, torn and crying in agony. Those who had managed to escape uninjured immediately began to help those who were in graver condition than themselves. Hundreds of people began to pour out of the various entrances of Union Station covered in dust, coughing and gasping for breath. It was the worst terrorist attack on American soil since the Twin Towers had fallen.

****

Hanaa Nazari was a registered nurse, riding the bus on her way to work at the ER but lost in thought, daydreaming about the special evening her boyfriend had planned. It was their first Valentine's Day as a couple. Hanaa was jolted out of her wistful reverie when she heard, and then saw, the explosion a block away at the Adams Street Metra entrance. An actual fireball raced out of the underground entrances, enveloping many of the pedestrians who were coming and going from the Metra. Hanaa's bus screeched to a halt, causing the passengers inside to lose their balance and reach for something to grab. As the bus stopped lurching forward, Hanaa got up from her seat and moved toward the door.

The bus driver was stunned in a frozen state of shock. "Excuse me, sir, can you open the door, please?" pleaded Hanaa.

The driver didn't say anything, but he did manage to pull himself together enough to hit the button so that everyone could get out. Almost all of the passengers rushed off the bus. Most of them began to run away from the direction of the blast, but Hanaa ran right toward it.

She saw numerous people writhing on the ground in agony and pain. Some people's bodies weren't moving at all and were clearly on fire. Hanaa ran toward the injured, wanting to help them. She was a nurse, after all.

She quickly surveyed the scene. The first order of business was to stop the flames on those who were still alive. She took off her winter overcoat and began to slap it down on flames to extinguish them. She saw a few people on the edge, staring at the scene in shock, and she cried out, "Hey! I could use your help. Can you help me put out these flames?"

A few of them seemed awoken by her call to action and began to help her blot out the fires. When the blazes were extinguished, she realized that although a lot of people had seen what happened, it was possible that no emergency responders had yet been notified. She touched the shoulder of a woman who had been helping her and said, "Thank you for your help. Can you call 9-1-1? I don't know if anyone has yet."

The woman nodded and pulled out her cell.

Once she was sure that additional help was on the way, she looked around to see what needed to happen next. There wasn't anything she could do for the dead, so she would have to leave their bodies to be taken care of by someone else. Some of the people had serious third-degree burns, but she didn't have any IV catheters or solutions hanging out in her bag. As Hanaa surveyed the injured, she found a few people who had severe abrasions. With what she found around her, she was able to MacGyver some fabric into makeshift tourniquets. That should at least hold them until help arrived.

One man had a head wound, and he was flipping out at the sight of his own blood. Head wounds are notoriously heavy bleeders. Hanaa signaled to one of the other people there who had been helping to come over. "I need you to apply pressure here," she directed, showing the man what to do. Then, seeing that her patient was possibly going to pass out, she quietly whispered to her new friend, "See if you can get him to drink some water, slowly. Then move him to the side and help him to lie down. Try to do what you can to distract him from thinking about the blood. Hopefully, that will keep him from passing out until the ambulances start to arrive."

The man replied, "You've got it," and then dutifully began to do as he was told.

Suddenly, a tall dark-haired man began yelling at Hanaa. "Hey, you! Raghead! You've done enough damage. Go back to your terrorist country and stay there!" He started to walk toward her in a menacing manner.

Hanaa suddenly felt very exposed. She was on the petite side and this man seemed to be twice her size.

The guy who had been guarding the head wound stood up quickly and put himself as a shield in front of Hanaa. "Hey, man, don't be an idiot," he said, putting out his hand as if to say, "Back up." "Not everyone that wears a hijab is a terrorist. She's a nurse. Don't you see the scrubs and the name tag? She's been helping people. She may have even saved some lives."

The man slowed down but still seemed angry. Another witness to the situation also moved himself between Hanaa and the agitator. "Hey, man, calm down. We need her help. Maybe you should be helping, too."

At that moment, the first ambulance arrived, and the man seemed to decide that Hanaa wasn't worth his trouble. He walked away.

"Thank you," Hanaa said, grateful for the two men who had stood up for her.

"I'm sorry that guy came at you like that. Thank you for helping all these people and showing us what to do."

There wasn't any more time to talk. Hanaa was needed to help the ambulances identify the patients who were the most critical. When there was a break in the action, Hanaa called her boss to let her know why she was late. She breathed a sigh of relief when her supervisor told her to do whatever she needed to do and just come in when she could.

****

Dr. Ibrahim Eliamam was sitting quietly at his desk in the office of the medical clinic. As he sipped his tea, he silently watched the seconds on the clock continue to countdown, until finally, the designated time had arrived. A few seconds passed, and Ibrahim hadn't heard anything yet. He began to think that their martyr might have been captured. Then he heard the thunderous boom as the bomb went off more than a mile away. He smiled inwardly, knowing that today marked the beginning of what was going to be a reign of terror on the Americans.

A few minutes later, one of the physician's assistants walked into his office out of breath and exclaimed, "There's been a massive explosion at Union Station! Quick, you should come see it on the news."

Outwardly, Ibrahim looked shocked, then horrified by the news. He quickly rose from his chair and followed the man down the hall to a waiting room that had Channel 9 News playing on the television. What they saw on the screen was horrendous. Bodies were lying everywhere: on the street, the sidewalks, and inside the lobbies of buildings nearby. Most of the glass faces of the structures around Union Station had shattered from the concussion of the blast.

A WGN Channel 9 news crew had been conducting a live report two blocks away when the explosion took place. Though their camera didn't catch a glimpse of the fireball escaping the Metra center from Adams Street, they were quickly on the scene, showing the devastation for all the world to see.

One of his physician's assistants immediately requested, "Dr. Eliamam, can I please head over there to help those poor people?"

An RN and a CNA joined in, "Yes, please. I want to go, too!" Several others could be heard making similar comments.

Ibrahim raised his hand, calling for calm. "I beg you, for your own safety, please stay here at the clinic. Right now, we don't know if there are other bombs out there. What if a second attack takes place? You will do no good to anyone if you are injured or killed yourselves."

The room was still restless, and Ibrahim could tell that his response wasn't enough to appease the group. "I will make some calls to the local hospitals, and we can take some of the patients who are injured but do not require surgery. I'm sure that the emergency rooms are going to be flooded. We can still help from here."

Everyone in the room breathed a collective sigh of relief, and they all started scurrying around, preparing trays for dressings, stitches and IVs.

The hospitals were very grateful for the help, and it wasn't long before patients were arriving at the clinic. Soon their rooms were filled with second degree burns, abrasions, and patients who were stable but in shock.

Ibrahim knew the next attack was about to take place, so he finished his last call with a hospital and returned to help his staff get ready to receive injured people from the terrorist attack he had so elegantly designed.

Chapter 15

First Responders

Upon hearing the details of their mission, John Osborn had insisted that his partner Zameer should join him at one of the indoor/outdoor gun ranges in the suburbs and practice how to properly operate the AR-15s they were going to use. He would spend the next four days teaching Zameer how to use the rifle, going over the equipment for it and imparting some basic fighting tactics. They both knew this was going to be a suicide mission, but that didn't mean they couldn't kill as many people as possible before they went to paradise. After several days of training, John was confident that Zameer knew what he was doing enough that at least he wouldn't get himself killed right away.

As John and Zameer sat in their truck, they saw that they had about five minutes until the bomb in the Metra station went off. They decided they had better get out of the van and try to look busy. They technically weren't supposed to park there, and they didn't need a police car coming along right at that moment, forcing them to move.

They exited the vehicle and began to take some measurements of the sidewalk. Then they sprayed some markings on it, as if they were identifying where future cables would be laid. As they continued to look busy, they heard the thunderous blast come from the Metra station just down the block. In seconds, they saw smoke rising from the station entrance and hear the loud screams of terror, agony and pain. For a split second, everyone just stood still, not sure if what they had heard was really a bomb.

From John and Zameer's vantage point, they couldn't directly see the Adams Street entrance, but it wasn't long before emergency response sirens rushed toward the scene of the attack.

John turned to Zameer. "Hey, it's time to get back in the van. We need to get ourselves ready for our part."

As they climbed back into the van, Zameer felt like he had a million butterflies in his stomach. He wasn't sure he could do this.

As John took his Comcast utility vest off, he saw the angst across Zameer's face. "Hey, man, take a deep breath and calm down. Everything's going to be fine," John reassured his partner.

Zameer did take several deep breaths to try and calm his nerves. He felt a little better, but he still had a million butterflies in his stomach. He looked at John and asked, "How are you not nervous? I feel like I'm about to throw up."

John just smiled. Once he finished strapping on his individual body armor, he checked to make sure that each of the six magazines he had was full and ready. "Zameer," he said, "I am nervous. I'm just controlling my emotions by focusing on the task at hand. You need to close your eyes and just focus on our assignment, going over what you're supposed to do and how you are going to do it. This will help to clear your mind."

Zameer nodded and did what John had suggested. When he opened his eyes a few seconds later, he felt a lot calmer. He felt ready. He got his own IBA on and checked his magazines, just as John had taught him. He then reached down between the seats and pulled his AR-15 out. Their AR-15s were identical. Each had a fourteen-inch short barrel with forward grips, EOTech holographic sights, and an adjustable butt stock. They both loaded their weapons and readied themselves.

Just as they were about to exit the van, John held up his hand and quietly said, "Wait."

Zameer felt panic creeping back up. "What's going on, John? What's wrong?" he asked, voice shaking.

John responded, "I just saw four ambulances pull up across the street, along with a couple of fire trucks. They look like they're setting up a triage tent. We need to wait a couple of minutes and see how this new turn of events unfolds."

"But the bomb is going to go off in twenty-three minutes now," asserted Zameer, glancing at his watch several times.

"I know, but we need to wait a couple of minutes. They will have their triage area set up soon." He turned to face Zameer adding, "In a few minutes, there will be thirty or more first responders at that makeshift aid station. Trust me, our attack will be a lot more devastating if we just wait a few more minutes."

John continued to watch the scene unfold as Zameer began to sweat profusely from the pressure of uncertainty. Then, a lightbulb seemed to go off over John's head. "Zameer, we're going to change the plan. When we get out of the vehicle and start our attack, we need to bum-rush the triage center and attack the people there. Now, if we can get beyond the triage hub and past the buildings on the next block, we could survive the blast of our truck. Then we could continue to attack civilians and emergency responders as well."

"This is a huge deviation from the plan, John," protested Zameer. "They want us to die in the blast so there is no possibility of us being injured or captured."

"I know, but if we are going to be martyrs, I want our sacrifice to count for as much as it can," replied John.

Zameer eventually nodded in acquiescence. John was the team leader, so he'd do as he was told.

John asserted, "I need you to stick with me. Move quick and continue to shoot. Don't get bogged down. We don't have much time. Once the van goes off, we'll reemerge and begin to attack the firemen, police and paramedics until we are killed. Don't let yourself be taken alive. Remember to use your cyanide tooth if you have to."

Although Zameer didn't feel comfortable straying from the plan, John seemed to know what he was doing, and Zameer was confident in following him. If his brother in the holy jihad had a better idea for killing more people, then he was all for it.

John checked his rifle one last time and then looked at Zameer. "We go on three...one, two, three."

With that, they both emerged from their vehicle and walked toward the triage center, no more than a hundred feet away. John took aim at a paramedic kneeling over a woman who was clearly in great pain from an arm injury. John took a deep breath. His heart rate slowed, and all he could see was the red dot where his gun was about to fire. He gently squeezed the trigger and his rifle barked. The paramedic was struck in the center of his chest, and he instantly fell backwards, away from the patient.

John shifted his rifle to the left and saw a policeman helping to carry an injured man. He centered his scope on the officer's chest, just below the neck where the police body armor didn't cover, and gently squeezed the trigger. The officer went down immediately, and so did the man he had been carrying to safety.

Zameer quickly calculated that John was picking people off to the left of their position, so he aimed toward the right. He saw several firefighters working to hook up a hose from their truck to one of the fire hydrants; he took aim at them and fired off a string of shots, hitting each of them multiple times. Then he moved his rifle to a group of civilians who were attempting to give first aid to some people who had been injured by falling glass. He aimed at the group of men and women and began to fire at them. Several of them were hit. A couple of them dropped to the ground or sought cover.

As John and Zameer approached the triage point, they had shot over two dozen people, mostly first responders. John saw several police cruisers heading toward their position down the road. He yelled to Zameer, "Quick, we need to get down to the end of the block! The van's going to go up in less than four minutes."

The two of them swiftly started to trot past the triage point. They moved down the sidewalk along South Wacker Drive, heading to the corner of Monroe Street and the Deloitte buildings. As they approached the corner, they saw a slew of cars stuck in traffic. Many people were standing outside their cars, pointing in the direction of the first bomb. They were completely caught off guard when John and Zameer came running toward them, until they started shooting at them. Several people were hit before the onlookers and pedestrians began to scream and run for cover.

John saw a Loomis armored truck stuck in the traffic jam and quickly pointed it out to Zameer, yelling, "We need to get to the other side of that armored truck!"

Zameer was out of breath, so he just nodded. They swiftly made it to the armored truck and placed it between themselves and the location of their utility van bomb that was about to go off.

At this point, a small group of police officers saw that the two gun-toting hostiles had hidden themselves behind the armored truck. They slowly moved in two groups. One group swooped in toward the front of the truck while the other group headed toward the back. They wanted to box them in and not let them run any further until additional police officers could assist them in taking them out.

John saw what the police officers were doing, and he didn't like it. They were doing exactly what he would do if the roles were reversed. He checked the timer on his watch and saw that they had less than sixty seconds before the van would explode. With that, he raised his rifle and took aim at one of the police officers. As the officer ran from one car to another, John squeezed the trigger and hit his target twice in the chest.

Then, as if on cue, the Comcast van exploded. The roar of the blast was deafening. John could hear the whizzing of thousands of ball bearings flying from down the block, some obliterating the vehicles nearby. Nearly all of the police officers who were in the process of surrounding them were hit by fragments from the blast. Several of the glass faces of the buildings around them shattered and rained glass down all around them.

John turned to look at Zameer to see how he was doing and found him lying on the ground with a bullet in his head, a pool of blood forming around him. Somehow, before the blast, one of the police officers trying to surround the armored truck had managed to get off a good shot.

It must've happened just prior to the explosion, he thought.

John quickly leapt to his feet and began to run further down Monroe Street. As he continued to run down the road, he shot everyone he came across. Many people raised their hands as if he would somehow take them prisoner. He just shot them instead. It wasn't until he got to the corner of Monroe and Franklin Streets that a group of police officers appeared from behind a bus and proceeded to unload their pistols on him. Most of the rounds hit him in his body armor; however, several hit his legs and both arms. He tried to pick up his weapon to aim it at them, but one of the officer's shots managed to hit him in the face. As he dropped to the ground, he had one final thought—the image of his wife's face.

****

The mayor of Chicago stood in the mobile police command center, not far from Union Station. He watched the screen as reports came in from the Metra attack. He was shocked and almost mesmerized; the images flashing on the screen were appalling. Fortunately, the city wasn't dependent on his actions alone. Dozens of emergency plans had been put forward for a multitude of scenarios, and people began to do the necessary work without much instruction.

The sound of a police radio interrupted his glazed-over pool of thought. "1071. Shots fired! Shots fired! Two armed men are shooting at the triage center we just set up near Willis Tower. Suspects are armed with AR-15s and are continuing to shoot at officers and rescue workers. They are running down South Wacker Drive, away from Willis Tower. Officers down! Repeat, officers down! Send additional ambos immediately!"

The mayor listened intently to the updates. After a few moments, one of the officers reported, "They're hiding behind an armored truck. We have them surrounded now. Our team is about to move in." Suddenly, the audio was interrupted by an incredible *BOOM!*

"What was that, Officer?" yelled one of the police captains into the radio. No response. They tried a few other signals. After a frantic couple of moments, the captain turned to the mayor and said, "Sir, it's no use. None of the men are responding."

The mayor turned to his police chief and shouted, "George, what in the blazes is going on?"

George Monroe, the newly appointed police chief, had been talking on his cell phone when the mayor yelled at him. He put up his left index finger as if to say, "Just one moment." When he finished a few brief words with the person on the other end, he hung up the phone and turned to speak to the now exasperated mayor.

"Sir, I apologize, but I was just talking with one of my captains who was near the Willis Tower. He told me that it appears a large vehicle bomb has gone off."

"Lord help us," gasped the mayor.

"From his immediate observations, it didn't look like there was any significant structural damage to the building that might cause it to collapse, but there are a lot of injured people. Most of the buildings around the area have had their windows blown out as well."

The mayor just stood there, dumbfounded by what was happening to his city. *How could this have happened?* he grumbled to himself. He immediately wondered what group could be behind such a terrorist attack.

As the mayor stood there like a statue, pondering what was happening to his city, Chief Monroe was trying to gather as much information as possible on how this had happened, who was responsible, and if there were any additional threats they should be worried about.

Police Captain Eddie Jordan walked up to the chief and said, "Sir, I just received a flash message from the FBI. They believe there may be a third bomb that's about to go off." His voice sounded remarkably calm amongst all the chaos.

****

Captain Eddie Jordan was an old-school cop. He believed in developing a network of informants throughout the city. He was highly regarded in the CPD circles, and just prior to the old chief being relieved of his duties for going against the mayor's refugee policies, Captain Jordan had been placed in charge of a new CPD intelligence unit. His group was charged to go after gangs and narcotics, but over time, as the mayor turned the city into a sanctuary city and began to accept tens of thousands of refugees a month, he had quietly formed a smaller unit inside his, to specifically infiltrate this community and keep a watchful eye out for any Islamic extremists.

Captain Jordan continued, "The FBI also sent us a passport photo of who they believe the Metra bomber was." He linked his tablet with the large monitor in the room and brought the photo and passport information up.

The mayor was the first to notice the entry date. "This Fahd al Saud just arrived three days ago. Did this notification from the FBI come with any intelligence on who he met while he was here?"

"Not yet, but now that we know what the bomber looks like, we may be able to go through some of our CCTV cameras and see if we can spot him," Chief Monroe replied. He didn't sound very optimistic about their chances.

Captain Jordan interjected, "I've told the officers in my unit to drop everything they're working on and to focus on this new information. We'll start scanning through the CCTV cameras and try to determine who he may have met with while he was in Chicago. He had to have had help, and my team will figure out who those individuals are."

The chief nodded his head. "Thank you, Captain Jordan. I want you to get your team to start working on who those two attackers near the Willis Tower were as well. Once the on-scene commander collects their biometrics and sends them to the FBI and CPD, you should have access to them, too."

After talking with a few other officers outside the command center, Captain Jordan reached into his pants pocket and pulled out his smartphone. He placed a quick call to his intelligence group's operation center. He needed to get more information quickly. When a female voice answered the phone, Jordan jumped right into the conversation.

"Officer Yates, have we found anything out about the two attackers at the Willis Tower? And has the FBI sent us any additional information?"

Yates responded, "Yes, Captain, we did find something. We just got their biometrics back from the FBI. Apparently, one of the attackers was a Dallas Police SWAT member, and the other was a part of the recent refugee program. The FBI said they have confirmed through biometric data that the SWAT member was John Osborn and the second attacker was Zameer Mandi."

Captain Jordan shook his head in disbelief at the realization that a police officer had been part of this dastardly attack. "That's good news that we were at least able to identify the attackers so quickly, but I can't get over the fact that one of them was a cop."

He paused for a second as he formulated his next course of action. "Yates, does the FBI have any additional information? Do they believe this was an attack by some Islamic extremist group? Has anyone claimed responsibility?" Jordan asked. He knew the mayor and the chief would be waiting on that information.

She responded, "The FBI says it appears John Osborn had converted to Islam many years ago, and he had recently traveled to Saudi Arabia. The FBI tells me that they're going to be making a public statement shortly about the attacks, but they do believe this to be a terrorist attack committed by an

Islamic extremist group. Right now, they're trying to narrow down which group."

Captain Jordan now had the information he needed. "Thank you for the quick work on this. By chance, has anyone reviewed the CCTV footage from Union Station to see if this Fahd al Saud had previously staked the place out before he blew himself up, or if he was accompanied there?"

"Actually, Jorge just finished looking over the footage, and he said they saw Fahd there yesterday afternoon with another man. They walked around Union Station and the nine-eleven platform, stopping briefly at what we believe was the point where the bomb went off.

"Before you ask," she continued, "we don't know who the second man was yet, but our camera got a good look at him, so we're confident we'll find something. We sent the image over to the FBI and Interpol. I'll call you back as soon as we find something."

Letting out a sigh, Captain Jordan responded, "Officer Yates, I can't thank you and Jorge enough for your hard work on this. You guys are clearly putting together a lot of information very quickly. Let me know as soon as you have some noteworthy updates." He didn't say goodbye but just hung up the phone. He knew Yates wouldn't take it personally; they were all too busy for formalities at this point.

As he terminated the call, he looked up to see several FBI agents walk into the mobile command center, walking toward the mayor and Chief Monroe. He immediately walked toward them so that he could hear what they were saying.

Captain Jordan didn't have time to relay any of the information he'd just learned before the FBI agents started talking. The newcomers were already making introductions.

"I'm Special Agent in Charge John Deeks, the agent in charge of the Chicago field office. We have some information we would like to share with you so that we can bring you up to speed." He gestured toward the table and chairs in the center of the expandable trailer, indicating they should all sit down.

As everyone took their seats, SAC Deeks proceeded to show them what they had discovered up to this moment. "As you may know, we've been coordinating with Captain Jordan's group," he said, nodding toward him, "and have identified the two attackers at the Willis Tower. The first of the two attackers at the Willis Tower was Zameer Mandi. He came to the US as a refugee and settled in Chicago about two years ago. By all accounts, Zameer had kept to himself and stayed out of trouble, so we had no reason to suspect he was a part of anything nefarious."

Captain Jordan felt a bit irritated that he hadn't been the one to break the news, but interrupting would have made him seem petty, so he kept his mouth closed.

"The other attacker was named John Osborn. He was a Dallas Police officer and member of their SWAT team. What we know about Officer Osborn is that he converted to Islam about five years ago, but we don't believe he was radicalized until the death of his wife. After she was murdered in that Dallas mosque attack a few years ago, he made a lengthy trip to Saudi Arabia, which is where we believe he came to hold extremist views." As SAC Deeks spoke, one of his fellow agents showed several pictures of Officer Osborn and Zameer on the screen in the room.

Agent Deeks continued, "We believe you're already aware that we've identified the first attacker that blew up the Metra station."

Everyone nodded. Deeks went on, "His name is Fahd al Saud. He was a Saudi national who had just arrived in Chicago from Riyadh three days ago. We aren't sure who he met or what kind of support he received, but we're fairly certain that he was a part of an ISIS terrorist cell operating here in Chicago."

The mayor interrupted to ask, "How do you know this is an ISIS cell and not some other terrorist organization?"

"Just prior to the Metra bombing, an ISIS spokesman broadcast a message on several jihadi websites, saying that they were about to carry out the first of a series of terrorist attacks against the city of Chicago today. Within five minutes of his posting, the Metra bombing happened. Then the Willis Tower bombing. We believe a third bomb is likely to go off today, and we're actively working to determine where and when it may happen, but as of right now, we have no leads."

Everyone in the room looked nervous, almost panicked as they waited for the other shoe to drop.

A third bomb…please, God, not another bomb, Captain Jordan silently prayed.

Chapter 16

Lower Wacker Drive

Mohammed listened studiously to the radio. His heart leapt when he heard the breaking news about the Metra bombing as he continued his drive into the city. About thirty minutes later, he heard an announcement about two men who were shooting rescue workers near the Willis Tower. Then a few minutes later, the broadcaster sounded exasperated as he announced that another massive bomb had gone off near the Willis Tower. There was no official tally of casualties, but so far, the death toll was expected to be in the hundreds, if not the thousands.

Mohammed continued to drive on Lower Wacker Drive, though the traffic was starting to get worse. He was concerned that he might not make it to his designated target on time. He still needed to turn on North Wabash, and judging by the traffic in front of him, it was going to be a little while before he got there. He reasoned that people must be trying to flee the city. Mohammed had driven this route at least a dozen times with the same truck, timing everything, but he couldn't account for the reaction to the previous attacks. As he approached the stoplight, the excitement Mohammed felt continued to grow. If things went well, his eighteen-wheeler just might cause one or more buildings to collapse.

Four months ago, Mohammed had been trained on how to drive a specialized tractor-trailer carrying liquid natural gas. He began to drive this trailer regularly, so he would become comfortable operating it. The unique trailer system held a capacity of up to 641,080 cubic feet of LNG. Essentially, the truck had been turned into a forty-ton mobile bomb that was now being driven into the heart of Chicago.

As Mohammed sat at the stoplight on Lower Wacker Drive and North Wabash, he began to sweat profusely. He was nearly to his target. His heart raced, and he felt as if his body was going to explode. To calm himself, he began to say prayers to Allah and recite various parts of the Quran. Finally, his truck moved between the Trump International Hotel & Towers and the Langham Hotel under Wabash Avenue. He reached down and grabbed the detonator. He held it tight in his hand as he moved his thumb over the red button on top. Then he slowly depressed the button until his world flashed and immediately evaporated with him.

His LNG bomb exploded between both towers, near the base of their foundations. The concussion from the blast was so powerful that it blew the road above him completely apart, sending dozens of vehicles that had been sitting in morning rush-hour traffic high into the air. The foundation of Langham Hotel was so compromised from the explosion that the whole building began to tilt to the east toward Trump Tower, until the upper floors of the hotel snapped from their own weight, falling toward the street below and striking Trump Tower. The foundation of Trump Tower had also suffered immense structural damage from the blast. The structure began to tilt to the west, causing nearly the entire glass face of three of the four sides of the building to explode and shatter, showering thousands of pedestrians with glass shards.

Mohammed had avenged his father's death and brought the ISIS fight to the streets of America. His name would be remembered long after his death as the man who had killed hundreds of Americans in a single day.

****

Back at the police command center, the group continued their discussion, trying to seek out any leads on where another bomb might explode. One of the officers turned away from the bank of computer screens he was monitoring, face white as a ghost. He cleared his throat and said, "Mr. Mayor, we just received reports of a third bombing. The report says the explosion detonated on Lower Wacker Drive, between the Trump International Hotel and the Langham Hotel." The officer's voice cracked with emotion as he spoke.

Everyone in the group looked at each other dumbfounded, not sure what to say or do next. SAC Deeks immediately grabbed his smartphone and tried to call one of his officers at the Trump International Hotel. On a hunch, he had sent an agent to the Trump Tower because it was the second-tallest building in the city. He had figured if the terrorists were going to attack another skyscraper, this would probably be the one.

It took a couple of rings before he got through, during which an entire lifetime seemed to pass by. When Agent Rodriguez picked up the phone, Deeks was clearly relieved. "Thank God I got you. Can you tell me what happened? What's your assessment of the damage?" The TV news crews hadn't moved any cameramen to the area yet, so they couldn't rely on the news for any footage.

Agent Deeks hit the speakerphone button on his smartphone and placed it on the table as the group gathered around. "Sir, you were right to send me to Trump Tower," began Agent Rodriguez. "It was clearly the next target. What I'm seeing, it's just unbelievable. We were in the process of evacuating the hotel, when suddenly, this enormous explosion happened. The glass façade of the building shattered, and suddenly it was raining glass down on everyone we had just told to evacuate. Then we heard a loud grumbling and the building started to shift. I'm standing across the street from the Trump Hotel right now, and it appears the hotel is leaning but still intact. The other hotel across the street on Wabash is nearly destroyed. Part of the top half of that hotel broke off and fell into the Trump hotel and the crater below, where the explosion apparently happened. It's horrible, Sir. What do you want us to do now?" Agent Rodriguez's voice was shaky, as if you could hear his knees knocking through his words.

"Just continue to help evacuate people away from the blast area to safety. Keep your phone close, and I'll give you a call in a little while to check in," SAC Deeks said before he ended the call.

The mayor put his head in his hands for a moment, dumbfounded. When he looked up, there was a fire in his eyes. "SAC Deeks, I just can't believe this. Is it over, or are you expecting more attacks?"

Deeks sat down, devastated at what was happening. "Frankly, Sir, we aren't sure. What intelligence we do have said there would be three attacks today."

"Well, I'll tell you one thing. There had better be some scalps for me by the end of the day," grunted the mayor.

"Yes, Sir. I think we all want that," responded SAC Deeks. Then he turned to the group and announced, "You heard the man...let's get on that."

Chapter 17
Scapegoat

McClean, Virginia

National Counterterrorism Center

Director Mallory Harper was furious. The terrorist attacks in Chicago were all over the news. The images of bloodied and torn bodies of men, women, and children lying dead in the streets were horrifying. Chicago looked like a war zone. Then the FBI released the names of the attackers and, sure enough, two of the four terrorists involved were refugees who had been vetted and cleared through her department. Now the White House was all over her about how this could have happened. She needed information, and she needed a scapegoat.

As she walked into the room, she barked, "Mr. Stone!"

At the sound of her voice, Mike felt like ice was running down his back. "Yes?" he answered cautiously, looking up from the conversation he had been having with some of the analysts in the bullpen.

"What information do we have on these two individuals? Who completed their vetting?" Mallory was furious that two of the people her department had vetted had just perpetrated the largest terrorist attack in American history.

Mike walked toward her and guided them away from the other analysts. In a quieter tone, he said, "Director Harper, just so you know, I'm also irate that another major terrorist attack happened on our watch. I'm still trying to track down who completed the vetting for the two individuals who were approved by our department two years ago. I do need a few more minutes, but I'll have more information for you shortly."

With that, Director Harper grunted and then turned to look for another victim until she could figure out a way to make this stink stick to someone else besides her.

A minute later, Julie walked toward Mike and handed him two folders. "These are the vetting folders of the two attackers and who screened them," she said. He immediately began rifling through the papers until he found what he was looking for.

Stone looked up at Harper, who was now about twenty feet away, talking to one of her favorite analyst team leaders, a person she had brought with her from the Senate Intelligence Committee. He signaled with his arm to get her attention. "Director Harper, I have the two attackers' vetting packages, and the name of the person who did the screening."

Director Harper began to walk quickly toward him, "What do you have?" she demanded.

He lowered his voice a little. "The vetting was originally done by George Lee. He had flagged both of them as having possible terrorist links. The files were then transferred to Dawn King, who approved them for the refugee program." As he finished speaking, Mike looked up at Mallory and then glanced back at Dawn, the analyst team leader Director Harper had just been talking to.

At first, Harper was visibly stunned that it had been her friend Dawn who had signed off on the vetting. She began to search her mind for how she could spin all of this so that all the blame wouldn't have to land on her friend. After some calculation, she muttered, "The way I see this, this is George's fault. He had the files first." She knew her argument was weak at best once she uttered it; she felt foolish for even letting the words out of her mouth.

Mike's face contorted as he obviously controlled his initial response to her statement. "You can't be serious," he asserted. "He's the one who flagged them as having potential terrorist ties. I know you think he's a problem child because he's flagging a lot of these people as having possible terrorist links, but he's one of the best analysts we have, if you ask me. Let's not forget, he tried to block them from being accepted into the refugee program. It was Dawn King who reversed his decision and allowed them in. She is the one who clearly screwed up, and I, for one, would like to know why she approved two individuals who George had assessed to have potential terrorist links." Mike's tone was accusatory, but Mallory couldn't tell if he was accusing her as well or just Dawn.

Mallory just stood there for a second, thinking about what to say next, what to do. She was under a lot of pressure from the White House to identify who had let these guys in. She didn't want to sacrifice her friend, but Mike was right. Anyone who reviewed the file would see that Dawn had overridden George on this one and approved their packages.

Sighing audibly, she replied, "You're right. I'm not sure what I was thinking." She tried to regain her composure.

After taking a deep breath, Mallory turned and walked toward Dawn, Mike right behind her. She whispered to Dawn for her to follow her to her office. When all three entered the room and the door was closed, Mallory said, "The White House is all over us to figure out how these two attackers were able to gain entry into the refugee program. Mike's been doing some digging into their electronic files, and we found their packets. We just finished reviewing the files of the attackers, Dawn. It shows that you approved these two individuals." She let that hang in the air for a moment.

Dawn defiantly replied, "No, I didn't. I don't believe you."

Mike handed her the folders, which clearly showed her name and signatures approving them for entry into the program.

Dawn looked up at Mallory with pleading eyes, begging to be saved. She began to cry. "You told me to approve those names. I was only doing what I was told." As she spoke, she looked from Mallory to Mike, as if he might somehow be able to help her.

Neither Mike nor Mallory said a word. After a very awkward moment, Dawn whimpered, "What's going to happen to me now?" She wiped away a tear from her cheek.

Mallory let out a deep sigh before responding, "For starters, I'll need your badge and ID card. You're going to be placed on administrative leave until a thorough investigation has been done. As for what will happen in the long run, I really don't know right now." She legitimately had no idea if her friend would just be publicly crucified or if she might actually be charged with some crime.

Once she had left the room, Mike turned to Mallory and asked, "What did she mean when she said you told her to approve their names?" He spoke in a tone that managed to be soft and full of accusation at the same time.

Mallory shot him a dirty look before responding, "Mike, I'm under a lot of pressure from the White House to ensure these refugees and asylum seekers don't pose a threat to our country, while still letting in as many of them as possible. We're all trying to do our best here. I'm not sure what she meant by her last comment, but right now, we need to focus on making sure no one else we screened is going to carry out another terrorist attack." Then she opened her office door, indicating that he should leave.

****

Following his conversation with Mallory, Mike made a quick call from his office to Trevor over at Langley. He was busy, of course, but he agreed to meet Mike for a quick coffee at a nearby Starbucks.

Thirty minutes later, Mike stood in line and ordered a grande caramel macchiato with an extra shot of espresso. It was going to be a long day so he needed the added caffeine. When his drink order was ready, he walked to the counter and grabbed his cup, hurrying to a table that had miraculously just become available. No sooner had he sat down than Trevor walked in and made a beeline to him.

"Sorry for the delay, Mike. I hope you haven't been waiting long," he said. He sounded a bit out of breath, which was unusual. Trevor was almost never in a hurry.

Taking a quick sip before replying, Mike shook his head. "No, not long. Just got my drink," he responded, his voice almost jovial.

The monitor near their seats was showing CNN coverage of the horrific attacks. Trevor's eyes strayed as he watched for a moment, transfixed. Then he turned back to Mike. "You said this was important—so, what is it?" he asked gruffly.

"Remember when I told you that Chicago and Baltimore were receiving an unusually high percentage of single military-age males through the refugee program?" Mike asked as he too watched the carnage unfolding on TV.

"Yeah, I remember. Our analysts found it odd and unusually high compared to the other cities. What of it? Did you find something else?"

Mike nodded softly so as to not give anything away. He then leaned in slowly and whispered, "Two of the four attackers were part of the refugee program."

"I already know that, Mike. The rest of the world is about to find that piece of information out as soon as someone in Congress leaks it," Trevor replied angrily.

"No, you don't understand yet. They were both originally flagged for having potential links to terrorism. They should've been denied entry, but their recommendation was overruled by one of the senior analysts and approved anyway. The analyst who made the final approval said she was just approving the names Director Harper had given her," Mike added.

Trevor shook his head slowly. This little piece of information painted an entirely different picture. "You have to be kidding me, Mike," he finally replied. "Are you sure this is correct?"

"Once we saw the ISIS videos and we learned who these guys were, we ran their information through the refugee screening program. Sure enough, two of them popped. We found the initial screening packets and dug into them. The original recommendation was to deny them entry into the program based on possible terrorist links. Something in their background was a red flag, a past associate or CELLEX or something. Either way, they failed the screening. Then the lead analyst overrode that decision and approved them anyway. Both of those analysts still work in the department.

When Director Harper and I questioned the lead analyst who approved their packets, she said she was just approving the names of the people Harper had given her. Before she could say anything else, Harper placed her on administrative leave until things could be sorted out. I tried to ask Harper about it, but she stonewalled me."

The two of them sat there silently for a moment, watching the TV footage as the other patrons in the Starbucks did likewise. A woman nearby wiped away some tears, while a man openly sobbed in a chair as he looked at his cell phone.

"Trevor, I think you're right," Mike admitted. "Something isn't adding up with Mallory Harper. I'm not sure what it is, but if she's approving people to be a part of this refugee resettlement program that shouldn't be, then something terribly awful is going on, and this may be the first of many dominoes to fall."

****

Washington, D.C.
White House, Oval Office

The President was in the middle of the worst day of his life. Thousands of Americans were dead, all on his watch. A meeting had been called at the Situation Room, but he had a little time before everyone assembled, so he went to his office to clear his head.

"For the next fifteen minutes, I don't want to hear from *anyone*, understood?" he said to his secretary as he opened the door to the Oval.

"Yes, Mr. President," she replied.

As he sat alone in the room, the silence was deafening. He was confronted by thousands of conflicting thoughts, some angry, some sad. At one moment he wanted to cry, and then he felt like punching a wall. None of these responses seemed to appropriately express what was happening that day. A few moments went by like this. Nothing was happening, but at the same time, everything was happening.

The buzzer rang. "Mr. President?" asked his secretary tentatively.

"Kathy, I thought I told you I didn't want to be disturbed," he shot back.

"I know, Sir, but it's Karen Philmore on the line. Do you want to take it?"

As much as he wanted to, he really couldn't refuse a call from the former Secretary of State, who was now the Democratic presidential nominee. He sighed. "OK, Kathy. I'll take it," he reluctantly responded.

"Secretary Philmore, you are on the line with the President," said Kathy, and then there was a click as she got off the call.

"Hi, Karen. What a horrible day, huh?" he began, not sure how to begin the conversation.

"Horrible doesn't even begin to describe it," she snapped. "How on God's green earth did this happen?"

"It's too early to be sure, but you know every agency is following all available leads right now," replied the President.

"Well, I want some heads to roll over this, do you understand? If we don't come down on this with an iron fist, then you might just have cost me the election," barked Karen.

"You think this is my fault?" he retorted.

"Well, it happened under your watch, didn't it? At the end of the day, that is how history is going to see this. So, you'd better make someone an example, or else you—and by proxy, I—will go down as the incompetent fools that allowed the death and destruction of thousands of innocent Americans." Secretary Philmore's voice dripped with condescension.

"I understand, Karen," the President snapped. "You'll have your head."

There was silence on the phone for a moment as both of them spoke anger without using any words.

"I have to go now, Karen. I have a meeting in the Situation Room."

"Good day, Mr. President," Secretary Philmore said in an overly sweet tone.

****

Having had his own moment, the President now fumed at his National Security Advisor, Leah Bishop. "You assured me the refugee program was secure, that we had the resources in place to make sure this type of attack could never happen!" As he shouted, everyone in the room tried to appear as small as possible to avoid being a target of his anger.

Clearing her throat, Leah defiantly replied, "Mr. President, with the exception of the Saudi national, none of the attackers recently came to the US. They had all been here for at least two years. They were clearly sleeper cell agents, which the FBI should have caught." She stared daggers at the Director of the FBI.

The President shifted gears, zeroing in on his FBI Director. "She is partially right. Why did these attackers go unnoticed?" asked the President, a bit more calmed.

"Mr. President, we're doing the best we can with the resources we have. The refugee program has brought thousands of questionable people into the country over the past three years. ISIS has also said on numerous occasions that they would infiltrate the US through the refugee programs. After today's attack, it appears they have successfully done just that."

The President was livid. He was about to go on national television to calm the nation and assure them that their government was doing everything in its power to protect them. He brooded, wondering if they really had done the right thing by accepting these refugees from the Middle East.

Every moral fiber of my being tells me this was right, though, he concluded.

The President huffed. "Listen, the public is going to want to know how this happened, and so is Congress."

He turned to look at Leah again. "I want a head to deliver them. Who's handling the screening for the refugee program?"

Before Leah could respond, the FBI Director replied, "Director Mallory Harper, at the National Counterterrorism Center."

The President couldn't help but notice that Leah was burning a hole into the FBI Director's head with her eyes.

She turned toward the President but didn't break her angry gaze at the FBI Director. "I was going to say that Mitchel Liam at the State Department is technically in charge of the program," she declared.

The President sat back in his chair. He couldn't just throw the State Department under the bus, not right now, with the election in full gear. His former Secretary of State was running to replace him, and any dirt that got thrown at State would certainly stick to her as well. His eyes focused as he made his decision.

"Take care of Harper," he announced. "I want her gone by the end of the day. Everything is to fall on her. Do you hear me, Leah?"

"Yes sir, Mr. President," she responded. The tone in his voice had indicated that she had better not challenge his decision.

Chapter 18

Not Over Yet

Undisclosed Location

Streaming Live

As the man only known to a small circle of people as "the Ghost" sat in the corner of the room, he watched the spokesman for ISIS, Taha Falaha al-Baghdadi, read the script for what must have been the tenth time. This was going to be a big speech; their first attack against the Great Satan had succeeded beyond their wildest dreams. This video would trigger the second wave, which would wreak further havoc on the Americans.

The Ghost and his backers were certainly getting their money's worth out of their venture with ISIS. As Taha walked over to the wall that had the black flag of ISIS hung across it, he could hardly contain his excitement as their elaborate plan was starting to play out.

The room became quiet and all eyes turned toward Taha. He signaled that he was ready to begin. The camera turned on and his compatriot gave him the signal.

"My fellow Muslims, may peace be upon you and his prophet Mohammed. Today, with the merciful help of Allah, our Muslim brothers struck a great blow against the Great Satan in the city of Chicago. The Americans have come to our lands to strip us bare of our resources, wage war on our people, and kill our women and children in the name of freedom—their deluded, misguided version of freedom. Today, we brought the war to them, just as they have brought endless war and conflict to our lands.

"Today, I want to announce to the world that the Islamic State now claims control of the city of Chicago. I call upon our fellow Muslims living in the lands of the Great Satan to rise up and join our forces in Chicago. I call upon you to use whatever means you have at your disposal: knives, weapons, and even your own vehicles can be used as a weapon. Brothers, Sisters, now is the time to rise in defense of your religion. To our fighters in America, the Islamic torch is lit."

The message quickly streamed across Twitter, Facebook Live and YouTube. The men in the room took down the props and packed everything up with a sense of urgency. It wouldn't take American intelligence long to track the IP address to this location in Yemen and send a drone their way. As Taha finished wrapping something up and placing it in his backpack, he walked toward the Ghost.

"Your message has been sent. Our fighters will carry out their orders," he said and then quickly walked out of the room. His entourage would escort him to a safe location where he would spend the next couple of weeks in hiding.

The Ghost got up and followed his bodyguard to their waiting vehicle. From there, they drove to a small airport where his private aircraft was waiting to take him back to Riyadh.

****

McClean, Virginia
National Counterterrorism Center

It had been a rocky three days at the NCTC. Director Harper had been relieved of her position by the end of the day of the attacks in Chicago. As the highest-ranking person in the department, Michael Stone had been placed in charge of the department until a more permanent solution could be found. He came in guns blazing. His first order of business was to recommend a temporary block on any new refugees coming into the country until his department could reinvestigate everyone who had entered through the program over the last three years. Then he requested that all the screeners and analysts currently supporting the program in Turkey and Jordan be reallocated to his department stateside to assist in processing all this additional work.

Despite some initial pushback from the National Security Advisor, his request had been approved. Congressional leaders were calling for inquiries and investigations, and some were calling for a complete end to the program. Mike managed to satisfy both sides by convincing the administration to take a pause while they focused on rooting out any potential terrorists that might have slipped through the program during former Director Harper's tenure.

As far as Mike could tell, the President's team didn't really have a choice in the matter, and Harper made for an excellent scapegoat. Any new people they identified could be hung around her neck. They had to agree to his proposal to save face if they hoped to salvage the program at a later date.

The casualty reports continued to roll in from Chicago. There had been 234 people killed during the Metra attack, then another 1,453 during the second attack near the Willis Tower. The third attack killed the largest number of people at 2,748 fatalities. The Langham Hotel had been virtually destroyed during the initial blast. An hour later, the Trump Tower had collapsed and fallen across Kinzie Street, destroying two city blocks of buildings, roads and shops. The fires caused by the collapse of the Trump Tower had taken nearly thirty-six hours to get under control and required twenty-six different fire stations to put them all out.

In addition to the more than four thousand people who lost their lives that day, nearly six thousand others had been injured. The number of first responders who had been killed had also been alarming, and that slowed down the city's abilities to treat all the victims of the attack. The hospitals in Chicago and the surrounding area were completely overwhelmed. Injured people were being flown to Milwaukee and other trauma centers in southeastern Wisconsin and northern Indiana. First responders from around the country were flocking to Chicago to help, just as they had during the 9/11 attacks so many years ago.

When ISIS issued their rallying cry and their assertion that they now had control over the city of Chicago, the President raised the terrorism alert level across the entire country. Additional FBI agents were sent to Chicago. Every terrorism tip that was being phoned in was checked and cross-checked. The tension in the air was so thick it was palpable.

Chapter 19
Don't Get Comfortable

University of Chicago Medicine
Emergency Room

The ER at Chicago Medicine was still busy, but much closer to the normal flow of patients that came in on a daily basis. The hospital had handled thousands of injured people during the terrorist attacks three days ago, but most of them had either been transferred to other hospitals or been discharged, so the tempo of the hospital was finally starting to slow down.

It was 5:34 p.m. when Mohsin Yousef slowly walked into the ER. As he entered the waiting room, he moved to a corner where no one else was sitting. He pulled his smartphone out and proceeded to place a call to the hospital switchboard.

Once he had gone through the prompts, a live voice finally answered, "University of Chicago Medicine, how may I help you?"

Quietly but clearly, Mohsin Yousef told the operator, "A bomb has been placed in the second floor of the hospital, near the location where the majority of those who were injured during the attacks a few days ago are recovering. Allah is not done delivering his judgment on the Great Satan." Then he hung the phone up and placed it back in his pocket calmly, remaining in his seat like any other patient waiting to be seen at the ER.

The seconds stretched by for what seemed like hours to Mohsin. Finally, he observed one of the security guards receiving a message on their radio; once he heard the speaker on the other end, the guard began to look around the ER frantically, as if he were trying to locate the bomber.

The hospital PA came on. "Attention! All patients and staff, please evacuate the hospital. This is not a drill. Please leave in an orderly fashion. Again, this is not a drill. We are asking all patients and staff to evacuate the hospital immediately."

A journalist from NBC News had been interviewing a hospital administrator not far from the ER entrance when the evacuation announcement began to play overhead. Suddenly, the story about the bravery of the hospital staff in the face of extreme adversity took a back seat, and the cameraman and reporter began to film the crowd of confused patients as they were evacuating what should be a place of safety and refuge.

Mohsin stood up, by all appearances confused about what he should do. Then, as the hallways filled up with nurses, doctors and other hospital workers who were assisting patients to leave, Mohsin suddenly walked right toward the crowd.

As he headed toward the group, he had that thousand-yard stare. He had been prepping himself for this very moment since he had first arrived in America. It had sounded so simple when he was back in Kosovo. He would apply for a student visa to the University of Illinois and then wait to be activated to carry out his attack. Nearly two years had gone by since he had been recruited by ISIS. Secretly, he had had doubts. However, he reminded himself that if he succeeded, his family back in Kosovo would be taken care of financially for the rest of their lives. If he failed, they would be killed. As he walked closer to where he was going to detonate his suicide vest, sweat started to pour down his forehead.

****

Jim had been working as a security guard at Chicago Medicine for three years while he went to school part-time for a Bachelor of Science degree in police science. Jim had wanted to be a cop since he was a kid. His uncle had been a police officer, with nearly twenty-six years on the job. He had really inspired Jim to want to serve his community. During the terrorist attack, his uncle had been helping injured people near the Metra bomb site when he had been shot by those two terrorists wielding AR-15s near the Willis Tower. His death had only further motivated Jim to become a police officer.

As Jim was helping an elderly man move down the hallway toward the ER entrance, he caught sight of a young man with an olive complexion, slowly walking toward them. Something just seemed off about the man, who was walking in the wrong direction, so he pointed the elderly man toward the exit and walked toward this suspicious-looking character.

As Jim walked toward him, he called out, "Hey, buddy, you all right? You need some help?"

Jim continued to walk toward the young man, but he noticed that the guy had suddenly spooked and begun to grab at something in his jacket. At that moment, Jim saw a loose wire hanging from behind the back of the young man under his coat.

Without thinking, Jim yelled, "Everyone run! He's got a bomb!"

A police officer who had just walked into the ER heard Jim's warning and immediately reached for his weapon. Mohsin, seeing the threat, raised his right hand and yelled, "*Allahu Akbar!*" as he depressed his thumb on the detonator.

In less than a second, the bomb went off, sending thousands of ball bearings in every direction. The explosion eviscerated everyone in the ER with shrapnel and fire. Because numerous oxygen tanks are always present in the ER, they also exploded, adding to the carnage already being unleashed and rapidly fueling the growing fireball.

The blast shook the hospital and caused numerous fires and secondary explosions. Gas and oxygen lines exploded. One patient ran out of the ER covered in flames, screaming for help before collapsing in a heap. Dozens and dozens of dazed and injured people staggered out of the ER, trying to escape the fires that were now gaining in intensity.

Outside the building, the NBC News crew caught much of the carnage on film. The scene was so disturbing that one of the boom operators vomited from the horror of it all. The rest of the country watched these images in utter shock, helpless at the sight of yet another terrorist attack.

Chapter 20
Down at the Station

Chicago, Illinois
District 19 Police Station

Still unaware of the most recent attack at the hospital, several police cruisers pulled up to the station at the end of their patrol, another long day almost complete. The officers got out of their vehicles and headed into the station to start their shift change. They all had at least an hour's worth of paperwork before they were officially off the clock. Most of them grabbed an extra cup of coffee before they headed to their desks, hoping to stay awake while writing reports.

They all wanted to do their best to finish their office duties so they could get home and see their families. Ever since the terrorist attacks a few days ago, most of them had been picking up additional shifts and racking up the overtime. Between trying to fill in the gaps of the officers who had been killed in the attacks and assisting the FBI in following up on the thousands of terrorist tips that were being phoned in, they were all extremely overworked and exhausted.

The tension in the city was so thick that one could practically cut it with a knife. Muslims and non-Muslims were wary of one another. Fortunately, no major incidents had happened yet out in the communities, but it felt like just a matter of time.

****

Down the block from the police station, Aslan Maskhadov checked his watch for the fifth time in the last twenty minutes. "Shamil, be on guard. Only thirty-six minutes left," he said to his partner.

"Brother, you need to stop with the countdowns," Shamil replied.

"You're right, of course," Aslan chuckled.

He and Shamil Troshev had known each other for a long time. They were from the same small village in Chechnya, just north of Grozny. They had fought together against the Americans in Afghanistan before returning to their home country and establishing training camps to raise up insurgent cells to fight against the Russian occupiers. Once the Islamic State began to seize and hold territory, they had become enthusiastic members of ISIS. They saw the territorial gains the organization was making as a real opportunity to create a country. Like any new country, though, it needed to be defended. This attack against America was the first step in forcing this barbaric nation into leaving them alone.

Unlike the other attacks that had taken place so far, theirs was not intended to be a suicide mission. Aslan and Shamil were experienced fighters and knew how to carry themselves in a gun fight, as did the other members of their cell.

The plan was simple. They would pull up to the District 19 police station on West Addison Street and conduct a quick hit-and-run attack. Six other teams of two, all of whom were fellow Chechens, would simultaneously carry out similar assaults on other police stations in the city and the neighboring suburbs.

After they had checked their weapons one last time, Shamil announced, "It's time."

"*Allahu Akbar*," said Aslan with a big grin on his face, the excitement of the attack written all over his face.

"*Allahu Akbar*," echoed Shamil with a snicker.

Several police officers exited the front door of the building. As they began to walk toward their personal vehicles, Shamil and Aslan jumped out of their black Chevy Tahoe. Aslan set his sights on the lead officer and fired two quick shots, hitting him in the upper chest, just above his body armor and below the neck. The officer instinctively grabbed at his wounds, then fell backwards, unable to move.

Aslan quickly took aim at the next officer and began to systematically target the rest of the group. Shamil followed their plan and ran quickly down the sidewalk to position himself six cars away from his partner. As he opened fire, the officers were effectively caught in a crossfire, boxed in between several patrol cars and their attackers. Aslan heard the sound of Shamil's empty magazine hitting the sidewalk as he reloaded.

One police officer ran toward Aslan's position, crossing the street while firing his pistol on the move. Shamil was impressed by the officer's brave heroics, but he had finished changing the magazine in his rifle and quickly took aim at him, shooting several quick rounds that hit the man in his side and knocked him to the ground.

Several bullets hit the vehicle that Shamil was using for cover, forcing him to duck back down. Just as he did, he heard the whizzing sounds of bullets sailing past where his head had just been. He moved several feet to the left before he popped up again and aimed for the officer who had just been shooting at him. Before his target could readjust, Shamil fired a single round that hit the officer in the head, dropping him immediately.

Then the front door of the police station opened up, and nearly a dozen police officers who had heard the shooting outside rushed out to try to protect their law enforcement family. They moved swiftly toward the vehicles in front of the station, seeking cover before they engaged the attackers. Aslan emptied almost an entire magazine at the newcomers, and several of the men and women dropped to the ground, hit before they managed to get behind shelter.

Aslan shouted to Shamil, "It's time to go!" He quickly reloaded his third magazine and laid down suppressive fire to give Shamil some cover as they rushed back toward the Chevy Tahoe.

Shamil jumped into the driver's seat, and Aslan continued shooting at the officers out of the passenger window as all of the cops focused their gunfire on the getaway vehicle. The windshield shattered and sprayed Shamil and Aslan with glass pebbles. Shamil floored it, and the Tahoe roared away, filling the air with the smell of burning rubber. Dozens of bullets hit the back of the vehicle as they drove away, smashing all the remaining windows.

Somehow, they managed to get down the street without losing any of their tires. They sped to a location five blocks away, where they had a second getaway vehicle waiting for them. Shamil and Aslan quickly ditched the Tahoe and jumped into the gray Ford Edge hidden down an alley. They had managed to survive their primary mission, and now they were headed to a secondary target, a local grocery store.

With the rush of adrenaline pulsing through his veins, Aslan felt the need to review the plan for the next attack as they drove. "Once we get there, you take the left entrance and I'll go in the right. We empty one magazine at the customers in the checkout line, and then it's back into the vehicle and off to the safe house."

"We've got this," said Shamil excitedly. They didn't say anything else until they arrived at their destination.

Aslan spotted the Jewel Osco, and Shamil pulled right up to the center of the pickup lane in front of the store. They were equidistant from both entrances. They quickly exited the vehicle, leaving both doors open and the engine running. Mechanically, and almost without thinking, they entered the store and began shooting everyone who was unlucky enough to be in their way. Between the pops of gunfire, panicked screams filled the air. There were several crashes as customers knocked over groceries while trying to seek cover from the melee of bullets crisscrossing the front of the store.

Aslan dropped his now empty magazine and slapped the next one in place. Just as he was about to leave the store, he saw Shamil walk several steps toward one of the checkout lanes and begin to fire the bullets in a second magazine toward the aisles in the store.

He should have emptied the magazine and left. What is he thinking? worried Aslan.

Just then, an off-duty police officer, who must have been in the back of the store when the shooting had started, emerged from one of the frozen food aisles and fired at Shamil. One of the rounds hit its mark, and Aslan watched in horror as Shamil dropped to the ground.

Aslan yelled in rage, charging toward his wounded comrade as he shot at the off-duty officer. The policeman was severely wounded but continued trying to reload his gun. Unfortunately for him, with each beat of his heart, blood poured out of a wound in his chest until the officer eventually went limp and the blood stopped flowing.

Shamil waved Aslan off and got up on his own. The two of them rushed off toward their still-running getaway vehicle.

They screeched away in their Ford Edge, leaving tire tracks in the parking lot. Two miles down the road, they found the small strip mall parking lot where they had stashed a third vehicle, a Nissan Pathfinder. As they switched cars again, Aslan finally felt that he had a moment to assess what had just happened, and he really looked at his friend.

"Are you all right? Are you bleeding?" he asked, genuine concern in his voice.

Shamil nodded. "Yes, I'm fine. The bullet hit my vest. I think I may have broken a rib, but I will live."

Aslan sighed. "That was close...too close. We strayed from the plan. We were just supposed to fire one magazine and get out of there. Why did you keep firing?" He wanted an explanation.

There was a moment of silence as Shamil stared out the window. Finally, he responded, "You're right. I didn't follow the plan and it almost got me killed. Honestly, I don't know why I did that. I think I got overly confident and felt like we were in a safe position to try and kill a few more people."

"You know that I love you like my own brother, but when we make a plan, we stick to it. Period. We do not deviate," Aslan lectured angrily. They rode in silence for the remainder of their journey, all the way out to a farmhouse outside of Elgin, where they would meet the rest of their cell, or whoever had managed to survive the missions.

Just before they arrived at their safe house, Aslan finally broke the silence. "That was intense back there. Are you OK?" Even though he was still angry with his friend, he wanted to make sure that he really was all right. The two of them had been through a lot together: they had grown up in the same village, gone to the same school, and both suffered the tragic loss of their parents on the same day when the Russians had killed them in the first Chechen war back in 1994.

Shamil continued to watch the road as he responded, "Praise Allah, we made it. I am good, my friend." He smiled slightly and briefly turned his head to look at his friend. "We struck a big blow against the Americans today," he said.

Aslan returned the smile and then let out a laugh that released the tension that had been hanging in the air. "We did indeed," he agreed. "Those police officers never knew what hit them. I just hope the others had as much success as we did."

Chapter 21
Not Just Another Day at the Office

McLean, Virginia
National Counterterrorism Center

Acting Director Michael Stone and most of his staff had been working feverishly, putting in enormous amounts of overtime as they tried to figure out who these recent attackers were. All they really knew at this point was that this new set of terrorists had not infiltrated the country in the same way, so there was little in the way of a paper trail to follow.

Stone was reading through a report about the attackers at a frenetic pace while a group of team leaders who were sitting around the table waited for him to give them the synopsis. "It would appear that we are now dealing with a new and separate cell that may have absolutely nothing to do with the original group that carried out the first set of attacks in Chicago. Does that fit with your assessments?" he asked.

George Lee, who up until four days ago had been relegated to the paperwork mound that no one wanted, was the first to speak his opinion. "Sir, that's the assumption I am currently working off of. I know others may not agree with me, but please hear me out."

Because he had not been a yes-man, Director Harper had sidelined George during her tenure. His opinion had not been asked or sought until now. When Mike had been given temporary command of the division, he had immediately promoted George to team lead, as well as Julie Wells, his senior analyst. Mike wanted to have people on his team who were willing to think independently, even if their ideas weren't popular.

George looked through some files on his tablet for confirmation of his facts before he continued briefing the group. "Of the six groups of attackers that assaulted the police stations across Cook County tonight, two of the men were killed and three were captured alive. The suspects that were apprehended have all stated that they were born in Chechnya, even if they haven't given us much else to work with at the moment. The two deceased attackers were in our biometric database, and we had their latent fingerprints on file from previous encounters with US forces in the Middle East. One set of fingerprints was linked to the remnants of a vehicle-borne IED that hit our troops in the Green Zone near Kabul five years ago." He linked up his tablet to the projector in the room and brought up images of the vehicle bomb attack.

"A second individual's fingerprints were found at the scene of a raid carried out by a Joint Special Operations Command team in Azerbaijan. Following the JSOC raid, the Sensitive Site Exploitation team discovered his fingerprints on a number of forged German passports." The monitor then flashed images of the captured intelligence.

"Tell me a little more about this raid," Mike instructed.

"Director Stone, about fourteen months ago, a series of terrorist attacks targeted several Russian military leaders and the Russian military base in Chechnya. As most of you know, the Russians had been using an airbase there as a waypoint for their operations against ISIS and the anti-Assad rebels. These were the first known direct attacks by the Chechens against the Russian military in nearly a decade. Well, the Russians managed to trace the rebels to a camp that was located just over the border of Azerbaijan in the Zagatala State Reserve."

George took a quick swig of coffee and then continued, "The Russians informed the Azeris that they were about to carry out a raid on the camp and exterminate the group, but the Azeris put up a huge stink and wouldn't give the Russians permission to enter their territory. At that point, the

Russians called the US embassy and informed us that either we were going to need to work with the Azeris and terminate the rebel camp, or they were going to unilaterally do it themselves.

"Two weeks later, the President authorized JSOC to carry out the raid with an observer from both Russia and Azerbaijan. All captured materials were to be processed and jointly shared so everyone could see what was going on. As you can see from the images, nineteen individuals were killed, and fifteen prisoners were taken. The Azeris didn't want the prisoners, so they were handed over to the Russians."

Several people in the room broke into interested side chatter. Stone let them talk for a moment and then raised his hand to get the group's attention again.

One of the other team leads, someone from ICE, spoke up. "Director Stone, if I can get a copy of the captured German passports, I can reach out to the Germans and see if we can get the batch number of the stolen passports. Then we can run the entire group of passport numbers against the EU, Canadian and US airport databases to see if any of them has been used. If so, we'll be able to track exactly when and where they traveled." She had just offered the group the best piece of news they had heard so far.

"Julie, speaking of passports, did we recover *any* identification on the attackers? Anything that might link back to these passports?" asked Mike.

"No, Sir. There was no identification or travel documents of any kind on the dead or captured individuals. We are currently running all the biometric data we've collected through the TSA to see if they had flown into the US. We have also passed the biometrics over to Canada and Mexico to be run against their systems as well. If they traveled through Canada, then they definitely would have been biometrically enrolled there. We should have a good idea of how and when they entered the country soon."

Director Stone nodded. Then he stood up, signaling for the rest of the group to stay seated. He paced briefly behind the group before he spoke. "Listen, I have a meeting with the National Security Advisor in eight hours. What I really need to know is where are these attackers *now*? And I'm sure that they're going to ask me if there are any other attacks planned, so if anyone finds any usable intel on either of those fronts, that's the priority."

He sat back down and took a sip of water before he went on. "There is going to be a lot of pressure on us to help find these guys. I need everyone to be on their A game, understood?"

"Yes, Sir," replied the group.

"Listen, until these guys are captured, we have to anticipate that they are probably going to launch another attack." He glanced at his watch; it was almost one in the morning. "We don't have much time to find something before I meet with the President's advisors, so I'm going to end this meeting so you all can get back to work."

Everyone got up and went back to their desks. It was going to be a long night.

Heads are already rolling, he thought. He didn't want to join that crowd.

****

A few hours later, Acting Director Stone was headed to the White House. He couldn't help but think back to what Dawn had said in Director Harper's office the day of the attacks.

I was just doing what I was told—what did she mean by that? Something just wasn't adding up. He knew he was going to have to dig into that further, once he was done putting out the current fire.

Also...I'm going to need to watch my back, he realized. What if they had help from the inside? Maybe even directly in the administration? He wasn't sure who to trust anymore.

****

Washington, D.C.
White House, National Security Advisor's Office

Leah Bishop was exhausted. It had been a long and frustrating week. The terrorist attacks in Chicago had caught the country completely by surprise. The President was fuming that a terrorist attack had taken place during an election cycle, and the Republicans were naturally going to go crazy, blaming the administration for allowing this tragedy to happen on their watch.

The firing of Director Mallory Harper had given the public and the President a sacrificial lamb, but it had cost Leah to keep her quiet. She had had to call in one of the favors she had been hoping to save for another time. A big donor to Leah's husband's congressional campaign offered a high-paying fancy lobbyist job to former Director Harper, with a start date a few months away to give the controversy time to blow over. In exchange, she agreed to stay silent about receiving names for special consideration from Leah. It was imperative that the President never find out that CAGIR had been providing her names of people of interest that they wanted to have accepted into the refugee program.

If Nihad Nassimi didn't have her over a barrel with evidence to ruin her reputation and squash her husband's political career, she would have used her office to crush him like a bug. As it was, she was now having to use her office to cover her own tracks. Her husband, Alexander, would kill her if he knew about all the campaign money that was coming to him from CAGIR, not to mention all the other major donors to him that CAGIR had influence over.

On top of the contributions to Alexander's reelection campaigns, there was the whole matter of the house in the Hamptons. Five years ago, one of Nihad's associates sold his palatial estate to the Bishops at a rock-bottom price, just after she had become the President's National Security Advisor. At the time, Leah hadn't realized that Nihad had ensnared her in a blackmail trap. Her husband had been a bit aloof as well—he'd just thought that these perks came to them because of their positions of power. Now the whole thing was a house of cards, waiting for one strong breeze to knock it all over. She had to do what she could to protect their future.

Her Chief of Staff, Trey Lima, knocked on her door frame, interrupting her thoughts as he poked his head into her office. "Acting Director Michael Stone just arrived. You asked me to let you know when he got here." He paused for a moment to see if she had any additional requests for him.

"Thank you, Trey. Have him wait near you and see if he wants some coffee. I'll buzz you when I'm ready to have him brought in," she directed. She needed a few more moments to work out her approach. What was she going to say? Mallory had warned her that he was sharp, good at what he did. If he dug deeper into what former Director Harper had been doing and found any kind of link to her, it would be incredibly problematic.

Twenty minutes went by before Leah buzzed Trey and asked for Stone to be sent in. When he walked into her office, it suddenly struck her just how much he looked like a spy from any number of movies. He was tall and naturally just a bit too good-looking, with deep blue eyes and an athletic build. He took his seat opposite her, waiting for her to begin the conversation.

Leah opened by trying to stroke his ego a little bit. "I want to commend you for taking charge of the department the way you have. Your group has done a superb job of identifying several other potential extremists before they were able to perpetrate their attacks."

Mike held up his hand. "I don't mean to interrupt, but there's something I need to inform you about."

"Oh, OK, go ahead. Then I need to pass along some information to you," she said reluctantly.

"On the day of the first attacks, when Director Harper and I confronted Dawn King, the analyst who had cleared the two men that turned out to be terrorists and let them into the country, she said that she was just approving the names she had been given." He let that statement hang in the air, observing her facial features carefully. She suddenly felt exposed. She knew the color had just drained from her face.

Leah just wanted to crawl under her desk in that moment. At least he hadn't figured out who had given her those names yet, or else they would be having a different conversation—one that involved her being arrested. She had to nip this in the bud quickly before he was able to draw any additional conclusions.

"This is actually what I wanted to talk with you about," she said, trying to regain her composure. "Director Harper had mentioned that comment during her outprocessing debriefing. I wanted to discuss it with you and let you know that I have opened up a special investigation into this and referred it to the Justice Department."

Stone's left eyebrow raised incredulously. "I wasn't aware that Director Harper had given an outprocessing statement. I would love to read it, if possible," he said, calling her bluff.

"Because of the nature of some of the comments she made, I have classified her statement and made that document a part of the investigation," Leah explained. "This is incredibly sensitive. I do hope you understand, Director Stone, that this needs to stay quiet while we let the investigators do their work. Emotions are running high, and we can't allow an investigation like this impact or affect the election."

She brought her glasses down the bridge of her nose like a schoolteacher. "Just so you're aware, I've moved this entire investigation into a closed special access program until it is completed."

Stone's forehead crinkled like old aluminum foil. "Why would you move this to a SAP right now? It's going to be next to impossible to do any sort of intelligence sharing as we continue to investigate this out." He was clearly annoyed.

Noticing his displeasure, but not really caring, Leah responded, "This is an election year. The last thing we need is for this investigation to become politicized. The National Security Council, in coordination with the FBI Counterintelligence Division, will be conducting this investigation. Your department is to provide whatever information they need and be available for interview, if needed." She was essentially ordering Stone out of the investigation.

Stone's face displayed a range of emotions before he settled into a stoic expression "Yes, Ma'am," he answered.

****

McLean, Virginia
CIA Headquarters, Langley

Mike hit the button for the seventh floor on the elevator. He wasn't wasting any time; he was about to meet with his real boss again. He had a serious problem, and he needed some guidance on how to proceed.

As he approached the door to Trevor's office, Mike saw several people walking out. He recognized one of them as a member of Leah Bishop's team. One of them wasn't watching where he was going and bumped into Mike's shoulder before he continued to the elevators. The man didn't apologize.

Mike brushed it off and knocked on the door. Through the little window next to the entrance to Trevor's office, Mike could see his mentor look up and smile at him; then he waved for him to come on in.

Once Mike was seated, Trevor said, "I'm sure you saw the group that just left my office." He didn't sound pleased.

"I did. I recognized one of them, Lars Lichtman. He works as NSA Bishop's deputy," Mike replied with a bit of disdain.

Trevor chuckled. No one really liked Lars; he was one of those yes-men that said and did whatever he was told, never thinking for himself. "Yes, Lars wanted to make sure the Agency knew that the NSC was going to be running point on the investigation into how the Chicago attackers managed to slip into the country," explained Trevor.

Mike leaned back in his chair and sighed. "I'm reading from your expression that you might already have a pretty good handle on how these guys slipped through, huh?"

One side of Trevor's mouth curled up in a smile. "It's clear that someone in Director Harper's office cleared the individuals. The question is who? And why?" He grabbed his cup of coffee and took a long sip.

Mike grunted. "I've been sidelined in the investigation. Bishop told me directly that my office is to focus solely on giving the individuals who had already been let into the country through the program a second review, approving them again, while her office and the DOJ focus on who in my department was aiding and abetting these terrorists." A vein suddenly became visible on his forehead. He was livid.

Trevor shrugged. "Mike, this is all part of Washington politics. It's called cover your butt. You and I know someone cleared them to enter. That individual has been identified and relieved of their position, and most likely charges are going to follow. However, the bigger question to ask is who directed them to do it? I would wager it came from someone in Congress or the White House."

Mike processed what his boss was saying for a moment. He knew Trevor was probably right. He didn't believe for a minute that the analyst fired was solely responsible for this, despite what the White House and the media were conjuring up. Julie Wells had told him that she suspected that the orders came from Director Harper, but even she had been removed. Word had it that she had been given an immunity deal to cooperate, and so far, she was laying all the blame on Dawn King and Constance Pool.

After a pause, Mike said, "On the day of the attacks, I told you what Dawn had said when we relieved her. Have you been able to find anything on that angle that might shed some light on what's going on?"

"Well, I would like to investigate Director Harper's connections to all of this, but as you know, the Agency is strictly prohibited from investigating or spying on US citizens," Trevor recited dutifully, and then he smiled mischievously. "But the NCTC has that authority," he said with a wink and a nod.

Mike laughed. "Oh, I would love to open up a counterterrorism investigation into Director Harper, Constance Pool, and Dawn King. However, I've been explicitly told to stay clear of the matter, not just by NSA Bishop, but by the Attorney General's office. Even my FBI liaison has been cut out of the loop on this one."

"They're circling the wagons, Mike," Trevor responded. He sighed. "I know you'd like to dig into this further—I can see it all over your face—but I'm telling you as a friend, and your boss, heed their advice. Stay clear. Focus on the task they have given you and find any other ISIS operatives that might have slipped through. Chances are, some very powerful people helped to get these individuals moved into the US. As much as you want to find and expose them, wait until you have removed any further ISIS threats. In doing so, you will also prove yourself to the powers that be, and you will be in a better position to ferret these people out down the road."

Mike let out a deep exasperated breath. "It just makes me so angry that there are people in our own government who could've aided these extremists in entering our country and killing our fellow citizens. I want to hunt them down and expose them as the turncoats that they are."

Trevor paused for a moment, apparently calculating his answer. "I know you're frustrated with this, but trust me, you will be better served by appearing to be a team player right now and gaining the trust of the powers that be. Look at this as a long-term infiltration operation. Gain the trust of those above you, figure out who can be trusted, ascertain their true intentions, and then, when the time is right, you can move to uncover the traitors in our midst."

Chapter 22
Phase Two

Paris, France

Sheikh Maktoum folded his newspaper and placed it on the chair next to him in the presidential suite of the Grand Hyatt Hotel. Prince Nawaf had notified him that they should meet personally with his agent to discuss the next phase of their operation; it was too important to discuss via any electronic means.

The man he wanted him to meet was known only as "the Ghost." Frankly, Maktoum didn't care what he was called, so long as he continued to accomplish his mission.

As the Ghost walked into the presidential suite, two of Maktoum's security guards moved forward and motioned for him to raise his arms. As he complied, they quickly patted him down and began to run a wand across his body.

The man voluntarily turned over his sidearm to the security guards, along with his cell phone, tablet and other electronic devices. The sheikh's men even examined his eyes to ensure the Ghost wasn't wearing any fancy spy contact lenses. Maktoum was paranoid about security. When he traveled outside the country, which was often, he always traveled with a highly trained security detail. Most of them had previously worked for various intelligence services or presidential protective details of various world leaders. They were expensive men to have on staff, but very good at what they did and above all else, loyal to him personally.

Maktoum signaled for the Ghost to sit down in the chair opposite him. "It's an honor to meet you. I have heard nothing but good things about you and your work," he said with admiration. Maktoum poured himself a brandy and then poured a second for the Ghost, who leaned forward, reaching for the glass with his left hand. As he sat back in the chair, he placed the glass of brandy on the table next to his chair. He pulled out a cigarette from the breast pocket of his jacket and proceeded to light it. Then he took a long pull from it, holding the smoke in his lungs for a second before exhaling.

"I am told you would like to discuss the next phase of the operation," he said, not giving away any particular emotion.

He would have to wait just a moment for a response since Maktoum had just lit a cigarette of his own. Once he'd taken a drag, Maktoum casually took a sip of his brandy before he asked, "Where do we stand with regard to phase two? Do you believe phase one has been a success thus far?"

As he spoke, he observed every mannerism and facial expression of the man sitting before him.

"Phase one was a success," the Ghost replied matter-of-factly. "As outlined in the mission plan, we launched an attack against the Chicago Metra station. We carried out a secondary mass-casualty attack against the Willis Tower that caught first responders and hundreds of civilians out in the open, especially as the nearby buildings began to be evacuated. Then, just as they thought the attacks were done, we collapsed the Trump Tower and the Langham Hotel two hours later, several miles away, ensuring no one in the city would feel safe. As requested, we achieved a higher kill and casualty rate than that of the 9/11 attackers."

The Ghost paused for a second as he uncapped his bottle of water and took a sip. "Our message of ISIS seizing control of the city of Chicago was successfully uploaded, and all of the major news agencies in the United States covered it, thus adding to the emotional impact of the attacks. When we then fulfilled the shootings at various police stations and grocery stores, we had the Americans resigned to a feeling of complete helplessness. Attendance at concerts, sporting events and other public outings is down dramatically. Some companies are even offering their workers temporary work-from-home options until 'things become safer.' They are crawling on their knees in fear."

As the Ghost finished, he placed a report on the table, outlining the specifics of everything he had just spoken about. He sat back and observed Maktoum's expressions, seeming very satisfied with himself.

When the Ghost had been selected to run this operation four years ago, he'd been given a very specific outline of mission requirements he needed to meet. He had also been given a very large expense account to make it happen, and numerous points of contact to help him along the way. Maktoum had to admit, the Ghost had performed his job marvelously. It had been a nearly impossible mission when they briefed him on it, but he had proven everyone wrong and achieved mission success. The bigger question was, could he replicate that success with phase two?

Sheikh Maktoum handed a folder to the Ghost. "So far, you have proven yourself to be as adept and clever as everyone has said you are. Now it is time for some real work to begin," he said with a grin.

The Ghost thumbed through the papers in front of him, a devious smile slowly spreading across his face. "I like how you think," he began. "I just want to be clear, though—do you want us to kill the presidential candidates, or not?

Obviously, with all the Secret Service, that would be a bit more difficult to achieve, but we can rise to the challenge if those are the orders."

Maktoum laughed. "No, that will not be necessary, although I appreciate your enthusiasm. The goal is not an assassination attempt, but to make it so that people are afraid to attend political rallies, because they never know if they're going to be attacked. We can also bog down the process by forcing them to set their perimeters much wider outside the events. That's why we want you to use a variety of methods to complete these attacks. This way, no screening method would be truly useful. By the time we are finished, the people will lack all confidence in the government and their ability to protect them."

The Ghost asserted, "I do have some contacts that can fulfill your vision of cyber-attacks on the voting machines that have been linked with internet access. When they finish, there will be more votes in those precincts than registered voters. However, I do caution that the majority of the machines are not linked to a network. In those cases, we would have to manually switch out or tamper with the chips, and that is definitely more difficult to achieve."

"Completing a switch of a memory device would not be absolutely necessary. Instead, you can find a way to attack the electronic transmission of the sealed voting tally where possible. Between that and the attacks on the network-enabled voting devices, the people won't be able to trust the outcome of the election. There will be protests and riots. Mass chaos will surely ensue."

"Yes, I imagine they would try to redo the election with old-fashioned paper balloting, but of course, that would be costly, counting all those votes would take time, and in the end, people would likely not trust the results as reported anyway...I like how you think."

The two men sat there for a moment, enjoying their brandy and cigarettes while the fate of the free world hung in their hands.

The Ghost chuckled. "I imagine you will be buying a lot of defense stocks very soon." He knew there was a lot of money to be made for the Knights of Islam.

Sheikh Maktoum nodded. "Yes, timing the market prior to each major event has enriched a lot of people. Don't worry, our cause will have plenty of money to continue further missions after all your work is complete."

Chapter 23
Coffee and Conversation

Washington, D.C.

Georgetown Java

As Mallory Harper picked up her order from the counter, she turned around and almost walked directly into Acting Director Michael Stone.

"Mike—whoa, how did you find me?" she asked, startled.

"You do remember where I started my career, right? It's Friday. I've never seen you go a Friday morning without your large latte with two extra shots of espresso and a chocolate-filled croissant. You are kind of a creature of habit," he replied, face lit with a playful smile.

"Well…what are you doing here?" Mallory probed. She looked around to see if anyone was watching them.

He gently ushered her over to a less-crowded area of the shop. In a quiet voice, he almost whispered, "Harper, things are getting weird. I know that they made you the public sacrifice and everything, but in my heart of hearts, I just don't think that you were the mastermind behind bringing terrorists into the country. I have my suspicions, but I don't want to act on anything without confirmation. I—"

"—Mike, let me stop you right there," interrupted Mallory. "I can't talk to you about this. You'd have to know that I can't talk to you about this."

"Look, I do know that. People are telling me to let it all go, but something is terribly wrong. I just want to protect other innocent people from getting hurt. Don't you want that, too?" he asked.

She put her coffee down and placed a hand on his shoulder. "Mike, as much as I like you as a human being, if I see you again, other than for a coworker's wedding, I'm going to get a lawyer involved. Is that clear enough?"

"Understood," he answered, and then he nonchalantly walked to the back of the line for ordering drinks.

"Aren't you leaving?" she quipped.

"Not before I order a coffee and a doughnut. I quit smoking," he said, lifting up his sleeve to show a nicotine patch, "and a man's got to find a way to cope."

"Well, OK then. Have a nice life," replied Mallory as she walked out the door.

Trevor would kill me for coming here, thought Mike. However, he had learned so much just by the way she had acted in that short interaction. Everything in him was telling him that she was just a patsy. Whether it was Leah Bishop or someone else she was trying to cover for, there was definitely someone else at the top of all this.

Now I just have to figure out a way to keep looking without getting caught.

Chapter 24

Digging Deeper

Washington, D.C.

Press Briefing Room

The Press Secretary had just finished cueing up Leah Bishop, and she took center stage at the podium. She pulled out the paper that she needed with her statement on it.

"Ladies and gentlemen, what we have just experienced as a nation has rocked us to our core. My heart goes out to each and every one of the victims of these awful terrorist attacks, and my prayers are with you and your families."

She paused briefly, as if giving respect to those who had fallen. "While these horrific events sadden my heart and greatly weigh on all of us, we cannot allow such isolated incidents to create another tragedy. There are still thousands of refugees, fleeing war-torn countries, victims themselves, who need to find a place of refuge. I believe that America needs to remain that shining beacon of hope, especially in these dark times."

Leah put up her hand. "Now, I know that some of you are going to say that the refugee program is just not safe, but as the National Security Advisor, I have reviewed the situation, and I am convinced that we have the proper procedures in place to prevent such a tragedy from occurring in the future. After a thorough review, two government employees at the National Counterterrorism Center, including the director of the refugee program, have been fired. New policies and procedures are being developed and implemented immediately to ensure that this never happens again.

"We cannot allow a few bad actors who were bent on attacking us destroy the chance these asylum seekers and refugees are seeking. We're better than that, and while I know what happened to us is a terrible tragedy, the perpetrators are not indicative of everyone who seeks a better life in our country.

"In conclusion, our refugee program is now safe once again. Please be assured that we have put every available resource into the program to ensure that it stays that way."

She stepped back from the podium, and the Press Secretary announced, "Thank you for your time. There will be no questions."

****

Julie Wells had been grabbing a cup of coffee when she heard Leah Bishop make her statement on the TV in the break room, which was always set to CNN. Her jaw almost hit the floor.

How on God's green earth could she possibly think that the program is safe after everything that happened? Leah wondered, gobsmacked. Something didn't smell right about this.

She took her coffee with her over to Acting Director Stone's office and knocked on his door. He smiled and waved her in.

"Mike, you're not going to believe what was just on the news. Leah Bishop just made a statement trying to exonerate the refugee program. She claims that those responsible have been fired, and it's completely safe. I'm sorry, but do you buy that?" she asked with an incredulous look on her face.

Stone shook his head. "No, I still think there are problems."

"I know you have me on reprocessing all the refugees that were already let into the country, but can't I dig into this for you?"

Mike's eyebrows furrowed. "No, please don't. I can't even look into this right now—none of us can. The investigation into how this all happened has been classified at SAP level. If you want to keep your job, you shouldn't touch this with a ten-foot pole."

Julie retorted, "Are you serious?"

"Deadly," he replied. "Believe me, I'm not happy about it either."

"Ugh, this is so frustrating. If we don't look at this, how are we going to stop all of this from happening again?" she exclaimed, exasperated.

"I'm still working on that." Mike sighed. "If you come up with something, please let me know."

Julie left the office, angry and confused. However, as she sat at her desk, drinking her cup of coffee, an idea came to her.

Leah Bishop should have known that the program is not safe, she realized. She might not be able to look into the program, but there was nothing stopping her from checking out Leah herself. She had to be tied to this somehow.

She got back to work, researching the refugees in the country like she was supposed to do, but for the next several days, she would work through every lunch and break, seeking answers to her questions.

Chapter 25

We the People

Washington, D.C.

The Mall

As far as the eye could see, there were demonstrators crowding into the lawn on the strip of park that sits between all the museums and monuments in the capital. Most of them were peaceful, holding up signs calling for greater national security, or opposing the President's stance on the refugee program. Those who were closer to the reflecting pool in front of the Capitol Building could hear some of the Republican Senators and members of Congress making speeches, calling for the President to shut down the refugee program and for greater scrutiny into the student visa procedures.

Policemen and women nervously lined the edge of the Mall, dressed in riot gear, just in case. The atmosphere around the country was tense. Similar demonstrations were popping up all across the nation, and while most them had been civil, a few had erupted in violence.

After a few hours, the main speaker for the event, the Republican nominee for President, David Garcia, took the podium. To a casual spectator, it might have looked like he was out in the open, in danger of being attacked by someone in such a large crowd, but a more astute observer would have seen the bulletproof glass surrounding the stage, and Secret Service agents on the roofs of every building.

A hush came over this enormous crowd, and people much farther back could suddenly hear what had just been a mumbling like Charlie Brown's teacher only a moment ago. "My fellow Americans, we stand here today in the wake of a horrible tragedy. More than four thousand innocent people were lost, and thousands more were injured, some in ways that will affect them for the rest of their lives. Some of these people—mothers, fathers, grandmothers, *children*—were gunned down while performing the simple act of buying groceries. Now, I ask you, do you feel safe?"

"No!" roared the crowd.

"The current President of the United States wants you to believe that everything is fine. He says that the refugee program is safe, that there were just a few people who were vetting the refugees that were incompetent, and that they have been fired. Do you believe him?"

"No!" the people shouted.

"We cannot allow this to happen again! I have talked to people working in the camps to vet the refugees, and they say that they are overrun. They work insane hours with no days off to interview as many people as they can, in as short a time as possible. Now, does that sound like a way to be thorough?"

"No!" the crowd jeered.

"If I become your President, I will not allow this unsafe program to continue in its current disastrous state."

The people burst into applause.

"I want each and every one of you to call your senators and congressmen and women. I want you to tell them that you will not stand for a policy that has forced thousands of people into our country without properly clearing them. Can you do that for me?"

"Yes!" came the refrain.

"Thank you for protecting our fellow Americans. God bless you, and God bless the United States of America."

The crowd erupted in thunderous applause.

Along the borders of the park, a few people started shouting at the demonstrators. "Racists! Fascists!" they called. There was a little pushing and shoving, but fortunately the police intervened before anything truly horrible happened.

****

New York, New York
CNN Recording Studio

Congressman Azim Rahal from Virginia sat in the television station, getting prepared for his interview. He was getting some butterflies in his stomach for sure, and part of him wanted to bolt from the room, but he knew that his message needed to be heard.

"We're on in two," said one of the producers, as the makeup artist finished a last-minute touch-up and whisked away. There was a scurry as people moved out of the way and everyone quit talking. "On in five, four, three…"

No one said, "two, one." Those were implied. Then the anchor of the program, Sarah Bridger, began her introduction. "Good evening, ladies and gentlemen. I'm here tonight with Congressman Azim Rahal from Virginia. Congressman, thank you for coming. I am very interested to hear your opinion on the recent events. As many already know, you are one of only a few members of Congress who is a follower of the Muslim faith. How does that shift your perspective on our nation's recent tragedies?"

Rahal cleared his throat.

No backing out now, he thought.

"Well, Sarah, that is interesting that you begin the discussion with that point. Yes, I'm a Muslim, and I am proud of it. However, my reaction is the same as I imagine any American citizen's would be. I am shocked and horrified at the atrocious attacks that have taken place throughout the Chicago area."

"Sorry, I only meant that, as a Muslim, aren't you concerned about the public backlash that has been taking place toward people of your faith?" Sarah pressed.

"Of course, I am always concerned about any violence or threats of violence toward any person in this great nation," Azim responded. "I do not justify or condone any such acts. However, I do feel that a lot of this animosity has been allowed to grow in that when such tragedies occur, the leaders within the Muslim community have been largely silent. We need to be out there publicly declaring that these horrific events are a perversion of the teachings of the prophet Mohammed. That's why I'm planning several regional meetings with various leaders of our faith to try to address this issue."

"Are you not concerned, then, about your own safety, and the safety of your religious leaders, given the current climate?"

"Of course I'm concerned. We will take appropriate actions to protect ourselves. I also know that it is critical that we as a community begin to identify those who may be marginalized and trending toward radicalism *before* they strike. I say to all my fellow brothers and sisters in the faith tonight—if you see something, say something. It isn't just a trite expression. It could very well save lives."

"Indeed...Congressman, there has been a lot of buzz, especially coming from the Republican Party, that the refugee program needs to be shut down altogether. Doesn't that disproportionately affect people of the Muslim faith?"

"Listen, I'm all for letting in refugees whenever possible. However, something has clearly gone wrong with our ability to safely vet those who are entering the country. It is obvious that something needs to be done to recalculate how people are cleared. Possibly, the departments that are performing the interviews might also need additional resources, but I don't think that it's wrong to take a step back and make sure that we are being thorough. Those attackers killed people from all walks of life—including Muslims. If you ask me, we need to be the most concerned about the people here first, and then bring in other people once we are absolutely sure that they are safe."

"The leaders of your party are conveying a very different message. Do you not have compassion for those poor souls who are just trying to leave war-torn nations?" asked Sarah. It was obvious that she was a little annoyed at the answers he had given thus far.

"My heart sincerely goes out to them, and I think that we might be able to pursue other ways to help protect them, such as establishing safe zones or working with our partners in the Middle East to accept more of the refugees from within the region. However, that doesn't mean that we have to accept subpar security here. I have never been about toeing the party line one hundred percent. Some things are just right."

Ms. Bridger seemed flabbergasted. She fumbled through a few more questions. Finally, Congressman Rahal ended the discussion by saying, "We all need to stand together as Americans. If you are a non-Muslim and you see someone with a head covering, don't assume they are a terrorist. They may be just as frightened as you are. Instead, say to them, 'If you are with me, then I am with you. How can we help support each other during this time?' If you are a fellow Muslim, and you see someone who seems frightened by you, try to go out of your way to get to know them. Show them that you are just as concerned about this country as they are and let them know that you abhor radical extremists as much as they do. We can fight this, but we need to be able to discuss it openly. We cannot be afraid."

There was a brief pause, and then a producer said, "That's a wrap."

Azim breathed a sigh of relief. He had done what he had wanted to do, no matter how unpopular it might be.

Chapter 26

Catching a Break

Chicago, Illinois

Police Command Center

Captain Jordan walked quickly over to Chief Monroe's office. His secretary stood up as he approached, ready to stop him from barging in and disrupting her boss.

"Lisa, I need to talk to him right away," barked Captain Jordan.

"You aren't scheduled on his calendar until this afternoon. He's in an important meeting right now and is not to be disturbed," she replied. Although the Chief of Police's secretary was much shorter and thinner than Captain Jordan, she wasn't intimated by his towering presence.

"Look, we may have found a break in the case concerning those Chechens that attacked the police stations," he asserted.

Lisa's eyes grew wide with surprise. She buzzed her boss. "Sir, I'm sorry to interrupt. Captain Jordan is here with some very urgent information."

There was a brief pause, and then the chief buzzed back. "I'll be out in one minute."

Everyone knew Chief Monroe hated being interrupted, which was not necessarily an asset in his line of work. However, he had come to know Lisa as being a very effective gatekeeper. If she said it was important, he trusted her.

A moment later, Monroe stepped outside of his office, his face tense. "Jordan, just please tell me this is worth my time. I've got that megachurch pastor in there—you know, the one that's always complaining about police brutality. I need to try and get him on our side."

Captain Jordan announced, "Sir, I think we've found a way to track down all of those Chechens that attacked our police stations."

Chief Monroe's expression softened. "I'm listening," he said.

"Our officers have reviewed every CCTV camera in the city, and we finally figured out how they were able to get away. After each police station massacre, the attackers that survived switched cars a short distance away. Then again, after each grocery store attack, there was another switch. They appeared to have the cars set up, waiting for them. Well, we're working on enhancing the images of the license plates, but we should have at least one readable plate within the hour."

"Well, this is good news," said Monroe. "Once you're able to identify the numbers, obviously, we want to put out a BOLO on any plates that we can read. If you can track it down to some kind of safe house, set up a raid with whatever SWAT resources you can throw at it. Don't be skimpy— these guys are heavily armed and obviously know how to fight. But let's try to move on it at night and see if there is any way to capture any of them alive. I want their intel."

"Yes, Sir," replied Captain Jordan.

"All right, is there more? I need to get back to it," said the chief.

"No, Sir. I will set out your orders right away, and I'll give you any updates as I have them."

Chapter 27
Bread and Bullets

Special Agent Yousif Mansour of the FBI had just finished loading his last thirty-round magazine for his M4 assault rifle. He made sure to place one tracer round halfway through the magazine and three more as the last rounds. This would help him know when he was about to run out of ammunition during a firefight. As he placed the magazine in one of the ammunition pouches on his IBA, he looked at the other members of his SWAT team. They all had the same determined look on their faces as they readied their equipment and weapons for what might turn out to be a real gunfight.

Through exceptional police work, the Chicago Police intelligence division had been able to identify and track down the location where the Chechen terrorists were currently holed up. The FBI had immediately dispatched several agents to begin surveillance of the location and to establish the details of who all may be there, and what the security for the facility might entail. The farmhouse that the Chechens were using was situated about six hundred yards back from a country road outside of Elgin and had a small barn structure about fifty yards from the main building.

Because the property was more set back, they would have a bit more work before they could be sure how to proceed.

After twenty-four hours of surveillance, it was determined that there were roughly eight members of their cell at this location. All but one of the getaway vehicles that had been used in the last attack appeared to be stored in the barn to help keep them out of sight. The main building was a two-story traditional-looking farmhouse with a wraparound porch, which had several rocking chairs peacefully sitting on it as though the house were full of cookie-baking grandmas. As part of the surveillance of the farmhouse, the FBI had deployed about a dozen miniature drones that were the general size and appearance of dragonflies to begin infiltrating the farmhouse and gather more real-time intelligence.

One of the dragonfly drones had flown into the barn and done a sweep of the inside to identify any potential booby traps and count the number of vehicles present. Two more dragonfly drones had settled into positions above each of the entrances to the farmhouse, providing exceptional views and audio of the people coming and going from the farmhouse. One of the terrorists had left an upper-floor window open, presumably to allow some fresh air in. With that new access point, the FBI sent several more of the drones into different points within the farmhouse, providing them with an exceptional picture of exactly what they were going up against.

Each of the Chechens had their own IBA. From the looks of it, each IBA was fitted with ceramic plates, which meant they would provide protection against high-caliber bullets and handguns. The SWAT team would need to make sure they were using armor-piercing rounds if they hoped to take these guys down. Every one of the Chechens was also armed with a modified short barrel AR-15, forward grips, tactical sights, and a pistol and knife strapped to one of their legs. The FBI didn't spot any explosives, but that didn't mean there might not be some present and not yet detected. They did spot two rocket-propelled grenade launchers, although they had no idea how many rockets they had for them. This was probably the one weapon that concerned them the most.

As Agent Mansour walked around to the briefing table and took his seat, he couldn't help but feel nervous. Their FBI SWAT team was one of the best in the country, but they had never gone up against a well-armed and determined terrorist cell. While they felt they had the proper training and equipment, they wondered if this might be a better mission for the military Special Forces guys to take on.

Special Agent in Charge John Deeks walked up to the front of the room, getting ready to address the crowd before him. In the room were a total of thirty-two SWAT members that would lead the assault against the farmhouse. Another thirty DEA agents would act as the second wave to back them up, should they need additional SWAT members. Deeks surveyed all of their faces, then seemed to puff out his chest in pride.

He cleared his throat. Everyone fell silent. "All right, listen up, everyone. Agent Bishop briefed you all on the layout of the farm, the location where the suspects are likely to be found, where their weapons are located, and the plan of action to breach the farmhouse. This is going to happen quickly. You guys will need to move swiftly and take them by surprise. They've already proven that they know how to fight and are not afraid to die for their cause."

Using his pen laser, he pointed to a projection of the farmhouse on the wall. "We will have sniper teams located here, here, and here. Once you guys throw your flashbangs in the house, our snipers will immediately engage any targets they can see. They'll look to take one suspect out each before you guys breach the house. When you go in, make sure you mark your targets and take these guys out."

Agent Mansour raised his hand to ask a question, and Deeks nodded for him to speak. "So, right now, the plan calls for us to approach the farmhouse on foot just after dark. While this is an excellent silent way to approach, it also means we are out in the open for a few hundred yards in every direction. If they have someone watching the perimeter or any night vision goggles, they'll see us and may be able to engage us before we can get into position. Do you think we can go in using the vehicles instead?" Several of the agents around him began to nod their heads in agreement.

"That's a good question and something that we too are concerned about," Deeks acknowledged. "That's why we've placed sniper teams in three different positions to provide an overwatch for the assault team. While it is risky having the assault teams move in on foot, our concern is that if we approach the farmhouse with vehicles, they will hear them coming and be more prepared for us. Due to the location and layout of the farmhouse in relation to the tree line and distance from the road, we believe this is the best way to approach the suspects." His explanation garnered a lot of nodding heads from the SWAT members. This was probably the best trade-off they were going to get.

"Anyone else have any questions?" asked Deeks, hoping to hear crickets. No one else raised their hand.

"OK then, let's go ahead and keep this briefing short. Everyone get your gear and weapons ready to move. We're going to be staging out of the Army National Guard armory in Elgin, and we'll leave in the next thirty minutes. So, make whatever final arrangements you need to right now, and let's do this."

Everyone dutifully began to grab their IBA and weapon cases to take to the waiting vehicles. Once they left the federal building in downtown Chicago, the team of FBI and DEA agents would have a ninety-minute ride to the Illinois Army National Guard armory in Elgin, which would place them no more than five miles from their target location.

As the federal agents drove to the staging area, twelve ambulance crews were pulled from around the area and told to report to the National Guard armory as well to act as medical support, should they be needed. The Illinois National Guard also had two medevac helicopters, which would be on standby at their armory locations closer to O'Hare Airport, ready to provide additional medical support in case of a crisis.

****

It was nearly 1130 hours when Jamaal Nassir and his coworker, Becky Hawkins, pulled up to the Army National

Guard armory on Raymond Street in Elgin. Their Panera Bread store had received a large catering order the day before from the National Guard unit, asking if they could deliver food to feed roughly two hundred and fifty people the following day for lunch. The Guard unit had placed similar orders with their store in the past, so they didn't find anything unusual about it. The owner's son was a member of this particular unit, so he often provided them half-off lunches or a number of free lunches to support the troops.

When they pulled up to the armory, it wasn't an ordinary day. They noticed nearly thirty black SUVs and dozens upon dozens of FBI and DEA SWAT members gathered in different groups around the armory, assembling weapons and talking animatedly amongst themselves. This was a lot of activity for a Thursday afternoon, especially since the Guard unit typically trained on the weekend, and usually the first weekend of the month, not the third weekend.

Jamaal knew exactly why they were there.

They must have found the farmhouse, he realized.

While he and Becky unloaded the food and began to get everything set up, his mind raced. He had to get out of there before these guys launched their raid, and he needed to warn the cell that an attack was coming without being detected.

It took him and Becky nearly thirty minutes to get everything set up for the government agents. Then the line formed, and everyone began to dig into the various sandwiches and soups that had been brought over. Now that they had completed the delivery, they were free to head back to the store.

Once they arrived, Jamaal told his supervisor that he was suddenly not feeling well and needed to go home early. Jamaal had always been a hard worker and had never called in sick before, so his boss let him leave without much resistance.

As Jamaal got into his vehicle, he saw it was already almost 1400 hours. It was still March, so it would be getting dark soon, in another two and a half hours, maybe three. He didn't have much time.

****

Aslan Maskhadov had just woken up from a short nap when his burner phone buzzed. He reached over and swiped his finger across the phone, unlocking it so he could see who had sent him a text message. At first, he didn't recognize the number. Then his eyes grew wide as he realized who it was. It was from one of the two outside observers they had established in the town to help monitor the area and let them

273

know if their cover had been discovered. The message read, "FBI, DEA agents at National Guard armory. They know where you are. Will probably raid tonight after dark."

This knowledge startled him. At the same time, he had known this would happen eventually. The Americans might be soft people, but they were incredibly resourceful and technically savvy. Aslan looked down at the phone again, thinking for a minute. He replied in a group chat to both observers. "I received Jamaal's message letting us know about the imminent attack on us. If possible, you two should carry out your own assault against the FBI agents at the National Guard armory before they reach us. Use the weapons that we gave you and try to catch them off guard."

Within a matter of moments, two responses rolled in. "Acknowledged. I know what to do," and, "I will comply," read the texts.

Aslan wasn't sure if the farmhouse was bugged or not, but clearly the FBI knew where they were hiding. He signaled for the others in the farmhouse to walk with him to the barn. As they approached the building, he signaled for everyone to pile into the Ford Excursion and to stay quiet until they were all in there. It was cramped, but all nine of them fit inside.

The grumbling noises grew until someone finally asked, "What's the problem?"

Aslan informed the group, "We've been discovered. An FBI raid is being readied and could happen at any time."

One of the members asked, "If we know they're going to raid the farmhouse, why do we not just get in our vehicles right now and try to make a break for it?"

It's a fair question, but clearly he hasn't totally thought this through, Aslan thought.

"Ishmael, the FBI has our location under surveillance. They know where we are and would probably ambush us if we left. No, we're going to use this information to our benefit. We know they're coming tonight, so here's what we are going to do…"

Aslan and Shamil had been the leader of their Chechen terrorist group for the past five years. They knew everyone in the vehicle and had trained and fought with each other in Afghanistan, Iraq, Chechnya and Syria. If this was going to be their last stand together, then they would make the FBI pay when they launched their raid. They spent the better part of forty minutes talking over the strategy, who would do what, where each of them would be stationed and how this raid would go down.

The farmhouse had a basement with two windows on each side of the basement. They would look to leverage the cinderblock windows and basement like a pillbox. They would position five shooters in the basement to fire out of the windows. The other four shooters would be positioned in a different corner on the second floor. This would allow them to provide clear lanes of fire and have a good view of where the FBI agents would be coming from. Just as they were about to leave the vehicle, Aslan made sure everyone understood that the farmhouse was most likely bugged. They needed to keep their chatter to a minimum. They also needed to move quickly; they didn't know exactly how much time they had.

As the Chechens walked back into the farmhouse, they spotted a dragonfly as it moved from a door frame to one of the ceiling fans. One of the members swatted at it and knocked it to the ground. Upon further inspection, he discovered it was a small mechanical device, not a dragonfly at all. Aslan barked, "Everyone, look and see if you can find any more of these in the house!"

In a matter of minutes, they found three more and destroyed them. With the FBI's drones gone, they immediately went to work getting the farmhouse ready for the assault. They moved furniture in front of the various doors and placed additional objects in front of some of the walls that they planned on firing from.

Three hours later, the sun had finally descended and it began to get dark. As the last glimmers of sunlight left the sky, the Chechens turned on their night vision goggles and waited.

****

Director Michael Stone walked up to SAC Deeks, who was talking with several of his agents. They were apparently pretty upset. Stone got the attention of his partner, Special Agent Jim Leary, and said, "Hey, something's up." The two of them approached Deeks to find out what was going on.

"Is everyone all right?" Stone asked, hoping everything was still on track.

Deeks ignored them for just a moment as he turned to his agents and announced, "I want everyone suited up and ready to go. We have to speed up our timeline."

Turning back to face the two outsiders from D.C., he admitted, "We have a problem. About fifty minutes ago, the Chechens all went to the barn and climbed into one of the SUVs to have a conversation. They must have discovered the place was bugged, because when they came back into the farmhouse, they found one of the dragonflies and destroyed it. Within a few minutes, they had found the others inside the house and destroyed them as well."

If the Chechens know we're coming, this isn't good. They'll be waiting for us, thought Stone.

"Agent Deeks, if they know the place is bugged and are now preparing for your assault, then I think we should reconsider our options here," Stone said.

Deeks sighed deeply before replying, "Director Stone, the subjects are trapped in that farmhouse. We know there are only nine of them, and we further know that they only have a limited supply of ammunition. I have thirty-two FBI agents and another thirty DEA agents for this raid. I am confident our sixty-two federal agents will either capture or kill these nine individuals," he asserted, agitated at being second-guessed, especially by someone from Washington.

Agent Stone narrowed his eyes and walked a bit closer to the special agent in charge. "Listen, Deeks, you may have numbers, but how many of those men are going to die tonight because you want to stick to your plan? You may think I'm some desk jockey who doesn't know what he's doing. Well, I spent eight years in Delta Force prior to joining Homeland. I've personally fought Chechens in Afghanistan. These guys are professionals, and they know how to fight. I'm telling you, no plan survives first contact, and whether you like it or not, the enemy has found out about your strategy. Perhaps someone tipped them off, but they know you're coming. I don't want to see any of your agents killed needlessly when we can prevent that. Do I make myself clear, Agent Deeks?" Stone asked with an air of authority in his voice. He hated to pull rank, but he didn't want to see a bunch of FBI and DEA agents lose their lives just because their SAC wanted to prove a point.

Deeks took a step back, almost like he had been punched in the gut. He surveyed the people around him and his face turned pale, as if he pictured losing some of the people he knew. Looking down at the floor for a second, then back up at Director Stone, he admitted, "You're right. If they know we're coming, then they'll be waiting for us, and my people won't have the element of surprise. What do you suggest we do instead, Director Stone?"

Looking around the armory, Mike spotted the man he was looking for. "Lieutenant Colonel Jacobs. Sir, can you come over here for a second?" Stone yelled.

Lieutenant Colonel Jacobs was the battalion commander for the unit that operated out of this National Guard armory. He had been talking with one of the DEA agents as they were doing last-minute checks on their weapons. He saw Director Stone in his khaki utility pants and a tactical shirt call out to him and wave for him to come join him and Special Agent in Charge Deeks from the FBI.

Jacobs stuck his hand out and introduced himself. "I'm Lieutenant Colonel Jacobs, the Commander for the 1st Battalion, 178th Infantry Regiment. And you are?"

"I'm Acting Director Michael Stone, from the National Counterterrorism Center Immigration and Refugee Screening Center. As the name implies, my department is responsible for the screening of immigrants and refugees entering the country—and yes, my department is the one that screwed up the screening of these terrorists. The previous director is no longer here, and I am now in charge," Stone explained.

Jacobs nodded and a slight smirk spread across his face. "So, Acting Director Stone, what can I do for you or Special Agent Deeks here?"

"Colonel, we have a problem. The Chechens know we're coming. I'm not sure how, and frankly it's irrelevant. The point is, they are now alerted, and that means we need to change our plans. Your battalion has Stryker vehicles, correct?" Stone asked.

"Yes. We *are* a Stryker battalion. What are you thinking of?" Jacobs asked.

"This group of terrorists are currently preparing for our arrival. They will most likely have the place fortified and ready for the assault. If we attack as we had planned, a lot of FBI and DEA agents would most likely be killed. What I propose is that we use several of your Stryker vehicles equipped with heavy weapons—the .50-cal. machine guns—to make our approach. We'll offer the terrorists an opportunity to surrender. When they refuse, I propose we light the farmhouse up. The .50-cals will rip the farmhouse apart and hopefully kill them. We can also make sure that more than half of the rounds are tracers. Those incendiary rounds will cause the farmhouse to catch fire and they will either have to surrender and come out of the house, or they will burn to death. In either case, we won't have to lose agents in a direct assault," Director Stone explained stoically.

At first, the colonel just stood there, not sure what to say. Then he looked at Agent Deeks, who also seemed somewhat dumbfounded at the suggestion that they use military vehicles and burn the building down.

SAC Deeks cleared his throat before he asserted, "Director Stone, while I appreciate your wanting to protect my men, we can't just commandeer military equipment like that. Plus, you're wanting to burn them out, and headquarters would never authorize that. It would be a giant scandal to use military vehicles on a civilian compound like that."

Nodding in agreement, Stone replied, "You're right that headquarters would never authorize this, but I can go above their heads. If need be, I can contact JSOC and have them be the ones to carry out the raid. If you'd like, I can make the call right now." As he finished speaking, Mike pulled out his government-issued smartphone.

The colonel laughed at first, until he realized that Stone was serious. He was silent for a moment as he made a mental calculation, and then he responded, "Director Stone, if you can get authorization, I'll gladly let you use as many of my vehicles as you need. As to the ammunition and heavy weapons, if you get the approval, we can make sure you get what you need."

Director Stone nodded. Before he excused himself to make a phone call, he instructed SAC Deeks, "Call off the raid. Keep the farmhouse surrounded, but don't approach until I'm done seeking authorization."

Stone made four phone calls before he was able to speak directly to the Secretary of Homeland Security. He relayed his plan to the Secretary, who agreed. "If you found an alternative plan that does not involve dozens of FBI agents getting killed, I'm all for it. I'll contact the White House for final authorization and get back to you."

Four hours went by as darkness descended on the city of Elgin and the farmhouse. The lack of activity was making everyone restless. Suddenly, Mike's phone buzzed with an incoming call. "This is Director Stone."

He immediately heard the gruff sound of the DHS Secretary's voice. "Mike, I just got word from the White House. They don't like the optics of the plan, but I convinced them that this was the right call to make and would save the lives of dozens of FBI and DEA agents. The Attorney General and the Director of the FBI also agreed that this is the best course of action. The President just signed off on your plan. You are to take full control of the situation as the onsite commander. A JSOC team is being flown in to your location as we speak. They'll operate the equipment and carry out the attack against the farmhouse. The FBI and DEA will assist you as needed. Is that clear, Mike?"

This was now his baby. If things went sideways, then it would be his head served up on the platter. If it worked out, then he would be hailed the hero. Stone let out a sigh of relief out before responding, "Yes, Sir. I understand. I'll get things coordinated on this end and we'll be ready. I'll keep you advised on the timeframe for when the raid will take place.

Chances are, it will be sometime tomorrow afternoon. Thank you again, Sir, for trusting me on this. I appreciate it." His voice was filled with genuine relief and gratitude.

"Just don't screw this up, Mike. I went out on a limb for this mission. We have to bring these guys to justice or kill them. Too many people died last week in Chicago. Just finish this thing," the Secretary proclaimed, and then he ended the call.

Director Stone looked at the four others standing with him. "They approved the mission," he announced. "A JSOC team is flying in right now and will be responsible for driving the vehicles and manning the heavy weapons. Colonel, I'm going to need four of your Stryker vehicles made ready and equipped with .50-cal machine guns. We'll also need those extra tracer rounds, like we talked about."

Turning to face Agent Deeks, Mike continued, "I'm going to need you to establish a wide perimeter around the farmhouse. I also want your agents to make sure any houses in the immediate area are evacuated. Set up roadblocks and checkpoints. No one gets in or out of this area," he said as he pointed to the farmhouse on the map and indicated a wide area around the property.

Then, as if a lightbulb suddenly got turned on, Mike spurted out, "Oh, I also want to make sure there are no media helicopters or drones flying in the area. Keep them back. If anyone spots a media drone, I want it disabled. If a news helicopter violates the airspace around here, I want that helicopter escorted out of the area. No media is to be allowed anywhere near this place until after the raid has been completed. Let's get the local sheriff and police brought into the loop as well. We're going to need their help closing down the roads in the area and assisting with the evacuations." His mind was racing a million miles an hour. He had a lot of things to get done, and not much time to make it happen.

The rest of the evening and into the early morning hours went by in a blur. The sheriff helped to get the various roadblocks and checkpoints set up, cordoning the area off. The police helped to get people in the affected areas evacuated to nearby hotels until they could safely return home. Around 0200 hours, the JSOC team arrived at the armory and settled into the cots that had been readied for them. They would sack out and grab a few hours of sleep before everyone got ready for the day's activities.

****

At 0600 hours, most of the people staying at the armory were awake and getting ready. Lieutenant Colonel Jacobs, true to his word had four of his Stryker vehicles ready at

0630 hours. All four vehicles had a .50-cal heavy machine gun set up and five hundred rounds of ammunition. Every other round was a tracer round, ensuring there would be more than enough incendiary rounds. At 0900 hours, the fire chief was scheduled to arrive at the armory, and they would bring him up to speed on what was going on and what kind of support they would need from him. Once the farmhouse caught fire, they would need to make sure the fire didn't spread beyond the house into the nearby trees.

Colonel Jacobs walked toward Director Stone, letting out a big yawn. "Nothing like the smell of napalm in the morning to wake the senses, eh?" he joked.

Mike chortled. "Yeah, you could say that, Colonel. Thank you again for your quick help in getting the vehicles ready. I know your guys would love to be the ones using them today, especially since we're going to kill those Chechen devils, but it's better if they aren't involved."

"I know you're right. We *are* disappointed, but then again, none of my guys want to have a fatwah issued on them, so we'll let the JSOC guys have that honor," he said, still keeping the mood humorous.

Stone chuckled.

Colonel Jacobs saw an alert on his phone. "Oh, just so you know, we have Panera being brought in for breakfast.

They should be showing up around 0730. One of the soldiers in the unit has a family member who owns the place. They give us a great discount, so we order from them whenever we have a large number of people to feed or for special occasions."

"Oh, man, I hadn't even thought about breakfast. We had planned on doing the raid last night, so we probably wouldn't have even been here today. Thank you for taking care of that, Colonel. If you'll excuse me, I need to go talk with the JSOC commander and get him up to speed," Director Stone said, shaking the man's hand again. Then he swiftly moved to find the next guy he needed to speak with.
****

After Jamaal received his instructions from the Chechen leader Aslan to attack the FBI, he met up with Muthana at his apartment. The two of them got their assault rifles ready and were discussing how they were going to attack the FBI agents when Jamaal's cell phone rang. He saw it was work and he almost let it go to voicemail, but at the last moment, he decided to pick up.

His boss was on the other end. "Jamaal, I'm glad I caught you. Are you able to come into work early?"

"I don't know…" Jamaal hesitated.

"The armory has placed a large breakfast order to be delivered in the morning."

In that instant, it dawned on Jamaal that the FBI agents must be staying there another day before they attacked the farmhouse. This would be the perfect opportunity to attack them. "Of course, I will come in early. Not a problem."

After he had established the schedule with his boss, Jamaal hung up and went over the attack plan with Muthana. Muthana would hide inside the back of their delivery truck, and once Jamaal backed the truck up to the armory bay to unload the food, he would emerge from the back of the truck with his rifle and start shooting everyone. Yes, this would work perfectly.

At 0400 hours, the two of them drove over to the Panera Bread, where Jamaal let Muthana into the back of the delivery van. They loaded in Jamaal's weapon and ammunition as well. Once he was situated inside the vehicle, Jamaal went to work getting the morning's breakfast ready. While mixing the muffin mix, he made sure to add in some rat poison, so if anyone actually ate the food they were delivering, they would get sick and hopefully die.

Time went by quickly. Jamaal and Becky finished the preparations for the morning delivery and began to load the truck. Jamaal made sure he was the one to load the truck while Becky focused on other tasks. Then the two of them jumped into the truck and headed over to the armory to make their delivery.

On the drive over, all Becky would talk about was a new guy she was dating and how excited she was about her big date she had that evening. Jamaal just nodded, his mind a million miles away.

As they approached their destination, they noticed a number of additional military personnel and several military vehicles being made ready to head out somewhere. Jamaal drove the van over to the back of the armory, where the tables had been set up for lunch the day before.

"Becky, why don't you jump out and let them know we're here? I'll stay with the truck and back us up to the bay entrance. Ask them to open it up so I can back the truck up to the door. That way we don't have as far to carry all the food, OK?" he asked his colleague.

"Sure thing, Jamaal. Thanks for helping out with this. I know you had to come in extra early," Becky said. Then she hopped out of the truck and began to walk over to one of the soldiers and an FBI agent.

As Becky was asking one of the men to open the bay door, Jamaal looked in the back of the truck. "Get ready, my friend," he told his partner. "Once they open the bay door,

I'm going to back up to get us inside. When I stop the truck and give you the signal, jump out and start shooting everyone you can see. I will do the same. *Allahu Akbar!*"

A minute later, the door began to open. Jamaal placed the vehicle in reverse and started to back into the now open bay. As the rear of his vehicle arrived at the entrance, he stopped the van, placed it in park and then yelled, "Now!"

Jamaal simultaneously reached down to the pistol he had in the backpack to the right of his seat. At the signal, Muthana opened the door and swung his assault rifle forward. He swiftly took aim at the first set of individuals he saw. "*Allahu Akbar!*" he screamed at the top of his lungs while firing into a group of soldiers, FBI and DEA agents who were gathered around a whiteboard.

Jamaal heard Muthana yell and the sound of his shots starting to ring out. He immediately brought his pistol up and shot the FBI agent that Becky had just been talking to several times in the chest. She screamed in shock and horror. He then moved his aim to the soldier who was standing next to him before he could react and fired several more times at the soldier. Just as he finished disposing of his coworker, Becky, an FBI agent who had been on the other side of the vehicle came around the front of the truck and shot Jamaal twice in the back, killing him instantly.

Muthana emptied his entire thirty-round magazine at the group of soldiers and FBI agents at the whiteboard and then moved to the side of the delivery truck to reload. He dropped the now empty magazine to the floor, and just as he had finished loading the next magazine and charged the bolt, one of the soldiers fired a three-round burst at Muthana. Two rounds struck him in the chest and one found its mark in his head, dropping him to the ground, lifeless.

****

Acting Director Stone and his deputy, Special Agent Jim Leary, had been in Lieutenant Colonel Jacobs's office discussing how they were going to use the Stryker vehicles to either kill or capture the Chechens. Director Stone wasn't going to let this turn into a prolonged bloody siege—the Chechens would either surrender quickly or die in a hail of bullets and fire. Everything was going according to plan until they heard the unmistakable yell of "*Allahu Akbar!*" coming from down the hall. Then all hell broke loose.

As the shooting started, Director Stone immediately reached for his sidearm and bolted out of the office toward the gunfire, with Agent Leary hot on his heels. LTC Jacobs was following, although he didn't have a firearm. By the time they entered the bay, the shooting had stopped. They saw the bloodied soldiers and agents clustered around the whiteboard. A few agents were rushing over to see if any first aid could be administered. An assailant lay dead on the floor with an AR-15 nearby.

Mike flagged down the first guy he saw and called him over. "I need you to call our standby medical team and have them send help right away. Tell them what kind of injuries to expect."

"Yes, Sir," he responded.

Several of the other soldiers and agents were swarming over the Panera Bread delivery vehicle where the attacker had emerged from. Stone headed over there as well. As he approached the truck, he also saw a second lifeless attacker sprawled on the ground near the front of the vehicle, along with two other bodies.

Although a puddle of blood was already beginning to form around the man's body, they were able to make out that he had been wearing a Panera uniform. An agent nearby had already removed his weapon and made sure the attacker was dead.

"What in the world just happened?" an exasperated Mike asked one of the FBI agents nearby.

"We're still trying to piece it all together, Sir. One minute, the truck was pulling up. The next minute some guy jumps out of the back of it and starts shooting everyone," the agent explained, still a bit shaken.

The colonel was beside himself when he saw the attackers had emerged from the Panera delivery truck. "Oh my God, this is my fault. I placed the order from them last night. If I had only gone with another place, none of this would have happened," he gasped, completely distraught.

"Colonel Jacobs, this wasn't your fault," Stone assured. "You had no idea they were compromised like this." He wanted to make sure Jacobs didn't let himself sink into a pit of despair.

Then Director Stone turned to the rest of the agents nearby. "I want to know who the heck these guys are as soon as possible, and I want agents at their house now!" Stone yelled. They immediately went to work searching the attackers for any signs of who they were, as well as anything that might connect them to the Chechen cell.

Stone began to walk toward the JSOC team commander to get things moving again, "Major Kiln, I want your men to saddle up. We need to get out to the farmhouse and get this perimeter set up and take these guys out. I want them neutralized by the end of the day. Is that understood?"

"Yes, Sir. We'll have this settled soon," he replied with conviction.

With the JSOC team getting ready, Stone walked back over to what was now a crime scene filled with a gaggle of FBI agents. "What have we found so far? Anything yet?" he asked no one in particular.

One of the FBI agents who had assumed command replied, "These guys must've been in a hurry, because they didn't take a lot of precautions to hide or mask their identity. We found their wallets and even cell phones still on them. We're cross-referencing the IDs now to make sure they are in fact their true identities. A couple of the JSOC sensitive site exploitation guys are dumping their phones right now. They'll check them against any known bad guys we have in the system."

"This is great news. Thank you for working through the JSOC SSE team—they have the equipment on hand, and we'll get results back a lot faster than if we had to fly them back to Chicago for examination. Please continue to stay on top of this and run down any leads. See if they somehow coordinated with the Chechens. Check cell towers and anything else you can think of. I'm going to roll out with a few of the agents who aren't immediately tasked along with the DEA guys. We'll be at the farmhouse location with the JSOC team. Once the area is secured, we'll let you know when to send the forensic team over."

When they finished surveying the scene, the brief thirty-second attack had resulted in the deaths of two FBI agents, one DEA agent, and three soldiers. Nine others had been injured in the attack. One of the FBI agents that had been killed was Special Agent in Charge Deeks.

****

An hour later, four Army Stryker vehicles and half a dozen other Army vehicles headed down the road toward the farmhouse and the location of the Chechen terrorists. The local sheriff and police had already cordoned off the streets and areas around the property, ensuring no civilians or nosy media types were nearby that could potentially get caught in the crossfire once the festivities started.

The sheriff's SWAT team, along with a number of DEA and FBI agents, had already established a perimeter around the farmhouse and had a good view of the house and the barn. They had spotted movement within the house, but nothing outside. Using various thermal devices, they were able to identify all of the attackers as being in the house.

Within an hour of arriving at the location, the JSOC soldiers had established their new command center and began to move the vehicles to their various attack locations. They were going to have two vehicles approach from the east, while another two vehicles would approach from the north. This would give them good fields of fire to support each other, while not creating a crossfire that could result in them shooting at each other.

Major Kiln was just about to order his vehicles to their positions when Director Stone walked into his command center and signaled that he wanted to talk with him privately. "Major Kiln, I want this situation solved soon. This morning's shooting is going to be all over the news shortly, and the sighting of these vehicles will only add further fuel to the stories and rumors. How do you recommend we approach the farmhouse to offer them the chance to surrender?"

Personally, Director Stone did not *want* to offer the Chechens a chance to surrender, but he knew politically it had to be done. He needed to cover his butt and also offer the enemy a chance to live so that they could gather further intelligence from them. If they chose not to surrender, then at least he couldn't be held liable for their deaths when the shooting did start. He had no plans of letting this standoff go on now that they had surrounded them.

Major Kiln paused before responding, "Sir, I think one way we could approach this is to drive one of the FBI up-armored SUVs with a white flag near the house. We can have whoever the negotiator is going to be get out of the SUV on the opposite side, and then shout the offer to them with a bullhorn. This way, if they do shoot at the negotiator, they have an armored vehicle to protect them and get them out of the area."

"That's not a bad idea, Major," Stone admitted. He scratched his chin. "OK, here's what I want to have happen. I'm going to have the FBI head out there like you said in one of their armored vehicles. Then I want your vehicles to head to their positions—but make sure the Chechens see your vehicles and heavy weapons. That way they'll know there is no getting out of this. We aren't even going to let them have a chance to shoot at our people. If they fail to surrender, then I want your guys to light up that house with the .50-cals and burn them out."

****

Ten minutes later, one of the FBI's up-armored Suburbans had a white towel tied to a pole on it and zoomed out to the farmhouse. As they approached the terrorist safe house and got within 100 yards, several shots rang out, hitting the vehicle. The agent driving the Suburban stopped and turned the vehicle so that only the passenger side of the vehicle was facing the house. The Chechens held their fire as the FBI negotiator got out of the driver's side of the vehicle.

Agent Schneider was the man who had drawn the short stick to drive out there and talk to the Chechens. He was still a little shaken up from one of the rifle shots that had struck the windshield right in front of him.

Thank God for bulletproof glass, he thought as he opened the door. He was a white-collar crime agent— certainly not used to convincing terrorists to surrender.

He crouched down a bit, making sure he could dive back into the protection of the vehicle if needed. Then he raised the bullhorn to his mouth.

"I'm Special Agent Schneider from the FBI. I have been instructed to offer you a chance to surrender. You have exactly three minutes to come out of the house with your hands up," he yelled into the bullhorn, making sure it was pointed above his head and in the direction of the farmhouse.

As he was speaking, he could hear, and then see, four Army Stryker vehicles moving to their positions about 200 yards behind him. He saw several soldiers manning the heavy machine guns. It was intimidating, and he hoped the sight of them would make these guys give up. They had no chance of surviving the attack if they didn't.

****

"Aslan, what are we going to do? Those are heavy machine guns on those armored vehicles," Shamil pointed out. "And look at their uniforms—those are soldiers, not FBI or police officers."

All eyes were on Aslan. His mind raced, trying to figure out what their next move was. He knew the farmhouse couldn't withstand the heavy machine guns on those Army vehicles. He also knew they couldn't surrender. They would be shipped off to Gitmo and never heard from again. That would be worse than death.

Suddenly, he had an idea. "Look, we can't stand up against those heavy machine guns on those vehicles, but it looks like they only have four of them. So, here's what we're going to do. Two of you are going to pretend to surrender. As you walk outside, I want our guys with the sniper rifles to get down in the basement. Identify the soldiers manning the heavy machine guns, and when I give the order, I want you to take them out. I want the two RPGs we have positioned on the second floor—you'll need to fire at the vehicles and try to take them out. Once you fire the first rocket, they'll probably start to move quickly, so you will have to remember to lead the vehicle when taking aim, just like we used to do in Iraq and Syria."

The men in the room nodded in agreement.

Aslan struck his chest as a sign of strength. "We are most likely going to die, but let's make sure we go out with a bang and take as many of them with us as possible. Is that understood?"

Everyone replied with *"Allahu Akbar!"* and began to get into position. They didn't have much time.

****

Agent Schneider was about to give up and head back into the vehicle when he heard a voice call out from the farmhouse. "FBI! Don't shoot. We are coming out. We surrender," the voice shouted from the farmhouse. Agent Schneider looked through the vehicle's armored windows and sure enough, he saw two figures starting to walk out of the farmhouse with their hands held high, holding a white T-shirt.

As the two men began to move toward the vehicle, Schneider shouted out, "Where are the others? Are only two of you surrendering? We need everyone to surrender!"

Something just doesn't feel right about this, he worried. *Why would only two people surrender?*

Just as he was trying to figure this out, two loud shots were fired. Then there was a whooshing noise as he saw something fly out of two different windows from the second floor. Then the two individuals who had been walking toward the SUV turned around and ran at breakneck speed back into the farmhouse.

Then the scene erupted into violent pandemonium. One of the Stryker vehicles lurched forward with amazing speed. An RPG hit where it had just been, exploding, but not doing any major damage to the vehicle. A second vehicle also lurched forward but was slightly slower; the other RPG round hit the rear of the vehicle as it exploded. The second Stryker wasn't destroyed, but it was disabled and powerless to move. One of the two loud shots that Schneider had heard hit one of the heavy machine gunners in the head, killing him instantly. The second shot just barely missed the other gunner.

Within seconds of the RPG rounds hitting and the two sniper shots, the heavy machine guns opened fire. They immediately cut down the two terrorists who had pretended to surrender. One of the Chechens was hit by enough rounds that his body was completely cut in half. For a split second, Agent Schneider saw the upper body of the terrorist attempt to crawl to the farmhouse before it just went limp. The other terrorist had one of his legs ripped off as he fell to the ground. Schneider jumped back into the vehicle just as it began to take heavy fire from the farmhouse. The driver immediately raced away from the house to get away from the incoming barrage.

****

Director Stone heard the shooting and immediately put the binoculars to his eyes to get a better picture of what was going on. As soon as he saw that one of the Stryker vehicles had been hit, he immediately ordered Major Kiln, "Send several of the other armored vehicles forward to help get anyone who has been injured out of that vehicle."

"Yes, Sir," he replied.

The other three vehicles were moving slowly, ready to dart to the right or left if they saw any additional RPG rounds. Meanwhile, the gunners were raking the house with .50-caliber rounds, tearing huge chunks of wood out of the walls and shattering all the glass windows in the farmhouse.

With every second round being a tracer, it looked like lasers were slicing into and through the farmhouse. Many of the rounds were punching right through the house and continuing into the trees behind them. As more tracer rounds hit their target, several fires started to pick up. Stone peered through his binoculars, squinting. He noticed a lot of the enemy gunfire was coming from the basement windows.

Smart—using the basement as an improvised bunker, he thought.

He turned to Major Kiln. "Major, have your gunners shift their fire to the basement windows. That's where the Chechens are firing from."

Major Kiln looked through his own binoculars, and sure enough, he saw muzzles flashing from the basement. He raised his radio to his mouth and began to redirect his guys.

As the machine gunners shifted their fire to the basement windows, they shot huge holes through the foundation of the house. The second floor of the house was already in flames at that point since they'd focused their initial fire where they had spotted the RPGs coming from. The only time they stopped shooting was to reload their .50-cals. A number of other JSOC members were using high-powered sniper rifles as well, and they continued to pour accurate fire into the various windows or areas that they saw the Chechens shooting from.

The intense gun battle went on for maybe five minutes before Major Kiln told his guys to cease fire. As the shooting died down, it quickly became apparent that the Chechens had either all been killed or were waiting for them to do something stupid to expose themselves. Smoke continued to billow out of the basement windows and the areas that the heavy machine guns had punched through, so clearly, fires had started down there as well.

Director Stone saw Major Kiln on the radio to his guys. "What's our casualties?" he asked.

Major Kiln held up a finger, saying he needed a minute. Then he placed the headset down on the table and turned to Director Stone. "One of my guys was killed by that initial sniper shot. He got hit in the head—nothing we can do about that. Two other soldiers got injured from that RPG, but other than that, no one else was injured." Looking at the farmhouse, which was now nearly completely engulfed in flames, he continued, "I think we got 'em all. Do you want to let the farmhouse burn to the ground or send in the firefighters?"

Mike thought for a minute before responding. "No, I want the farmhouse to burn. We can't guarantee that they're all dead, and I don't want to risk the lives of any of the firefighters. We've already lost enough people today. You all did a great job. Keep your guys in place until that house is burnt to the ground. Once it is, then I want your guys to provide cover for the firefighters as they go in and put the remaining flames out, in case someone somehow survived," Stone directed.

As they were talking, they heard helicopters approaching. They both looked up and saw two TV helicopters fly into their restricted zone, probably looking to capture some images of the farmhouse and the military vehicles. With one of the Stryker vehicles damaged and smoldering, and the farmhouse ablaze, it would have made for an amazing scene from the air.

"What do you want me to do about the news helicopters?" Major Kiln asked.

Agent Stone snickered for a second and then, completely deadpan, replied, "Shoot them down." Then he laughed and said, "I'm just joking." The others around him started to crack up at the idea of shooting the news choppers down. No one on either side of the political spectrum was particularly fond of the media. They were about on par with the Congress in terms of popularity.

"Tell the police to get their helicopter over there and shoo them away. They can wait their turn for us to release information on the raid when we're ready," Stone directed. He then turned and walked toward the FBI and DEA agents. He wanted to get an update on the investigation at the armory and see if they had found anything new.

The FBI agents brought Stone and his deputy Agent Leary up to speed on what they had discovered so far. After triangulating the cell phone calls with the local towers, they were able to determine that several text messages had been sent between the man known as Jamaal and the Chechens at the farmhouse. They had obtained a copy of the text messages and it was clear that they had been working together.

After further digging into the backgrounds of the two attackers, they discovered that they were both American born. They came from Muslim families, although nothing obvious stood out to indicate they had left the country or attended any formal training by any militant groups. The only thing they had found of interest was the YouTube and Twitter activity of Jamaal and Muthana. They had apparently been radicalized via those social media platforms and had sworn their allegiance to ISIS. The strange part was none of their online activity had been flagged by any federal agency.

Director Stone scratched his head at that knowledge. He was going to have to dig into that when he got back to D.C. and find out why these radicalized individuals had never been identified and placed on a watchlist.

****

George Town, Grand Cayman

BAC International Bank

The Ghost was waiting in the lobby for the appropriate person to lead him back to his safety deposit box, when he noticed the news ticker at the bottom of the television read, "Nine suspected terrorists killed in raid on safe house in Elgin, IL. Men were believed to be responsible for the attacks on police stations and grocery stores in the Chicago area."

His heart sank. His mind filled with a sea of troubled thoughts. Those men were supposed to help him attack the political rallies.

How did they get caught? What am I going to do now? he wondered.

Nihad Nassimi had told him that the NCTC was all over the other refuges that had been let in; it was only a matter of time before his remaining men were caught. He'd have to harvest all his old contacts, and if that didn't work, then he'd have to go back to Mecca and see if he could get some more Americans on board…

"Sir…are you OK?" asked a woman standing near him, who had probably been trying to get his attention for a little while. She was ready to lead him into the back.

"I'm fine," he said, brushing off her concern. However, it was the first time in a long time that the Ghost had felt mildly panicked.

Chapter 28

Bending the Rules

Alexandria, Virginia

Constance Pool's Condominium

Mike knew that he couldn't talk to Dawn King. He had already pushed the limits by speaking with Director Harper, although he was certain that as long as he didn't continue to frequent the Georgetown Java, Mallory would never speak a word of their conversation to anyone. With the whole investigation classified at the SAP level, there really wasn't much he could do without sounding alarm bells. However, there was one person who he could speak with that was not technically a part of the investigation into the Chicago terror attacks.

Acting Director Stone didn't have to knock on Constance's door; he found her outside with her dog, in a part of her condo community that must have become the de facto dog park. He caught her line of sight and nodded to her. Constance nodded back and slowly made her way over to him.

"So, I hear congratulations are in order, Mike," she said with a leery smile.

"Oh, that. Well, I'm just acting director. Who knows who they'll appoint to be the permanent director? How did you hear about that?" he asked jokingly.

"Well, I keep my ears to the ground. There's not much else to do while I'm on administrative leave," she responded. "So...why exactly are you here? Do I need my lawyer?" she asked defensively.

"I don't think so. Do *you* think you need your lawyer?" he queried.

"That depends on where this conversation goes," she answered cautiously.

"Here's the deal, Constance. We didn't know each other very well before you left. I hadn't learned that much about the quality of your work. I've done some research since then. My current theory is that you are actually a star employee who is very loyal—so loyal, in fact, that you might have followed some orders from someone that got you in the current situation you are in. So, do you want your lawyer involved?" he asked slyly.

"I think we're good for now." She looked around, just to make sure that no one was watching them talk, and then she leaned in, lowering her voice as she continued. "I will go to jail before I state this publicly, but Mike, I was only following a directive from Mallory Harper."

"Why wouldn't you want to clear your own name?" he wondered aloud.

"The answer to that question is too long for me to explain in one sitting, but I've known Mallory for a *long* time, and we've been in the trenches together. I don't believe that she would purposely tell me to let someone with terrorist ties into the country. There is a greater game afoot, and that is what I want you to uncover," Constance explained.

They spoke a little longer and then parted ways. Mike wasn't sure if he'd made a mistake by coming.

Every step I take confirms my suspicions, but I still don't have any proof of anything, he thought. He wondered if he was just walking into a trap.

****

Washington, D.C.
National Counterterrorism Center

It had taken a significant amount of work, but Julie Wells finally had something she felt was worth bringing forward to her boss. As she grabbed her folder and walked toward his office, she stood up tall and straight, full of confidence.

Mike waved her into the office. "What have you got for me, Julie?" he asked, indicating toward her folder with his hand.

She sat down and slid a spreadsheet in front of him. "They say you should always follow the money," she began with a smirk.

"What am I looking at?" Mike asked mischievously.

"That is a listing of campaign donations to Alexander Bishop's most recent congressional campaign—well, not all of them, just the ones that seem to pose a problem," she announced, obviously satisfied with the work she had done.

His mouth dropped open as he read.

"Now, before you discipline me for disobeying orders, you need to know that I didn't spend any of my actual work time doing this research. Also, although everything about the investigation into the terror attacks has been classified, no one said we couldn't look into publicly available information about the National Security Advisor's husband. And, yes, those are all CAGIR donations or CAGIR-affiliated organizations—I would definitely say there is something going on there."

"OK, I should be mad at you for doing this, but I'm not," Mike said. "You and I both know something fishy is happening. However, you can't tell *anyone* else about this. I promise I will look into it, but there aren't many people we can trust. Do you understand?"

"You've got it, Boss," she said half-jokingly.

"No, but really, watch your back," Mike emphasized.

More somber now, Julie replied, "OK, I will."

****

McLean, Virginia
CIA Headquarters, Langley

Trevor smiled. "Mike, I'm kind of glad to see that you haven't lost your ability to think around a situation, but I already know about this."

"You do?" Stone asked incredulously.

"Yep. Did you guys find out about the house in the Hamptons yet?" he inquired.

"Wait—what house?" Mike shot back.

"Oh yeah, she bought an estate at a price that was so low, it clearly smelled of payoff," Trevor replied.

"How are you so happy about all this? Why didn't you come forward, if you already knew this?" Mike wondered in disbelief.

"Michael, what are we going to do? She outranks us. She has power that we can't even put measures on right now.

If you want to go forward, it's going to have to be with an airtight case that can't be refuted. What are we going to do, take her to a black site? You know we can't do that," Trevor explained.

"So what are we supposed to do?" asked Mike, feeling like the wind had just been taken out of his sails.

"Right now, you need to be patient. I know that isn't your strong suit, but we need to continue to gather a case."

Mike felt defeated. He left the meeting with a great sense of injustice. He would have to go back to the drawing board.

Chapter 29
Loose Ends

Arlington, Virginia

Mallory Harper's House

Now that she was unemployed, Mallory found great comfort in her daily rituals. Mike was right, she was very much a creature of habit. Most mornings, she took a run and then sat in her cozy breakfast nook with her cat and a cup of coffee while she read through the entire newspaper, cover to cover. She knew it was old-school, and she didn't care. She felt a lot was missed by listening to pundits on twenty-four-hour news cycles.

Mallory had never been married, although she'd come close a few times. She had a habit of being too dedicated to her work to continue any sort of meaningful long-term relationship of the non-feline kind. Being off work was driving her crazy, even if she knew it was only temporary. She was doing irrational things, like trying to learn Mandarin with Rosetta Stone, just to keep her mind sufficiently occupied.

The morning was going just like any other, until she hit about page twenty. Buried in the lower right-hand corner was a short story about the reported suicide of a government worker. Then the name jumped off the page—it was Dawn King. She read the article again. Yes, it was that Dawn King, *her* Dawn King. That was her neighborhood. The words on the page said that she had been found with a pistol in her hand, but that seemed entirely ludicrous to her.

This is all wrong...she would never kill herself. She didn't even own a gun, she thought. Wild thoughts swirled through her head and then she wondered if she was next.

Suddenly, the guilt that she had been keeping herself from feeling overwhelmed her. She felt the weight of all those people who had lost their lives on her shoulders. Even though she hadn't acted knowingly or with intent, those terrorist attacks were at least in part her fault. The heaviest weight though, was realizing that she'd played a part in the death of her friend. She collapsed on the floor, sobbing. She had never cried this hard in her life, and there was no stopping it.

When she had managed to collect herself, she called her friend that came to cat-sit when she was traveling. Once she had confirmed that her beloved Chester would be taken care of, she took the battery and SIM card out of her Galaxy 6, breaking the SIM card in two. Mallory shoved all the necessary items in a backpack for a week away from home, and then she headed out the door.

Just a block away was her local bank. There she pulled out a significant amount of cash. She didn't want to use her credit or debit cards for anything else until she was truly sure she was safe. She managed to find a pay phone that hadn't been torn down yet and called a taxi company. Once she got in the cab, Mallory kept looking back at the cars behind her to make sure she hadn't been followed. She switched taxis twice more, and then eventually stopped about a mile away from her destination. Harper walked in a very indirect route, making stops in various stores and coffee shops to make sure that she wasn't being tailed. Finally, she arrived at the one place where she felt truly safe.

****

Rosland, Virginia
Michael Stone's Studio Condominium

Mike had traveled a lot these past several years, so his condo was really more of a landing pad than anything else. He didn't have any decorations or fancy possessions to speak of, minus a few small trinkets from his travels and a picture of his deceased daughter and his ex-wife. In case he ever needed to move, he could be packed up in less than a day. Even still, he enjoyed coming home to his little nest away from work, especially with the lovely view he enjoyed. The main window he had looked out over all of D.C., and he could see the top of the Capitol Building and the Jefferson Memorial along the Potomac.

Stone was juggling a small bag of groceries as he tried to get to his keys. Just then, he saw a courier ride up on a bicycle. The man slipped something into his mailbox and then turned and raced down the stairs toward his bike.

"Hey!" yelled Mike. "Who sent you?" But he was already long gone.

Michael put his groceries down and pulled out the key to his mailbox. Inside was a manila envelope. He cautiously opened the top. When he found there was a single paper inside, he put the envelope in the bag of groceries and headed upstairs to read it.

The groceries waited on the counter while he pulled out the letter. It read, "Mike, I'm ready to talk. Please come to St. Andrew Apostle Catholic Church in Silver Spring, MD, at 8 p.m. tonight. M.H. Oh, and this should go without saying given your background, but burn this letter, come alone, and don't bring your cell phone. Make sure you aren't followed."

Stone looked at his watch. He didn't have much time. He put away his ice cream and milk, made himself a peanut butter and jelly sandwich, burned the letter, and he was out the door.

****

Silver Spring, Maryland
St. Andrew Apostle Catholic Church

Mike looked around. At first, he didn't see anyone, but then he saw Mallory lighting a candle. He quietly joined her, and whispered, "Is there a wedding here I didn't know about?"

Harper smiled weakly. "No, and I don't have a lawyer here, either." They quietly made their way to the pews, him sitting one row behind her as if they were just there to pray.

"Don't take this the wrong way, but I didn't have you pegged as a church person," said Mike as he eyed her suspiciously.

"I haven't been for a long time, but I have a second cousin who's a priest here. We don't talk much, but I knew I would be safe here," she replied.

"So, you said you're ready to talk, right? What do you have to share?"

"Mike…they killed her," she began, her voice betraying the fact that she was barely holding it together.

"Killed who?" he asked.

"Dawn King. I read it in the paper. The article said she committed suicide, but she would never do that," she insisted, exasperated.

"How do you know?" he queried.

"They said that she shot herself. You don't understand—Dawn didn't own a firearm, and her politics would've kept her from ever getting one. There's just no way. If it had been pills, I still wouldn't have believed it, but it just doesn't make any sense for her to have killed herself with a gun." She lowered her voice to a low whisper. "I think they're coming for me next."

"Well, if you have some information to share, they can't kill you for it if it's already out there," Mike asserted.

"I don't know who I can trust anymore. If I talk to the wrong person, I'm sure I'll end up dead," Mallory whimpered.

"You can trust me. You believe that, right? Isn't that why I'm here?" Mike asked as he tried to reassure her.

Mallory nodded as she wiped a tear away.

"If you tell me what you know, I will find a way for you to come forward safely. I have connections. We can get you a new identity, get you out of the country, whatever it's going to take," he assured her.

Harper handed him a list of twenty-three names on a piece of paper that looked like it had been ripped out of a diary. As he glanced over it, two names immediately stuck out. "Is this what I think it is?" Mike inquired incredulously.

"That is a list of names that Leah Bishop asked me to clear through the refugee program," she responded.

Stone couldn't believe what he was holding in his hands. "I'll find a way to keep you safe," he asserted.

"Thailand is nice," she said wistfully. "If I'm going to disappear, at least I think I could be happy there."

"I'll see what I can do," he replied. Then he quietly got up and left the church.

Chapter 30

Power of the Conscience

Working with Trevor, Michael did manage to arrange a way for Mallory to disappear, but only after she testified to some people that he knew could be trusted at the FBI. Her intel was condemning; she carefully laid out a case against Leah Bishop, explaining when and how they would meet. After her written and video-recorded depositions, Mallory flew away to a tropical beach hut on the other side of the world, never to be heard from again.

Each of the men on the list was obviously going to be investigated, and likely deported. However, this was far from over.

Mike knew something was wrong when Trevor showed up at *his* office. "What happened?" he exclaimed.

"I wanted to tell you this in person, Michael. The Attorney General has decided not to prosecute Leah Bishop," Trevor explained.

"What!" Mike questioned, practically shouting. He stood up and began pacing.

Trevor put his hand up as if to say, "Calm down." He understood the reaction, but it wasn't going to help solve the problem. "I know. I'm almost certain this is political. A scandal like this would really hurt Karen Philmore's chances at the ballot box, and it's already September. We can hope that the AG would move forward after the election."

"And what if he doesn't?" Stone bellowed.

"The investigation won't die. The FBI still has all the information needed to successfully prosecute Leah Bishop. We just have to wait. Another Attorney General will come along, and she will have her justice," Trevor reassured.

Mike stopped pacing. He sat down and put his hands in his head for a moment as he thought. He just couldn't believe that Leah might get away with this.

Trevor gave him a moment to be upset. Then he cleared his throat. "Twenty-one potential terrorists are going to be removed from the country—Mike, that's a win. And Leah isn't going to convince *you* to clear any names for her, so the extremists just lost their steady conduit into the United States. You just helped save potentially thousands of innocent American lives."

Stone picked his head up and straightened himself out. "So…what do we do now?" he asked.

"We wait."

****

Allison O'Brien tossed and turned in her bed until she sat straight up, screaming.

"Allie, what's wrong?" called her husband, still half-asleep.

"Babe, I'm sorry. It was just another nightmare," she said. She lay back down, hoping to get some rest.

"You've been having a lot of those lately," he asserted.

"I know. It's just some things at work," she explained.

"Do you want to talk about it?" he asked.

"I really can't, Honey, but thank you. It'll be OK," she responded.

Except, she wondered to herself, *will it?*

Allison had been plagued for a week by dreams about the terrorist attacks in Chicago. In each one, she ended up being the one that pulled the trigger on the guns, or detonated the bomb, or drove the explosive truck near Trump Tower. She watched the victims die, over and over.

This isn't my fault, she tried to convince herself. Technically, she was right—she hadn't participated directly in any of the attacks. However, as Deputy Assistant Attorney General, she was a part of this horrible plan to allow Leah Bishop to get away with her role in all of this.

She tossed and turned for a few more hours, until finally, at 4 a.m., she'd had enough. She made herself a pot of coffee, slammed two cups, and got ready as if she were headed directly to the office. Allie left her husband a note, explaining that something had come up for work and that she was going to have to go in early.

She walked down the street to a local coffee shop that she knew had computers and free Wi-Fi and logged in to a website where she could send text messages through the internet from an unknown number. She looked through the contacts in her phone until she found what she was looking for—the number of the one reporter who she felt was trustworthy.

"Angela, it's Allie C. at the Capital Café. URGENT. Please meet me here as soon as possible." She hoped Angela would get the message and show up. She didn't want to be late for work and draw suspicion.

Fifteen minutes later, Allison watched Angela Lapin roll out of an Uber, dressed in brightly colored athletic wear from head to toe. She quickly made eye contact with Allison and joined her in the corner.

Allison was on her third cup of coffee since entering the coffee shop, and she was starting to sweat. Angela must have noticed. "Wow, you don't look that great. Are you OK?" Angela asked, genuinely concerned.

"I haven't been sleeping that well," admitted Allie.

"Ahh. Well, I hope this is good, because I did interrupt my run for you this morning. I'm training for a half," said Angela, looking at her Fitbit.

Allison looked around, then leaned in and whispered, "We have open-and-shut evidence to put away a person who was passing suspicious names through the refugee program at the NCTC, including two of the Chicago attackers...and my boss is just sitting on it."

Angela's eyes opened wide as saucers. "Who was it?" she asked.

"The National Security Advisor, Leah Bishop," whispered Allie.

A moment of stunned silence followed. Finally, Angela managed to say, "I'm going to need some of the information to corroborate your story. When we go live with it, I want to make sure that there are a lot of the facts and supporting evidence to back this all up."

Allison nodded. The two of them chatted for a little longer, filling in the details of the story and working out a way to pass documentation back and forth without being tracked, and then they parted ways.

****

At work, it was business as usual. As far as anyone else could tell, she was just fulfilling her role as Deputy Assistant Attorney General. Casually though, she was getting Angela the information she needed.

She went home that evening, unsure if she would have a job when she woke up. Ms. Lapin wasn't going to name her as the source within the DOJ, but it would be pretty obvious to her boss where the information had come from. Then she decided that she didn't care. Her conscience was clear. She slept soundly that night, whisked away in a world of peaceful dreams.

Chapter 31

The Reset Button

The next day, headlines splashed over the front page of the *Washington Post*, and soon every reputable news outlet was covering the story nonstop. The White House, in order to try and cut off the cancer of this scandal, announced that the Attorney General was being asked to step down immediately and would himself be investigated for improper conduct. The new Acting Attorney General, Allison O'Brien, immediately arranged for Leah Bishop to be arrested.

Although the race had been pretty close up to that point, Karen Philmore's poll numbers summarily tanked. Even though she wasn't the one who had appointed a corrupt National Security Advisor, or an Attorney General who was willing to overlook justice on behalf of politics, the people felt that she now had a stench of dishonesty just by association with the President and those people surrounding him.

****

When the Ghost heard the news, he completely lost his temper for the first time in more than a decade. He threw expensive vases and other fragile items against a wall, causing a ruckus that made even his gardener leave for the day. Every single person that had been brought into the United States through the refugee program had now been compromised, and a friendly Attorney General had been removed from power. He was so angry that everything in his vision appeared red for hours.

Fortunately, he didn't have to be the one to share this news with his employers. There really was no avoiding it, since every reporter worth a grain of salt came running toward the word "scandal" like a dog salivating at the prospect of red meat. When Al Shabah had finally calmed himself enough, he logged in to the dark web and found the discussion board were players discussed exploits and cheats for a popular massively multiplayer online (MMO) game, which was how he and Sheikh Maktoum communicated.

Skimming through the different threads, he finally found the specific one he was looking for. There it was—a message from Maktoum. "Things are too hot now. Abort phase two. Reassess at a later date."

The Ghost breathed an enormous sigh of relief. At least he still had his life, and he wouldn't have to try and piece together a new plan under such challenging circumstances. "Acknowledged," he wrote back.

****

A few months later, David Garcia won the presidential election. The results weren't even close. Karen Philmore had tried to backpedal and explain that she wasn't a part of the salacious stories that were out there, but the more statements she made, the more people just grew to distrust her. Something about her constant clarifications and overly-metered speech made the voters feel that she wasn't genuine and that she had something to hide.

Although Mr. Garcia was incredibly busy selecting his cabinet and other key positions, he didn't completely exit campaign mode. He made several speeches after the election on his intended path after taking office. Given the atmosphere of fear that was permeating the very fabric of American life, the President-elect decided that one of his most important roles was to reassure everyone that there was a path for the nation to be more secure.

"My fellow Americans, I am honored and humbled that you have chosen me to be your next leader at this pivotal time in our nation's history. As you watch this tonight, many of you are sitting around your kitchen table, afraid to leave your homes. I want to work to restore the faith and trust that you once had in the government to fulfill its first and most important duty, to protect its citizens.

"When I take office, one of my first actions is going to be to propose a new agency within our government, a counterterrorism unit designed specifically to combat this problem. Now, I am not generally a fan of adding anything new to the government, but there is a hole that needs to be plugged. Right now, if a person of interest is being monitored by the CIA and then comes in our country, they become lost in the shuffle. Why? Because once they hit our soil, the CIA is no longer authorized to monitor them on American soil; they have no charter to spy in our country. And the FBI is only supposed to investigate actual crimes, so they are not going to continue to monitor a person without probable cause sufficient enough to lead to an immediate arrest. The NSA is only allowed to monitor foreigners on US soil with a court order. As you can see, we have a problem.

"The new counterterrorism unit will be independent of the CIA, the FBI, and the NSA, but will cooperate with those entities. They will work directly for the National Security Council and report to the National Security Advisor and the President. What they will be able to do that no one else is allowed to do at this time is to follow cases from start to finish, across jurisdictions. They will be able to operate both internationally and domestically. Also, I plan to have several Treasury Department agents attached to this group, because I believe that if we can track the money, we can stop the terrorists.

"I ask you all to call your Senators and Congress members and tell them that you want to support my proposal of a counterterrorism unit. As they begin to hear your voice, I am sure that they will be moved in the right direction. Thank you, and God bless America."

Chapter 32
Hunted

Ever since the news about Leah Bishop's arrest had been made public, Yasser Najjar had been in hiding. He was so paranoid about being caught that he hadn't even returned to his apartment to get any clothes or supplies. Unsure of where to go, he had wandered in the doors of a homeless shelter.

"Please, I just need a safe place to stay tonight," Yasser begged.

"Are you alone or with family?" the social worker at the door asked.

"I'm by myself," he answered.

"Well, then, you're in luck," she responded. "We just had a few more vacancies open up for the single male shelter. I just need a copy of your ID, I'll help you fill out a couple of forms, and then you can have a nice warm spot for the night."

"You need an ID?" Yasser asked in despair.

"Yes, it's a state requirement," she explained. "If you don't have one, that's OK. It's still early in the day, and we have a program where we can help you get one for free. What's your name?"

"I'm sorry—uh, I've got to go," he said, and then he turned and walked out the door.

****

The social worker wasn't shocked. She'd had the same conversation before. As she picked up the phone to alert the police to a possible criminal in the neighborhood, she wondered why this one was on the run.

He looks too clean for there to be a warrant related to drug charges. Maybe he stole something? she pondered.

She gave the police a basic description, and they thanked her for the tip. Then, five minutes later, someone came in completely drunk and threw up all over the floor, and she forgot all about it.

****

Mr. Najjar had gotten lucky that day. The police were too busy handling active cases to follow this tip from a social worker at a homeless shelter. That night, he drove his car to a church parking lot and slept in his vehicle. He knew it wasn't a permanent solution, but he would have to come up with a better plan the next day.

In the morning, Yasser found a spot near a hardware store where men congregated to find day labor. He needed a way to get money, and he was too paranoid to try and draw anything out of his checking account with his ATM card. He got picked up by a man who needed help digging irrigation ditches at a corporate farm conglomerate nearby. It was brutal hard labor in the cold, but at least he had on his winter coat and gloves. The man fed him a sandwich at lunchtime and provided him with water throughout the day, and when it was time to leave, he was rewarded with cold hard cash. It wasn't the worst day of his life.

Yasser found a cluster of people who were living in an abandoned building that evening. After bringing some cigarettes and cash, he was allowed safe passage to stay there.

Mr. Najjar might have gone on living that way indefinitely, but one day, ICE decided to do a raid on the place where he stood to wait for day labor.

As the immigration officials rolled up, one of the men yelled, "*La migra viene!*"

Yasser didn't understand Spanish, but he understood the panicked running that followed that announcement and took off as fast as his legs would carry him. Unfortunately, around the corner was another group of ICE agents, waiting to catch everyone who had dashed off.

They were all handcuffed and placed in the back of a bus. As they were driving off to a detention facility to be interviewed, the thoughts swirled inside his head.

Why didn't I get rid of my wallet? he thought with regret. They were going to know who he was right away. Maybe part of him had just wanted his family to know what happened to him if he died.

Is there any way out of this for me? he wondered in despair.

The more Yasser thought about it, the more hopeless he felt. He envisioned himself being tortured in a dark hole somewhere. Eventually, he knew what he needed to do. There was only one choice to make.

If only I had completed my mission, he thought in regret. Then he bit down on his cyanide tooth.

"*Allahu Akbar*," he managed to say before he began foaming at the mouth and convulsing.

The other men inside the bus began yelling and trying to get the attention of the driver, but the man wouldn't stop until he got to the station. He'd heard people make a fuss in the back before, and it was usually just a trap to try and escape or attack him. This time, when the driver opened the door to the back, there was a dead man waiting for him.

******

Acting Director Stone just got off the phone with ICE, and he was livid. He had barely managed to contain his response enough to keep from cussing the agent out, but he knew there was nothing that could be done now. Yasser Najjar was gone, and all his information and intelligence had died with him. They were still no closer to figuring out who was pulling the strings behind this giant puppet show.

When he had taken a moment to calm down, he drafted some memos to all the interagency partners. Mike wanted to make sure that the FBI, ICE, and any of his other partners would be aware that any of the remaining refugees that still needed to be detained might be outfitted with a cyanide tooth or other suicide technology. Maybe through cooperation, he could keep this from happening again.

****

Baltimore, Maryland
McElderry Park Neighborhood

Daoud Khalil still had nightmares about his time fighting in Syria with ISIS. The atrocities they had committed, that *he* had committed, haunted him in his dreams. He could still hear the screams of the Christian woman as he'd pounded the nails between her wrist bones to the wooden cross they had built. They had crucified 104 Christians in the small village of Tal Erphan, Syria, near the Turkish-Iraqi border, and it was one of the things that disturbed his thoughts every day.

Daoud was different than most of the fighters he had been surrounded by. He was educated at the University of Aleppo in electrical engineering and had worked for a power company in the city. When the Syrian civil war had erupted, he'd found himself caught between a rock and a hard place. He'd tried his best to stay on the sidelines, away from the fighting, and then one day, his portion of the city had been captured by ISIS. Once it was discovered that he knew how to operate and run a power plant, he became a man that they needed.

ISIS wanted people who could get the oil fields up and running and return power to the areas they controlled. They put Daoud to work doing just that. They also made sure he was well compensated and paid him in gold and US dollars. Daoud was not an ideologue. He didn't believe in their radical version of Islam but kept his mouth shut out of fear.

Then, one day while he was fixing an electrical problem at one of the substations near the city of Al-Hasakah, one of his bodyguards received a phone call telling him they needed to head over to the village of Erphan. Daoud and his two other companions went with their bodyguards to the city, only to see a dozen fighters standing guard over a large crowd of civilians.

When they approached the ISIS commander, he told Daoud, "We rounded up all the Christians in the village. We plan to crucify them if they don't renounce their faith and convert to Islam. I know that you three engineers are not fighters, but we will need help to crucify this many people."

Unspoken, but completely understood, was the message that Daoud and his colleagues didn't have any choice in the matter, at least not unless they wanted to share the Christians' fate.

In the year and a half Daoud had found himself working for ISIS, he had never had to participate in any killings or anything like this. It horrified him what he was made to do, but he had no choice unless he wanted to die himself. Secretly, he prayed to Allah that he would forgive him for his part in all this madness. After that horrible day, Daoud was desperate to find a way out of ISIS.

One day, while he was working at the power station outside of Ar Raqqah, a man walked up to him at the control room and asked, "Could I buy you coffee?"

Daoud was a bit startled. He didn't know the man at all. He tried to put him off. "I have another hour on my shift before my replacement arrives and I can leave," he responded, hoping the stranger would go away.

The man just smiled and said, "I will just sit down with you then and wait for your shift to end."

As the two men talked, Daoud could tell he was a foreigner, most likely from Saudi Arabia, based on his accent. Daoud had traveled to the Kaaba once, two years before the civil war had started, so he recognized the accent.

While they spoke, the man said to him, "I'm looking for an educated electrical engineer to help me accomplish a secret mission."

Daoud was intrigued but didn't want to become involved with ISIS any deeper. He just wanted to stay alive long enough to escape.

The man sensed his hesitation. "Mr. Khalil, I wanted to invite you to coffee to talk with you about an opportunity. I suppose we could talk about it here, since no one else is around, at least while we wait for the end of your shift."

Daoud looked at the man quizzically, then replied, "I am just a simple engineer. My place is here, working to keep the lights on for the people in the city."

Smiling warmly, the man responded, "That is why I have chosen you for this mission. You see, I run several businesses around the world. I also work with men who run even more. We are in need of someone with your skill set."

Daoud snorted before responding, "What skill set is that? I just operate a power station."

"Not just any power station," the man asserted. "You operate a natural gas power station. I talked with several members of the ISIS leadership. They tell me you are reliable and a hard worker. That is exactly what we are looking for...am I mistaken in my assessment that you would like to leave ISIS-controlled territory?"

Daoud's face froze. He had been so careful to mask his true feelings.

Has someone somehow figured out that I want to leave? he thought in horror.

"I'm not sure what you mean. I'm happy doing the work I'm doing," he responded, trying to speak the truth very selectively so as not to give himself away.

"Daoud, don't be afraid. I haven't told anyone in ISIS that you wish to leave. I told them that I believe you are special, that I may have a special mission for you. Do you want to know what the mission is?"

"I suppose listening can't hurt," Daoud stated cautiously.

The Ghost smiled briefly, then returned to business. "Good. I need to send someone to the United States. I want that someone to be you. Are you interested in going to America?" he asked.

Daoud tried to hide his emotions, but he couldn't help the smile that was now spreading across his face.

America, he thought warmly. The idea of going there one day had certainly crossed his mind, but he could never get there on his own—he lacked the money and the means. Then his happy expression melted as he remembered the reality that he was not there but trapped in ISIS-controlled territory.

"What would you need me to do?" he asked.

"A business partner of mine owns a company that manages an electrical substation facility in the American state of Maryland. He needs an experienced engineer who has experience managing electrical substations. You have that experience, which is why I am talking to you," the Ghost explained.

"You didn't answer my question. What do you want me to do?" Daoud insisted.

A smile curled up at the corners of the Ghost's lips. "You are perceptive. I want you to assimilate into America. I want you to work for this facility and not to attract attention. One day, you will be contacted by either myself or one of my associates. When we do, we will want you to perform a specific task or set of tasks for us.

"All I can tell you is that one day, we will most likely ask you to shut down the facility—shut it down in a manner that would make it impossible to turn back on again."

"If I do that, then the Americans would know it was me who did it and arrest me. Why would I willingly sacrifice my life, my freedom, for a cause that I don't believe in?" Daoud asked. Then he thought he might have crossed the line and given away his true feelings.

"Mr. Khalil, we have thought about that as well," the Ghost answered, completely brushing past Daoud's other comment. "We're going to give you a thumb drive to insert into one of the computer terminals at the facility. Once you do that, the virus will take care of everything for you. You won't have to do anything. No one will know it was you, and you won't be discovered. Once that task is done, you will be free—free to live as an American for the rest of your life, if you choose to."

It all sounded so simple, almost too simple. But it also presented Daoud with a chance to escape, and he desperately wanted out. "OK. I'll go along with this plan. Once I insert the virus, I am done. I'm not going to do any further work for you or anyone else. I will do this in exchange for my freedom and a new life in America." Daoud felt more like he'd just made a deal with the devil than finding his freedom, but the alternative was no more attractive.

****

It had been nearly fourteen months since Daoud had arrived in America through the refugee program, and slowly, he was working to forget about his experiences with ISIS. True to his word, the man with the Saudi accent had arranged for him to get a job at a company that managed an electrical substation plant in Maryland, just outside of Baltimore. Daoud did as he was instructed; he found an apartment in the McElderry Park neighborhood of Baltimore and kept mostly to himself.

Then, one Friday, while he was attending a Baltimore Orioles game, he was contacted by someone from his past, his original handler from when he had first moved to the States. The man bought a couple of hot dogs and slipped him a thumb drive in the packaging of one of them. Between casual bites of his own hot dog, the man told Daoud, "You have a week to place the drive in one of the computer terminals at work. After that, you will be free, and you can leave this company or stay if you choose."

The man left after the seventh-inning stretch. Daoud had thought about this day for a long time and pondered what he would do when it finally came. He had been researching where he would like to go when he could leave. He had determined that he would look for work in either Wyoming or Montana—somewhere out west, away from people, where he could just live a quiet life and forget about the past. Daoud looked down at the thumb drive and determined that he would bring it to work with him on Monday and be done with it. He wanted to move on with the rest of his life.

****

What Daoud didn't know was the man that gave him the thumb drive had been under surveillance by the FBI. While Daoud went about his weekend plans and business, the FBI had been busy digging into his background. When they'd discovered he had immigrated to the US through the refugee program, his name had been cross-referenced against the names that former Director Mallory Harper had given to Director Stone. His name matched, which meant he was placed in the US to carry out some sort of attack. An arrest warrant was issued and a plan was born to bring him in on Monday morning as he left his home for work.

****

As Daoud left his small one-bedroom apartment, he walked down to his car and fumbled for his keys. As he placed his key into the door to unlock it, he suddenly heard footsteps moving very quickly behind him. He turned around to see who was approaching him, but he felt a pair of strong hands grab him by his shoulders and slam his body against the driver's side door of his car.

"Are you Daoud Khalil?" asked a man he still couldn't see. What he did notice was several black SUVs pulled up near his vehicle and additional men in black suits and badges hanging around their necks gathering around.

"Who are you? What is the meaning of this?" Daoud shot back in broken English, not answering the man's questions.

"I'm Special Agent Mark Lavine from the FBI. Daoud Khalil, you are under arrest for suspected acts of terrorism," the man said to Daoud's genuine surprise.

"I have no idea what you are talking about! I have not committed any acts of terrorism. I fled the Middle East to escape terrorism," Daoud exclaimed as he was handcuffed and then turned around. The FBI agents began to pat him down and search his vehicle. One of the agents felt around in his pocket and found the thumb drive. He held it up for the others to see.

"Really? Then I suppose we won't find anything incriminating on this thumb drive, will we?" the agent asked sarcastically.

Daoud was loaded into one of the SUVs and driven away to the Baltimore field office. After arriving there, he was held in a private room for nearly thirty minutes before he was told he would be transferred to another facility. An hour went by and still no one had spoken to him. Daoud asked to speak with a lawyer when one of the FBI agents brought him a glass of water and a sandwich.

The FBI agent told him, "Lawyers are for citizens— people who have rights."

When another hour had gone by, he was transferred to the roof of the building, where a helicopter whisked him away to an airport. The helicopter landed at a hangar near a small Lear jet. He was quickly escorted aboard. As he entered the plane, he saw two men sitting in leather chairs, drinking a soft drink. They beckoned for him to join them, and they offered him a soda and some food. Then they removed his handcuffs so he would be more comfortable.

Daoud was confused. He could tell that these men, whoever they were, could probably kill him with their bare hands and not even break a sweat.

"Where am I? Who are you?" Daoud gasped.

"Well, those are good questions, Mr. Khalil. My name is Mr. Smith, and this is my colleague—you can just call him John. We work for the Central Intelligence Agency...I'm sure you've heard of our organization." As he finished his introduction, the plane raced down the runway and then lifted off.

"Where are you taking me, Mr. Smith?" Daoud squeaked. He saw the ground disappear below them as their plane began to gain altitude. He was starting to be more than a little bit concerned because he had heard horror stories of CIA black sites, how people went to them and were never heard from again.

"We're flying to Guantanamo, Cuba," Mr. Smith explained. "We should arrive in about three hours. Once we get there, you will simply cease to exist, Mr. Khalil. That is, unless you cooperate. We can place you into the witness protection program and take you to someplace quiet, like Idaho or Montana."

Do they know me? Daoud wondered. He was in awe that this man in front of him seemed to know about his plans to disappear into the mountains.

"We have some questions for you. First, we want to know what was on the thumb drive, and who gave it to you. If you are honest and upfront with me, we can help you. If you lie to us, then things are going to go badly for you. My friend here, John, is going to hook some equipment up to you. He is a very skilled polygrapher. We're also going to give you a shot that will help to calm your nerves."

As Mr. Smith spoke, John got up and began to walk Daoud through the process of what he was hooking him up to, and what each part of the machinery did. He also set up a camera that was mounted on a headset that he placed on Daoud. This would measure his pupils and eye movements. Lastly, he gave him a shot of some medicine that would relax him, and also make it more difficult for him to lie.

Once the equipment was in place, Mr. Smith went through a series of questions to establish a baseline for Daoud. With that complete, the questioning began.

"Mr. Khalil, what was on the thumb drive?" Smith asked.

"Um, I don't know for sure. I was only told to insert it into one of the computers that was networked to the computer system at the facility," Daoud responded honestly.

John and Mr. Smith looked at the readouts on the machines and mumbled something to each other.

"What were you told would be on the thumb drive, Mr. Khalil?" Smith said, changing the wording of his question.

"I was told it would most likely have a virus on it, and that the virus would shut down the facility when it was activated," Daoud replied candidly.

Smith smiled. "Who told you about the virus on the thumb drive?" he asked.

John was glued to the screen, analyzing data. Mr. Smith glanced over to him and he nodded.

"I'm not sure of his name, but his Arabic had an accent," Daoud answered. "I believe he was from Saudi Arabia. I know he was well-educated. When he spoke English on his cell phone, I noted that he spoke with a British accent, not an American one."

"Can you describe him for me? What does he look like?" Mr. Smith asked.

****

The conversation with Daoud went on for several more hours, with the CIA men getting a very good description of the Saudi who had recruited him and of the entire process Daoud had gone through to get into the US. What they found most helpful was how he had communicated with his handlers through the dark web. The MMO game exploit blog was genius. Daoud explained how he had been caught up by ISIS and forced to work in the power plants and oil fields to keep things running for them, how he had wanted to get away, but until the Saudi had offered him this chance, he had been trapped.

Daoud was still hooked up to the polygraph machines as he told his story, so they could see he was telling them the truth. After several hours of flying, Mr. Smith had them land the plane back at the municipal airport where they had originally begun their journey. Daoud sat with a sketch artist, and they further refined the description of the man who recruited him.

After a few more hours, Mr. Smith finally ended the interrogation. "Mr. Khalil, we will be placing you in the witness protection program since you cooperated with us and you have not willingly participated in extremism. We will keep in contact with you and may ask you further questions while your placement into the program is approved."

Daoud began to cry. "I can't believe it," he muttered between tears. "I'm finally going to be free. A quiet life in the middle of nowhere—it's all I've ever wanted."

Chapter 33

New Administration

President Garcia held true to his word. Within the first one hundred days of his administration, he managed to get both the House and Senate to approve his plan for a new counterterrorism unit, or CTU as the government folks who were so fond of acronyms called it. As the different appointments within the organization began to be filled, Michael Stone found that he had a job offer to consider as a Deputy Director of Field Operations. Apparently, Trevor Cole had put his name forward.

Mike didn't think about it very long. He was excited to be a part of a unit that wouldn't have its hands tied in terms of jurisdiction. However, they were still going to have to wait a couple more months while the details of Patriot Act 3 were negotiated in Congress, allowing them to more freely monitor those within the United States given "reasonable concern."

In the meantime, he planned to become pals with some of the agents that had moved over from the Treasury Department, until he could put together some intelligence that was actionable. The President was right—if they could follow the money, they could find the terrorists.

Although Mike was happy that Leah Bishop was on trial for her part in all of this, he knew that she hadn't acted on her own. Clearly, she had been paid off. CAGIR was involved in the scheme, but exactly who within the organization knew about it, and were they a puppet in a much larger scheme?

Stone sat down next to one of his new friends and explained his theory. "Simone, I'd really appreciate it if you could do what you could to look into the funding of CAGIR. I know that they bribed Leah, but I don't know where they get their money from. I need to know where exactly they fit in the food chain before we can really take them down."

"Yeah, sure thing," she replied nonchalantly. "You just want me to let you know when I have something useful?" Simone asked with a wink.

"Yeah, that works…wait, this isn't going to be as easy as you just made it out to be, is it?" Mike asked with a chuckle.

She shook her head. "No, Mike. This won't exactly be a piece of cake, but I'll get on it for you."

He headed back to his office to work on some theories. After a while, he grabbed a corkboard and pinned a title at the top of it: "Wish List." Then he added his first Post-it note below: "Nihad Nassimi."

Twenty minutes later, his supervisor was walking past his office and pointed to his new creation. "What's that?" he inquired.

"I'm starting a list of people I want to track once we have Patriot Act 3 on board," Mike answered.

"Oh, good idea. Looking a little empty, but you've got to start somewhere," he said, half-joking.

****

Riyadh, Saudi Arabia

Prince Nawaf had been called into the Minister of Foreign Affairs's office for a meeting with the Americans. He hadn't been briefed about the contents of the meeting, but his was not an unusual occurrence. Prince Nawaf's English skills were superb, and although there was always an official translator in the room, he had traveled so much that he sometimes caught nuances in the culture that would otherwise have been missed.

As he walked into the room, he recognized two of the Americans sitting there. One was an undersecretary for the Secretary of State, and the other was a part of the US intelligence community. The prince figured this must have something to do with the refugees they had been shuttling into the States. He eagerly waited to see the depth of information that they would share.

Everyone shook hands and engaged in the compulsory amount of small talk. Tea and a few snacks had been brought in as well. Prince Nawaf was feeling impatient as they muddled through these perfunctory formalities. Finally, though, the real meat of the conversation began.

The Undersecretary of State was the first to begin. "Gentlemen, as you know, we have been trying to recover from the brutal terrorist attacks that took place on our nation. Part of that effort has been tracking down the individuals who were pushed through the refugee program's vetting process by corrupt individuals within our government."

Everyone nodded. They all had been watching the trials and hearings taking place in Washington.

The intelligence officer spoke up next. "Now that we have captured several of these men, we're harvesting what useful intelligence information we can from them. Which brings us to why we are here. Two of the refugees we interviewed claimed to have been approached by a man with a Saudi accent. We were hoping that you could assist us in identifying and locating this man."

The intelligence officer pulled a couple of sketches out of a folder he had brought with him. He held up two different drawings that bore some resemblance in the prince's mind to someone he knew, although he wasn't positive who it was just yet.

"Of course, we would like to help you. However, why do you have two different drawings if you are looking for one person?" asked the Minister of Foreign Affairs as he exchanged looks with Nawaf.

"We believe that this man is very adept at using disguises but is the same man. As you can see by comparison, the general facial structure is basically the same—wide eyes, narrow lips and high cheekbones. However, when he met with one man, he had long hair and a mustache, and when he met with another, he was completely bald and had no facial hair. We were unable to find a match with our facial recognition software, but we were hoping that you could run it through your own databases and see if you have some investigations of your own against this man," explained the intelligence officer.

"We will do what we can, of course," assured the minister. He turned to Nawaf. "Prince Nawaf, would you please escort these men over to our own intelligence offices, to make sure that they are taken care of?"

"Of course, Your Grace," answered the prince with a smile.

As they left the room, Nawaf knew exactly who was in those sketches, and he contemplated what to do. He could kill the Americans himself, but definitely at least the Undersecretary of State would be missed, and that might create a bigger problem.

Hmm…I suppose I can make sure there will be no official matches to return to the Americans, he thought, more calmly. He was going to need to contact Al Shabah soon—he'd need to be careful.

That night, the prince sent a message to the Ghost on their dark web chat room. "The Americans are getting really close to figuring this out. I would just hang back if I were you."

****

Washington, D.C.
Counterterrorism Unit

The last few days had been slow for Mike at CTU. He didn't really have a solid lead to work from yet, and forensic accounting wasn't really his strength, so he was going to have to wait on Simone to help him with that piece of the puzzle. He tried to work the connections as best he could, but so far, all he had was a whiteboard with a bunch of photos attached by different-colored yarn.

He yawned and reached for his coffee. Then someone knocked at the door. Mike turned away from his arts-and-crafts spiderweb to see Simone standing there, bleary-eyed and holding her own cup of joe. He eagerly waved her in.

"Just the person I wanted to see."

"OK, well, I'm glad you're a visual person, because I brought along a few charts to help explain this one," Simone said as she placed her coffee on his desk and pulled out a printed PowerPoint presentation. She began to tack some of the slides to his corkboard.

Mike suddenly realized that he had found the perfect overachiever to help him in his quest.

"What have you got for me?" he asked.

"The first thing I noticed is that CAGIR received an influx of money following each terror attack. See here?" she questioned, motioning to several highlighted transactions.

That's odd, thought Mike.

"Where did it come from?" he muttered aloud.

"Well, these donations all seem to be from front companies, because they all cease to exist a few months after the donations are made to CAGIR," Simone explained.

"Yikes. Tell me there's some good news," he asserted.

"Well…it gets a little complicated here, but basically, I realized that many of these front companies are all transacting out of the same bank in Singapore. I did a little more digging and noticed that there are a *ton* of Bitcoin transactions happening between that bank and another bank in the UAE," she said, pointing to spreadsheets and charts as she spoke.

"OK, but don't most banks transact in Bitcoin now?" asked Mike with a raised eyebrow.

"They do, but not at this level. Here are the latest reports of Bitcoin transactions from Wells Fargo, just for reference," she instructed. "So, then I started to investigate this UAE bank a little more and researching who it is they interact with. Lo and behold, the front company that purchased Fahd al Saud's plane ticket to the US used this bank for the purchase."

"Seriously?" he asked. "Well, we definitely need to examine this organization. What's the name of the company? And do we have anything else on them already?"

"It's KIDL Investment International. There's not a lot out there about them, which makes sense. However, they also have a US subsidiary, KIDL American Investments, that donated a substantial amount of money directly to Alexander Bishop's congressional campaign," Simone concluded.

She stood back and smiled. She obviously knew Mike was impressed.

"This is really, really good work," Mike said. He traced his fingers across some of the people, connections and other pieces of information. His mind was already racing with new leads.

He turned to face her. "I'm going to direct our team to start investigating each of the board members at KIDL. I'm pretty sure that if we can put a tail on each of them, we'll soon have something pretty concrete to work with."

Chapter 34
Closing In

Lucerne, Switzerland

So far, the teams monitoring the board members of KIDL International had managed to watch their marks without being spotted. Each team of four to five agents was working around the clock, keeping careful tabs on their targets and utilizing electronic surveillance when possible to help keep their distance. Some of the teams were having a very boring week, watching their assigned board member look at spreadsheets and stock prospectives on their computers. Others were on the move so much that they barely had time to take shifts to sleep.

The team assigned to Marwan Kattan felt like they had hit the jackpot. So far, they had spent their entire week in beautiful Switzerland, surrounded by mountains and looking at gorgeous Lake Lucerne. In between shift changes, they had even had a chance to sample some famous Swiss chocolate. Their mark was apparently conducting a series of banking transactions; he had traveled to three separate banks so far but had otherwise been on his own except for his morning trip to the local bakery for a freshly baked pastry for breakfast and a coffee. In the evenings, he had taken a few strolls along the sidewalk, seemingly to enjoy the view of the reflections of the city lights in the water. Even with all the hypervigilance necessary to adequately perform this job, the agents were relishing the scenery.

As they observed, the agents had also been quietly collecting biometric data. One of the agents, Diana Green, had managed to collect a very good set of fingerprints from one of the morning coffee run cups. Another agent, Micah Wolf, had used a series of mirrors to collect a photo of Marwan's face that was good enough to run against the facial recognition database. So far, both sets of data had come up dry against any known biometrics in the United States. That was somewhat suspicious, considering that someone at that level would have most likely traveled into the United States at some point and been biometrically enrolled into the system.

One night, Marwan broke his normal routine. As he took his stroll along Lake Lucerne, he suddenly changed course and entered the Zunfthausrestaurant Pfistern, a well-known fondue restaurant. Diana was on shift that night, and she got a bit excited when he walked in—it meant that she was going to be able to be able to munch on some fancy Swiss fondue on the government's dime.

She talked into the mic in her sleeve, "Hey, Micah, I need another half to a couple. Head on inside Kornmarkt 4. Hope you like fondue."

Soon they were sitting about ten feet away from Marwan, holding hands and looking very much like a couple in love. Diana had placed a pen with a directional mic in it on the table, nestled in the pages of a notebook. She was hoping that they might be able to pick up some audio, although so far, he was just dining alone.

Ten minutes later, another man joined the table. Diana was at a better angle to see his face than Micah. She did a double take, then slowly stood up and whispered something in her partner's ear before excusing herself to the powder room.

In the bathroom, she pulled out her phone and woke up the members of her team that were on the "off" shift. "Guys, I'm sorry to pull you out of your sleep, but Marwan is talking to Nihad Nassimi—yes, that Nihad Nassimi, from CAGIR. Please notify CTU and be prepared join us out in the field. We are currently eating at Zunfthausrestaurant Pfistern located at Kornmarkt 4, and we will let you know when we head out."

"Acknowledged," came a sleepy voice on the other end.

When she walked back inside, Micah was taking advantage of the giant table of breads that customers would cut off for themselves. It seemed like a good idea to Diana— Micah managed to get a better view of Marwan, and also, what else was a man supposed to do while his date was in the bathroom?

They finished their meal slowly over the rest of the hour. Meanwhile, the two men were still talking. Since they had essentially finished eating and had at least one cup of coffee, they couldn't really stay in place any longer without looking suspicious, so they got their check and exited the restaurant.

When they left, they needed to quickly find another reason to hang around the area, so they bought coffees from a nearby spot that had a view of the lake and would also allow them to see when Marwan made his way out.

Diana was having a great night: fondue, coffee by the lake, an adventure, and she had to admit that she enjoyed holding Micah's hand. It was hard to spend all that time pretending to be in love without feeling anything. She sighed.

Maybe someday...but I've got to keep this professional right now, she thought.

"You OK?" asked Micah.

"Yeah, I just don't want to lose these guys," she responded as she snapped herself out of her daydream.

"Hey," he said, squeezing her hand slightly, "we've got this."

Ten minutes later, Marwan and Nihad left the restaurant, headed in different directions. Diana sent her teammates toward Nihad, and she and Micah continued to stay on Marwan. He walked in an unusual pattern, probably to throw people like them off. Fortunately, he wasn't walking very fast.

Diana and Micah managed to pull out a few new accessories to change their appearance a bit. She put on a gray shawl that was the very same shade of gray that six in ten Europeans seemed to be wearing, and Micah donned a hat and pair of nonprescription glasses. Things seemed to be fine. They kept their distance and ducked into shops as needed. Then, Marwan suddenly looked back when there was nowhere for them to hide. Micah swooped Diana to the side of the building, his body tight against hers as he planted a big kiss on her. She might have even kissed him back.

When their kiss had lingered long enough, Micah pulled away. "Woo, that was close," he said. "He almost caught us."

Almost bewildered by what had just happened, Diana quickly added, "That was quick thinking there, Micah. I'm not sure I would have thought to do that." She winked at him with a mischievous grin on her face.

Blushing now, Micah quickly tried to recover. "Diana, I'm so sorry for grabbing you like that and kissing you without asking. It was the only thing I could think of to keep Marwan from spotting us and blowing our cover."

She shook her head. "It's OK, Micah, you made the right call. The mission comes first. Let's see where he continues to lead us."

Another hour went by as they continued to follow Marwan as he made a serious of cutbacks between streets, alleyways and stores, continually checking to see if he had a tail. Eventually, they finally tracked him back to the same hotel he had been staying at and then prepared to listen to the tapes they had collected during the dinner.

****

Not all of the audio was usable, but that was to be expected. There was definitely some interference from the waiters and other patrons who were occasionally rising above the normal din of chatter. However, they could understand the gist of the conversation. Apparently, the two men had an established working relationship, and Marwan was essentially telling Nihad that he needed to take a step back from their enterprise. They established a new back channel for communications and discussed finances. Nothing too exciting for as long of a conversation as they'd had, but Nihad was apparently trying to take full advantage of having someone pay for the check, because he had continued to come up with a whole lot of nothing to talk about while they had more drinks and desserts.

A few clips were good enough that they decided to run it through the voice recognition database. It would take more than a few hours to run that data comparison, so they wrote up their reports and decided to get at least some sleep before the morning activity of D.C. would eventually catch up to them.

****

Washington, D.C.
Counterterrorism Unit

Mike walked into his office and immediately saw the flashing light on his desk phone that indicated he had a voicemail. He had already read a bunch of emails on the way into work, so he was fairly certain that he had received a call regarding the recording in Lucerne last night.

He picked up the phone and followed the prompts. "Good morning to you, Michael Stone, this is Elizabeth Cole from the Scotland Yard. Please call us as soon as you get in. We have some very important information for you, and we don't want to miss you today because of the time zone difference," said the voice on the recording before leaving the appropriate phone number, extension and reference number for him to use to call back.

Stone wasted no time. After dialing the litany of numbers necessary to make an international call, he was soon speaking with Elizabeth. Her British accent and tone of voice reminded him of his ex-wife, and he felt a twinge of pain at the memories of his previous family life.

"Glad we were able to talk today," she began. "We had a match on that voice recording clip that you sent to us."

"Oh?" inquired Michael. "Who did we find?"

"The man in the recording is a former MI6 agent, and we have an outstanding warrant for his arrest. His real name is Omar Bishara, but we have recently had reports of him being referred to as Al Shabah, or 'the Ghost.'"

"No kidding," said Mike, trying to keep his voice from betraying his excitement. "We've been looking for a man that goes by that moniker for some time now."

"Well, you might have to get to the back of the queue. We've had an outstanding warrant for his arrest for years. We came close to capturing him one other time, but the Saudis intervened. They gave him a new identity, altered his fingerprints and gave him facial reconstruction surgery to help evade our matching software. That's why his prints didn't come up when you searched. Please just tell me you haven't lost him," she pleaded.

"As of right now, my team is still on him. Do you want us to bring him to Gitmo, or do you have a special place in mind you'd like me to bring him?" asked Michael, hoping they could jointly interrogate this guy.

"I think we would prefer if you could bring him to us. We have ways to make him talk and a lot less rules involved, if you know what I mean," she answered wryly.

Chapter 35
Birth of a Ghost

Omar Bishara wanted to be one of those men in history that would influence and help shape the future. The problem was, although he came from a rich family, he wasn't a member of the Saudi royal family. His ability to rise within his country's government would be greatly curtailed because of his lack of birthright.

In the 1980s, his father took a position with British Petroleum and moved their family to London. Omar's father had worked hard to become a well-respected oil executive in Saudi Arabia, but when he was offered a senior position with BP, he jumped at the rare chance to increase his family's influence and wealth. In his pursuit of creating more upward mobility for his children, Omar's father also worked very hard to get the family dual citizenship.

While attending the University of Oxford, Bishara would often walk the halls of the Shmolean Museum on Beaumont Street when he needed to clear his head or think. It was a beautiful institution that displayed a lot of unique pieces of art and explained key elements of British history. Seeing the various images and styles of art helped him link ideas together to find solutions to problems. During his naïve university days, Omar would marvel at the rich history of Britain and how this country had so influenced the formation of the modern world.

In his final year at Oxford, Omar had planned on returning to Riyadh and entering the diplomatic corps. His father had become close with an attaché at the Saudi Embassy, who had offered to help Omar gain a position in the prestigious agency. Then, one day while sipping a cup of coffee at the rooftop café of the Shmolean Museum, Omar was approached by a mysterious man.

"You're Omar Bishara, right?" inquired the gentleman as he walked up to the table.

"I am, but how do you know me?" he asked, confused.

The man pulled out the chair opposite him and sat down. "I'm a part of an organization that knows quite a bit about any number of people," the man said, pulling out a badge. On it was his name, Denton Holt, his picture, and below the government seal was the title, "MI6."

Now Omar's curiosity was piqued. "So, what's your interest in me?" he asked.

"It's very simple, really. We need smart, educated people from the Middle East who can help us to interpret not just the language, but the nuances of the culture, politics, and religion in the region. With your studies at Oxford and your family's background, you are our ideal candidate," replied Denton in a very matter-of-fact tone.

"I won't lie and tell you that I'm not interested," admitted Omar, feeling his heart race at the thought of being an actual spy. "However, I am supposed to be returning to Riyadh. My father helped me to secure a position in the Saudi diplomatic corps, and it is really a prestigious opportunity. If I were to turn that down, I would have to present him with a glowing alternative."

Denton did not seem concerned at all by the initial dismissal.

"I'm quite certain that we could arrange for a cover story that would be acceptable to your family, Mr. Bishara," he explained.

It wasn't long before Omar's protests were completely dismantled, and he agreed to delay his journey back to Saudi Arabia.

True to his word, Mr. Holt did help to organize a very impressive opportunity for Omar to present to his parents. MI6 placed Omar into a promising position with the Royal Bank of Scotland, which came with a large signing bonus. The cover story was that he was being groomed to become a banking executive at RBS, which was planning on establishing a presence in Saudi Arabia and other locations in the Middle East. This provided him with a plausible reason for turning down the diplomatic corps and an explanation for his extended training in the UK before he would return to Saudi Arabia.

When Omar told his father, the conversation couldn't have gone any better. The opportunity to rise in the financial ranks of a global bank was just as significant to him as working in the diplomatic corps of their home nation. It would open up all sorts of new opportunities for Omar, and he couldn't have been prouder.

Once Omar had completed his two years of training with MI6, he received another six months of intense training in investment banking and analysis. Two and a half years after graduating Oxford, Omar was transferred to RBS's new Middle East office in Riyadh, where he began his first overseas assignment as a spy. Omar's career was moving along quickly, both at RBS and with MI6. He had successfully recruited fifteen sources, several of whom were senior officers in the Saudi military and two of whom were in the diplomatic corps.

Then, in 1996, a terrorist organization called "The Base," or Al Qaeda, carried out a terrorist attack against the US forces who had been staying at the Khobar Towers near the King Abdulaziz Air Base. It was one of the largest terrorist attacks in the kingdom's history. MI6 tasked him with trying to find out what he could about this organization and its leader, a man by the name of Osama bin Laden. The bin Laden family was very wealthy and influential in the kingdom, so they needed to tread lightly.

Omar wasn't exactly a devout Muslim, but tracing information about Al Qaeda would require a fervent adherence to Islam. Not having the necessary skills to personally infiltrate the organization, Bishara set out to identify those who could. Over the next several years, he recruited several individuals who were successful in joining the organization. They provided him with valuable information on the formation of some terrorist training camps in the Sudan and Afghanistan.

Then, during one of Omar's meets with a high-level source in the diplomatic corps, he was arrested. He fell into a counterintelligence trap set by the Maslahat Al-Istikhbarat Al-Aammah, or General Intelligence Department of Saudi Arabia. The Saudis had been conducting their own infiltration of Al Qaeda, and one of the individuals they had arrested, tortured, and turned had been one of Omar's sources.

As a dual Saudi-UK citizen and spy for another nation, Omar knew that he wasn't in a particularly good situation.

After a few weeks of beatings to soften him up, a man named Prince Nawaf bin Abdullah came to visit him in prison.

"I think you know what kind of trouble you are in," he began. "They wanted to kill you, of course. However, I saw that you might still have some value in this world. Do you want to live, Omar?" he asked, putting a briefcase on the table.

Omar gulped, then gasped, "Yes. Yes, I want to live."

Nodding his head, Nawaf said, "Excellent choice, Omar. I have another decision for you to make. You can either work for me in the GID as a double agent, or you can face execution."

He paused for a moment, either for dramatic effect or to let the information sink in. "So, what do you choose?" inquired Prince Nawaf.

"I want to live," Bishara answered without hesitation.
****

Thus began his life as a double agent. While the decision was easy to make, the actual reality of life as a spy within MI6 was very challenging to pull off. After four years of living as a double agent, a few people at MI6 started to suspect that perhaps Omar's loyalties were no longer pure.

They ran a parallel collection operation, giving Omar the same information to collect as two other trusted sources. He failed the test on multiple occasions, which ultimately sealed his fate.

Fortunately for Bishara, the GID had a mole within the UK's Ministry of Justice, who intercepted a discussion about an arrest warrant for "an MI6 agent who had been identified as a double agent." With his cover blown, Omar was whisked away and given a new identity before the British were able to make their arrest.

Right from the get-go, Omar began to work directly for Prince Nawaf within the GID. Most of his work seemed to benefit a specific firm, Gulf State International. He was given projects ranging from corporate espionage, sabotage, and occasionally, assassinations.

Then, in 2003, with the advent of the US-led invasion of Iraq, Omar's role as a spy morphed once again. He received orders to gather intelligence and infiltrate the Al Qaeda in Iraq organization. His identity was changed more permanently this time, as he underwent more advanced facial reconstruction surgery and fingerprint alteration. He began to successfully cultivate sources within Al Qaeda in Iraq and the various terrorist and insurgent organizations fighting the Iraqi government and the Americans. Over the next four years, Omar had developed the persona known within the circles of Islamic extremists as "the Ghost." He developed networks to acquire weapons, explosives, smuggle people, narcotics and nearly every other skill that made him indispensable to a terrorist organization. By the end of the Iraq war, Omar had become a rather influential leader while still being a secret informant to the GID.

The intelligence he gathered had led to the capture or death of numerous Al Qaeda leaders across the Middle East and around the globe that posed a threat to the kingdom. Their deaths had also facilitated his continued rise within the organization as he was effectively killing off his competition.

This undercover position came with incredibly peril to his own safety. He was nearly killed by numerous US drone strikes and several US-led capture missions, but Prince Nawaf had also helped him stay one step ahead of the Americans. From what Omar could tell, the Americans knew Prince Nawaf had a source high in the organization, but they had not identified him as the source. This anonymity had worked to his benefit and only further added to his mystique as "the Ghost."

In addition to the facial reconstruction surgery, Bishara implemented numerous additional safeguards to keep himself from being detected and captured. When traveling through airports, he used special contact lenses that not only changed the color of his eyes but gave him a different iris image. He also used fake fingerprints to help him evade the biometric sensors being used for those entering the UK and US from foreign countries. Omar had an American identity he would use when he needed to travel to the US, UK or EU, which enabled him to bypass the need for travel visas and additional vetting. For trips to other regions, he could pull out his Canadian or Saudi passports.

The Ghost was living the spy's life, and frankly, he was exceptionally good at his job. If he were entirely honest with himself, he even enjoyed it. In the occasional quiet moments though, he did long for the freedom to do whatever he chose to do. Which was why he took great pride in controlling whatever he could about his life, no matter how small it was.

Prince Nawaf recognized his natural talents and slowly began to groom him for something new after the Iraq war ended. Each mission he completed as the Ghost now came with a healthy bonus. He began to become very wealthy in his own right. Then one day, he was given an offer he couldn't refuse. If he worked with the Knights of Islam and completed their missions, he would be a free man, allowed to retire and use his money as he saw fit, or grow his position within the organization if he chose to stay and be inducted in.

Now, hiding out in Lucerne, the Ghost was truly afraid--not frightened of being caught or killed, but of losing his one chance at freedom. The only thing he wanted in the world was to break free of his many masters, and he saw it slipping away from him.

Chapter 36
Joint Mission

Lucerne, Switzerland

After Marwan's meeting with Nihad, he stayed in Lucerne one more day and visited the Grand Casino Luzern on Haldenstrasse, which had a spectacular view of Lake Lucerne. He spent most of the day playing poker and other card games with a variety of people.

At first, Diana didn't think anything of it. It made sense that a spy would enjoy a sport that was all about reading and manipulating people. She slowly nursed a martini at the bar and tried to keep observing without being too obvious.

Suddenly, Micah's expression changed, and she knew he'd spotted something. He walked around the bar to her, held her hand, and then whispered in her ear, "Diana, Marwan is meeting some of his sources while he's here."

Her left eyebrow rose, and then she whispered back, "How do you want to proceed?"

Micah wasn't much of a poker player, but he bought into the table that Marwan was playing at and made sure his lapel pin was transmitting the images of the people his target was interacting with. Diana then left the bar and moved over to the café in the casino, which had a better angle on the poker tables. She deftly set up her pen camera and directional mic at the table and began monitoring what Micah was seeing and parsing out the audio of the various people at the table.

Pulling out her smartphone, she logged in to the casino's Wi-Fi and established the secure VPN link to their team's makeshift office at the suite where they were staying. She also made sure the data was streaming back to CTU.

She almost chuckled at the sight of Micah as he continued his best effort to fake it at the poker table, but all the while, the images his lapel pin collected were being cross-checked against all the government intelligence databases to see if they could find a match.

Marwan moved on to a different table and seemed to be talking with someone else there. Diana grunted. Micah would have to continue to play poker for a while so as not to draw suspicion.

A few minutes later, Diana's laptop notified her that she had a new email from CTU. She had barely finished reading the subject line when her phone buzzed. In her twenty-second conversation with someone from Washington, she learned that they had been given the green light to apprehend Marwan immediately.

Diana spoke in hushed tones into the mike on her sleeve. "We have a live capture order for our subject," she announced. "Micah and I will keep an eye on the Ghost. George, it's time to rent a van. Bring it to the casino parking lot. Ashley…it's time to do your thing."

The team acknowledged her directions and set into motion.

A few minutes later, Ashley entered the casino in a tight-fitting slinky skirt and a low-cut top. Many of the males in the room seemed to suffer whiplash as they watched her move gracefully around the card tables toward the bar. Clearly, she had their attention.

A waiter at the bar was finalizing the drinks to be brought to the card table that Marwan was sitting at when he looked up and noticed the stunningly beautiful woman who had suddenly appeared before him. Smiling as he finished loading the drinks on the tray, he paused to see if she wanted him to fix her one before he left. She motioned for him to come closer, then reached out and took his hand, whispering something flirtatious to him in Swiss German. The guy's cheeks flushed, and they exchanged a few hushed words.

While the waiter, bartender, and other patrons at the bar were distracted by her interplay with this now bewildered young man, Diana walked near the waiter's drink platter and placed something in the drink that was meant for Marwan. It helped that he always ordered the same thing.

The waiter stammered for a minute, then Ashley, apparently put off by his blubbering mannerisms, pushed him away and told him that she just wanted a gin and tonic. She sat at the bar, turning a bit so that the men at the card tables could see her. As she crossed her legs, the slit in her skirt showed off more of her athletic legs.

Diana smiled as she walked back to her laptop in the café. She noticed that Ashley was having way too much fun playing the honey pot as she worked the room to make sure all eyes stayed on her. When she noticed Micah gazing at her just a little too long, she got a bit miffed, but then she reminded herself that he was a man, and all straight men seemed to be trapped when a woman showed a little too much skin.

The waiter brought over the drinks to Marwan's table and handed them out to their respective owners. Marwan had also been watching Ashley, so when he received his drink, he unknowingly took several gulps before returning to the business at hand. After ten minutes, during which the men of the casino continued to ogle Ashley, Marwan suddenly got up to head to the restroom.

As he headed toward a sign that read "Toilette," Diana closed her laptop and placed it in her bookbag. She got up and walked toward the powder rooms as well. Out of the corner of her eye, she spotted Micah collecting his chips and cashing out. He too began to amble toward the restroom. As the rest of the patrons of the casino continued to watch either Ashley or their cards, Diana and Micah both converged on the restroom Marwan had gone into. Micah took up a position near the pay phones just opposite the entrance and waited.

Then, Marwan exited the bathroom looking a little pale. Diana bumped into him. "Oh, dear me. I'm so sorry. I didn't see you. Please excuse me," she said in a British accent, trying to distract him briefly while Micah went in for the kill. Before Marwan could respond, Micah stabbed a needle through his target's shirt into his deltoid muscle. He quickly pushed the plunger down, slamming the drug rapidly into his body.

In seconds, Marwan's world went black and he collapsed into Micah's arms. Diana reached over and picked up Marwan's left arm and placed it over her shoulder and around her neck to help Micah as they carried him toward the exit at the end of the hall.

From an outsider's perspective, it would look like Marwan had had too many drinks and his friends were helping him home. However, as they exited the building, George pulled up with the white van and opened the side door. In seconds, Marwan was inside the van, along with Diana and Micah.

Diana spoke into her sleeve. "Ashley, we have our mark. It's time to head for the airport."

"Roger that," came the reply.

Diana pictured her colleague chatting away with wealthy men. She must have caused just as much fanfare on her way out as she had coming into the casino. Diana tried not to feel jealous about just how good a job she'd done as the distraction.

Focusing her attention back on the task before her, she and Micah checked over Marwan's body for any possible weapons or bugs and then hoisted him into a large ski carrying case. They had purchased this bag in advance, knowing that it should be big enough to hide Marwan inside, but breathable enough to keep him from suffocating.

As they approached the municipal airport, they pulled up to the Lear jet that would whisk them away once they had everyone on board. As they got out of the van, two men grabbed the now-quite-heavy ski bag and loaded it into the cabin of the aircraft, along with their other suitcases and equipment. Twenty minutes later, Ashley arrived and walked over to the aircraft as well.

She flashed a devilish smile. "That was fun. Now stop staring at me, you guys—where are my clothes?"

Micah and Diana chuckled uncomfortably. Diana had never really noticed her colleague's figure before—she tended to wear clothes that kept it well hidden while on the job. She handed her a small duffle bag and they all boarded the plane.

As their aircraft took to the air, the pilot announced, "We're flying to the London City Airport, folks. Your charge will be handed off to a joint interrogation group with MI6 and CTU agents."

The flight wasn't a long one, just a few hours, which gave the team time to decompress and begin to write up the mountain of paperwork from their operation. As the aircraft descended, they caught a great bird's-eye view of London as they came in on their final approach. When their plane landed, it was escorted to a nondescript-looking hangar near the end of the airport, where several blacked-out vehicles waited inside. The pilot began the process of shutting down the engines while a couple of attendants moved to chock the wheels.

George, their wheelman, reached over and unlocked the aircraft exit, pushing it forward and then down as it turned into their stairs to leave the plane. As he exited the aircraft, Micah followed suit, each of them carrying half of the ski case. Ashley and Diana exited next as several people approached their group.

A woman in a formal business suit appeared to be in charge. She stepped forward to extend her hand to each member of the team and introduced herself. "Welcome to London. I'm Laura Taylor, Director of Operations," she began.

"I cannot tell you how long we have been after this guy. He used to be one of ours, before he was turned." She bent down and unzipped the ski bag. She looked at Marwan, who was still out cold, briefly touching his face with her hand, which Diana found odd. She then zipped the bag up and thanked their team again.

Micah, who was the official head of their detail, commented, "We're glad we were of assistance. Has Director Stone said who would be supporting you in his interrogation from our end?"

She smiled as she responded, "Yes. He has a team that is en route as we speak. I was told you would accompany me and the prisoner until they arrived for the formal handoff.

Director Stone was insistent on having someone from his team present with the prisoner at all times," she said candidly, clearly not at all offended by his persistence.

****

With that, Micah left the rest of his team as he headed with the MI6 Director to wherever they were going to take Marwan. Micah was a bit envious of his team—they were now going to sit tight in London while they were waiting on him, enjoying some much-needed downtime in yet another spectacular European city. As they drove toward the city, one of the MI6 men handed him a folder.

"This is our background information on Omar Bishara, the man you call Marwan Kattan. I suggest you take some time to read up on him as we will begin questioning him shortly after our arrival," the agent explained.

As they approached the MI6 building, a frantic call came over the radio from the vehicle they were following, the one that had Marwan in it. "Director Taylor, the prisoner is dead! He must have had a cyanide capsule in his tooth. We heard some rustling from the bag and then he just started to shake violently, so we opened it up, only to find him foaming at the mouth and convulsing," the agent said, disheartened.

The MI6 Director looked at Micah with an accusatory glare. "Did your team not check to see if he had a false tooth?"

Micah felt his face begin to turn red. "Ma'am," he said softly, "I don't know what happened, but we *did* check for that."

The Director just hung her head down. She took one long, deep breath and then looked up at Micah. "Dead men tell no tales. I'm afraid we aren't going to get anything useful out of him now, are we?" she remarked, disgusted. "Your team failed, and I'm going to make sure Director Stone knows why. That was an amateur mistake, something that never should have happened." Her cheeks were hot and red, and he could tell that she was containing what would have otherwise been a much more enraged response.

Micah felt horrible. There was nothing more he could say or do other than hang his head low and stay quiet.

Did we really miss that? I know we checked his mouth, he wondered. He couldn't figure out what had gone wrong.

He did keep reading the rest of the file as they continued to drive to their intended location. What he read was truly amazing. This guy had really been a spy's spy. After some time had passed, he dared to ask, "Could I keep the dossier for our own records? Maybe we could see if we could use anything from it to help with our own ongoing case."

The MI6 Director just grunted. "Why not? He's dead, so it's of no use to us now."

As Micah continued to pick apart every detail of the day in his mind, he couldn't help but think about the strange moment at the tarmac when Director Taylor had touched Marwan's cheek. It had just seemed odd.

Is there a possibility that she slipped him the cyanide? he wondered. He didn't know if he was just creating a conspiracy theory, but something just didn't add up.

****

Several hours later, Laura Taylor was finally headed home for the day. She needed to grab a few things for dinner, but rather than stopping at her regular grocery store, she made a detour at an out-of-the-way location. She purchased her soup, bread and a few miscellaneous items, and then at the last minute, she added a disposable cell phone.

Those cheap phones didn't work very well, but it didn't matter. She only needed to send one message. She disposed of the packaging before she climbed into her car, and then quickly typed out, "Nawaf, the Ghost has been neutralized. LT."

As she drove home, she dropped the phone out the window inside a roundabout. She was confident that the busy traffic would effectively demolish any evidence of her communications.

Chapter 37

Beginning or the End?

Sheikh Maktoum poured Prince Nawaf a glass of brandy and opened up a nice box of cigars. He figured his friend might be a bit down and need some cheering up after their recent setbacks.

"My friend, I'm so sorry to hear that we have lost our 'Ghost,'" said the sheikh, offering to light his friend's cigar.

Nodding slowly, Prince Nawaf replied, "I'm disappointed to lose him as well. He really did some great work in Chicago. However, I am very pleased that my source made sure everything was taken care of so he wouldn't give away any incriminating information after his capture."

"True. At least we're not in any danger ourselves," asserted Maktoum. He paused a moment. "How much do you think this will set us back? Do we have to pause our activities for a while now?"

Prince Nawaf smiled mischievously. "I'm sad that you would have so little faith in me," he retorted. "I have a few up-and-comers that I have been working on for quite some time. We are still in business."

From the Authors

Miranda and I sincerely hope you have enjoyed this book. If you are hungry for more, we are now working on a modern civil war series, and the first book, *Rigged*, is already available for preorder on Amazon.

In the meantime, we do have several audiobooks coming out. *Battlefield Ukraine*, *Battlefield Korea*, and *Battlefield Taiwan* have all been released in audiobook and the rest of the books in the Red Storm Series are currently in production. The first three books of the World War III series are available on audiobook now, and the final book should be released by the end of the year.

If you would like to stay up to date on new releases and receive emails about any special pricing deals we may make available, please sign up for our email distribution list. Simply go to http://www.author-james-rosone.com and scroll to the bottom of the page.

As independent authors, reviews are very important to us and make a huge difference to other prospective readers. If you enjoyed this book, we humbly ask you to write up a positive review on Amazon and Goodreads. We sincerely appreciate each person that takes the time to write one.

We have really valued connecting with our readers via social media, especially on our Facebook page https://www.facebook.com/RosoneandWatson/. Sometimes we ask for help from our readers as we write future books—we love to draw upon all your different areas of expertise. We also have a group of beta readers who get to look at the books before they are officially published and help us fine-tune last-minute adjustments. If you would like to be a part of this team, please go to our author website: http://www.author-james-rosone.com, and send us a message through the "Contact" tab. You can also follow us on Twitter: @jamesrosone and @AuthorMirandaW. We look forward to hearing from you.

You may also enjoy some of our other works. A full list can be found below:

Nonfiction:
Iraq Memoir 2006-2007 Troop Surge
Interview with a Terrorist

Fiction:
World War III Series
Prelude to World War III: The Rise of the Islamic Republic and the Rebirth of America

Operation Red Dragon and the Unthinkable

Operation Red Dawn and the Invasion of America

Cyber Warfare and the New World Order

Michael Stone Series

Traitors Within

The Red Storm Series

Battlefield Ukraine

Battlefield Korea

Battlefield Taiwan

Battlefield Pacific

Battlefield Russia

Battlefield China

For the Veterans

I have been pretty open with our fans about the fact that PTSD has had a tremendous direct impact on our lives; it affected my relationship with my wife, job opportunities, finances, parenting—everything. It is also no secret that for me, the help from the VA was not the most ideal form of treatment. Although I am still on this journey, I did find one organization that did assist the healing process for me, and I would like to share that information.

Welcome Home Initiative is a ministry of By His Wounds Ministry, and they run seminars for veterans and their spouses for free. The weekends are a combination of prayer and more traditional counseling and left us with resources to aid in moving forward. The entire cost of the retreat—hotel costs, food, and sessions, are completely free from the moment the veteran and their spouse arrive at the location.

If you feel that you or someone you love might benefit from one of Welcome Home Initiative's sessions, please visit their website to learn more: https://welcomehomeinitiative.org/

We have decided to donate a portion of our profits to this organization, because it made such an impact in our lives and we believe in what they are doing. If you would also like to donate to Welcome Home Initiative and help to keep these weekend retreats going, you can do so by visiting the following link:

https://welcomehomeinitiative.org/donate/

Abbreviation Key

ACLU	American Civil Liberties Union
CAGIR	Center for Advancing Global Islamic Relations
CELLEX	Cellular Exploitation
CIA	Central Intelligence Agency
CNA	Certified Nurse's Assistant
CPD	Chicago Police Department
CTU	Counterterrorism Unit
ER	Emergency Room
EU	European Union
FBI	Federal Bureau of Investigations
GID	General Intelligence Department (Saudi version of CIA)
GSI	Gulf States International
HR	Human Resources
IBA	Individual Body Armor
IC	Intelligence Community
ICE	Immigration and Customs Enforcement
IED	Improvised Explosive Device
ISIS	Islamic State in Iraq and Syria
JSOC	Joint Special Operations Command
LNG	Liquid Natural Gas

M & A	Mergers and Acquisitions
MMO	Massively Multiplayer Online (Roleplaying Game)
NCTC	National Counterterrorism Center
NSA	National Security Advisor, OR National Security Agency
NSC	National Security Council
RBS	Royal Bank of Scotland
RN	Registered Nurse
RPG	Rocket-Propelled Grenade
SA	Special Agent
SAC	Special Agent in Charge
SAP	Special Access Program
SOG	Special Operations Group
TF	Task Force
UAE	United Arab Emirates
WMD	Weapons of Mass Destruction

Made in the USA
Lexington, KY
23 April 2019